Praise for *A Ranger's Trail*

Carefully blending fact and fiction, Darlene Franklin brings one of the lesser-known eras in Texas history to life in this powerful story of love and vengeance, family and faith. For a realistic look at the way the Old West really was, don't miss *A Ranger's Trail.*

—AMANDA CABOT, author of *Summer of Promise*

Darlene Franklin has taken a dark time in Texas history and turned it into an intriguing tale of family loyalty, self-preservation, and love. She weaves together the lives of two people who don't realize the ones they love are in the middle of the fight. How the differences are resolved and peace restored makes a compelling drama that will keep you turning the pages. Another winner in the Texas Trails series.

—MARTHA ROGERS, author of the Seasons of the Heart series

Darlene Franklin immerses the reader into the bitter Hoo Doo War through her passionate characters and exemplary research. In *A Ranger's Trail* she explores the struggle between family loyalty, vengeance, and justice, yet examines both sides of the conflict without partiality. Thoughtful and challenging, *A Ranger's Trail* is an experience that continues long after the last page.

—REGINA JENNINGS, author of *Sixty Acres and a Bride*

TEXAS
TRAILS

⟵★⟶

A RANGER'S TRAIL

DARLENE FRANKLIN

A
MORGAN FAMILY
SERIES

MOODY PUBLISHERS
CHICAGO

Powell River Public Library

© 2012 by
DARLENE FRANKLIN

All rights reserved. No part of this book may be reproduced in any form without permission in writing from the publisher, except in the case of brief quotations embodied in critical articles or reviews.

Edited by Pam Pugh
Interior design: Ragont Design
Cover design: Gearbox
Cover images: Masterfile, VEER, and Photos.com
Author photo: Motophoto

Library of Congress Cataloging-in-Publication Data

Franklin, Darlene.
A ranger's trail / Darlene Franklin.
p. cm. — (Texas trails : a Morgan Family series)
ISBN 978-0-8024-0587-6 (alk. paper)
1. Cattle stealing—Fiction. 2. Vigilantes—Fiction. 3. Texas—Fiction.
4. Domestic fiction. I. Title.
PS3606.R395R36 2012
813'.6—dc22

2011032809

We hope you enjoy this book from River North Fiction by Moody Publishers. Our goal is to provide high-quality, thought-provoking books and products that connect truth to your real needs and challenges. For more information on other books and products written and produced from a biblical perspective, go to www.moodypublishers.com or write to:

River North Fiction
Imprint of Moody Publishers
820 N. LaSalle Boulevard
Chicago, IL 60610

1 3 5 7 9 10 8 6 4 2

Printed in the United States of America

This book is dedicated to my biggest fan
and number one (and only) son, Jaran Franklin.
Together, God has taught us how to forgive the unforgiveable
and has restored us to each other.

Above all, I want to dedicate A Ranger's Trail
to the God who sought me
and died for me while I was still His enemy.

NOTE TO READER:

Range wars are an ugly part of the history of the American West. The Mason County, or "Hoo Doo," War is an example of range wars at their worst. German settlers felt they were denied justice when A. G. Roberts and M. B. Thomas were acquitted of cattle rustling. They decided to administer rough frontier justice to several key figures of the Anglo community, including Tim Williamson. Unfortunately for the Germans, Williamson was a close friend of former Texas Ranger Scott Cooley. Cooley vowed to see everyone involved in Williamson's murder brought to justice. Other historical characters who appear in the pages of *A Ranger's Trail* are Major John B. Jones, Sheriff John Clark, Henry Doell, Rev. Johann Stricker, Johann Wohrle, James Cheyney, Capt. Dan Roberts, August Keller, Ernst Jordan, Peter Jordan, Miles Barler, Dan Hoerster, and Captain Neal Caldwell.

Unless otherwise noted, quotes are taken from:

The Lucia Holmes Diary 1875–1876: The Hoo Doo War Years by Lucia Holmes (Mason, Texas: Mason County Historical Society, 1985)

The Mason County "Hoo Doo" War, 1874–1902 by David Johnson (Denton, Texas: University of North Texas Press, 2006)

Names have been spelled uniformly for the sake of simplicity, although there is some variation in original sources.

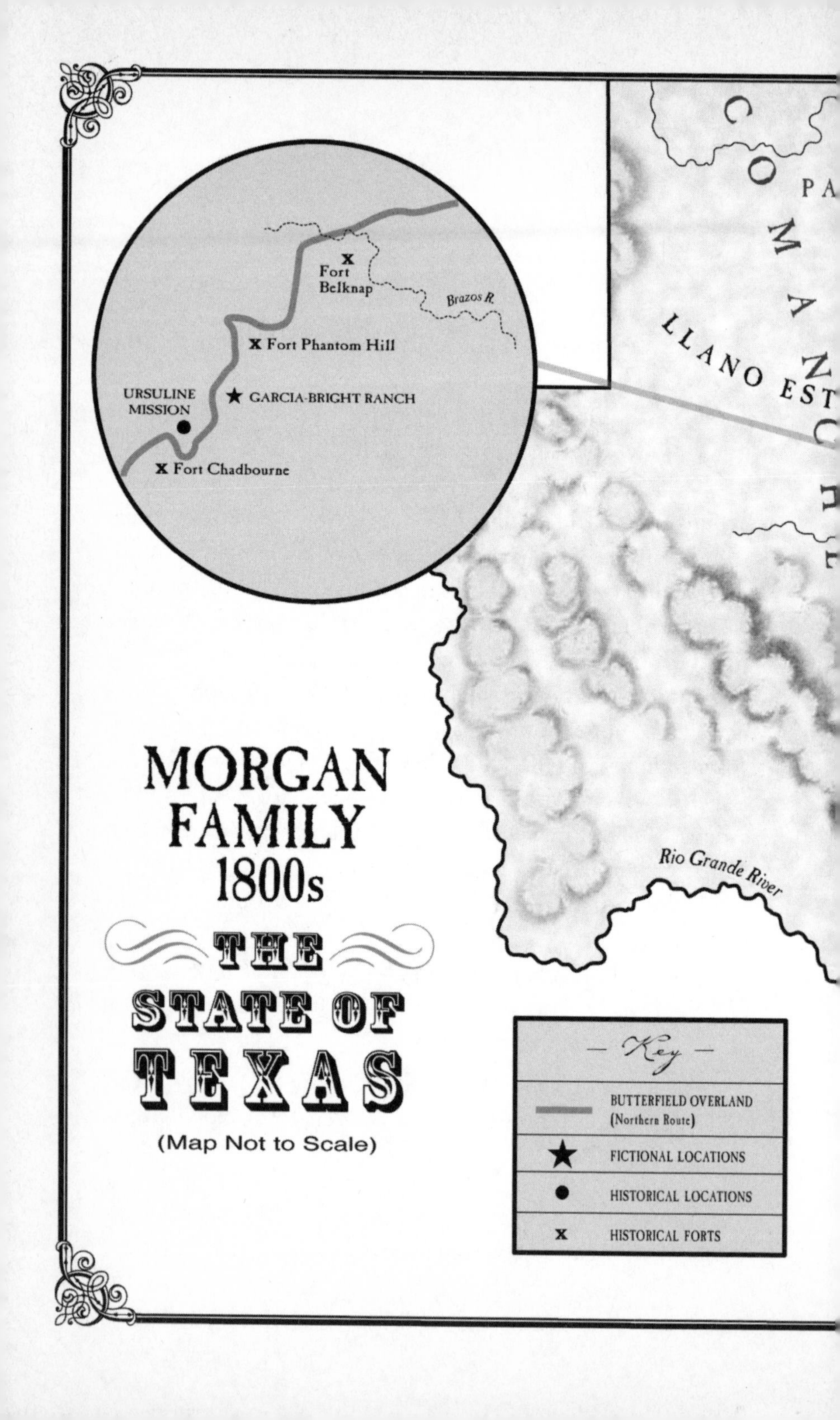

Fort Belknap
Brazos R.
Fort Phantom Hill
URSULINE MISSION
GARCIA-BRIGHT RANCH
Fort Chadbourne
LLANO EST
PA
Rio Grande River
MORGAN FAMILY 1800s
THE STATE OF TEXAS
(Map Not to Scale)
Key
BUTTERFIELD OVERLAND (Northern Route)
FICTIONAL LOCATIONS
HISTORICAL LOCATIONS
HISTORICAL FORTS

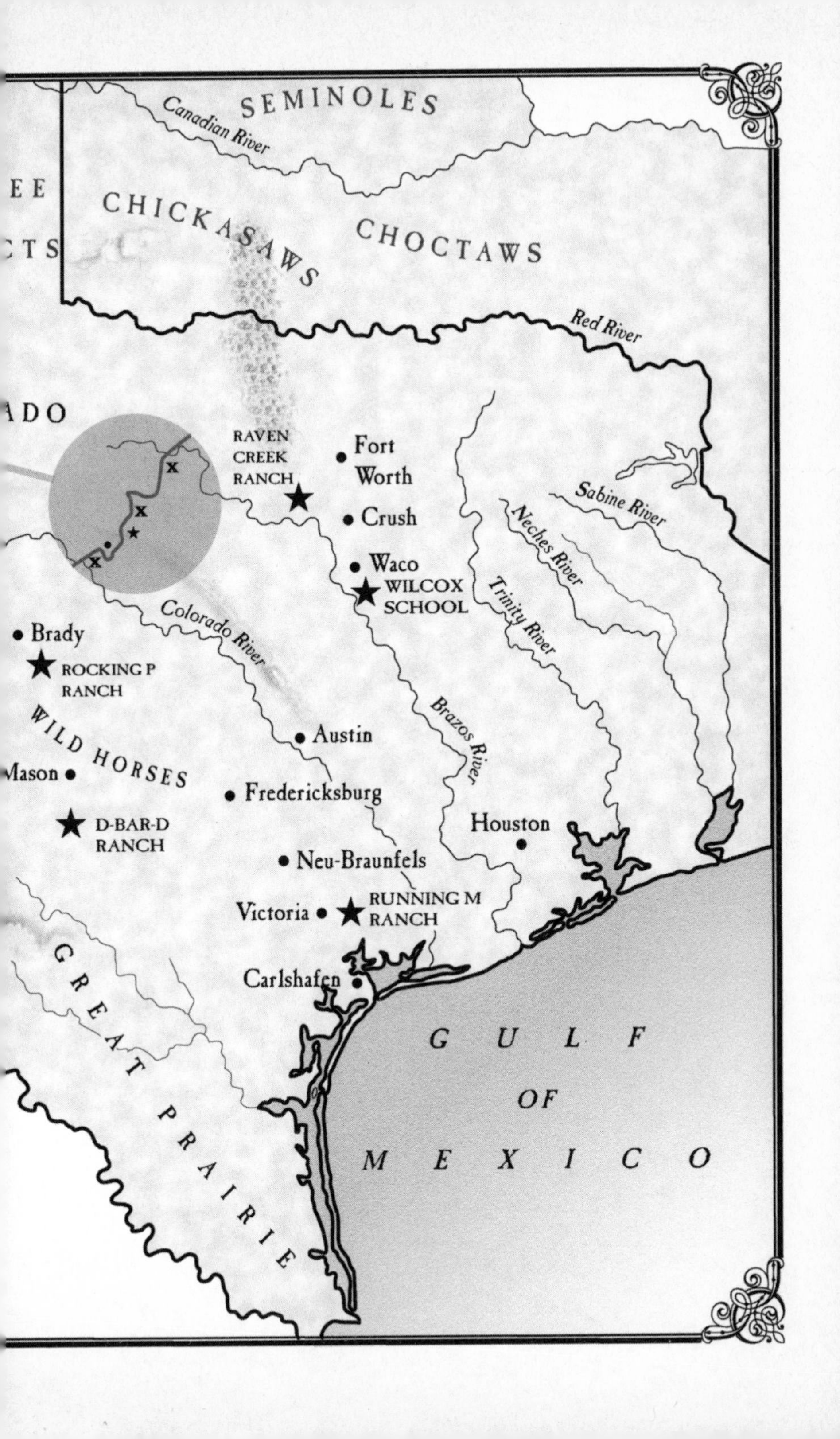
SEMINOLES
Canadian River
EE
CHICKASAWS
CHOCTAWS
CTS
Red River
ADO
RAVEN
CREEK
RANCH
Fort
Worth
Crush
Waco
WILCOX
SCHOOL
Sabine River
Neches River
Trinity River
Colorado River
Brady
ROCKING P
RANCH
WILD HORSES
Brazos River
Austin
Mason
Fredericksburg
D-BAR-D
RANCH
Houston
Neu-Braunfels
Victoria
RUNNING M
RANCH
Carlshafen
GREAT PRAIRIE
GULF
OF
MEXICO

PROLOGUE

HOUSTON DAILY TELEGRAPH
March 3, 1875

We are able, thanks to a gentleman who was present, to define the deliberations that took place under the spreading branches of a live oak a little more definitely. Some unknown parties (many citizens probably) seized upon the five men who were suspected of being horse thieves, and succeeded in elevating three of the five, when the sheriff put in an appearance . . . So instead of five men being hung, only two were hung, and one was shot. For the sake of the reputation of Mason as a law-abiding community, we hope this correction will be made.

Mason County, Texas
August 1874

"Found not guilty of any wrongdoing. Praise the Lord." Derrick Denning lifted his cup of coffee in a mock salute to his wife, Leta. "As the Good Book says, 'Thou hast maintained my right and my cause.' Though I feel bad about the fines the other fellows have to pay."

The Denning family sat around the table enjoying a celebratory dinner in their cabin on the D-Bar-D Ranch. Young Ricky clapped his hands on the table, although he didn't know what they were celebrating. Leta looked into her husband's eyes over their son's head and smiled. The baby inside her stirred, as if contentedly joining in on the joy.

"I'll read up on that new law about transporting cattle over county lines before I go on any more cattle drives. Right and legal aren't always the same thing, and we want to be sure we stick on the side of the law."

"It's not right, the other men getting fined." Leta's brother Andy stopped shoveling beans into his mouth long enough to grumble. "They didn't do nothing wrong. The cattle belonged to Mr. Roberts and Mr. Thomas."

When her husband was arrested for helping M. B. Thomas and Allen Roberts take their cattle to Llano County from Mason County, the ordeal filled her with anguish. Local German cattlemen had accused both Thomas and Roberts of stealing cattle. In the court case, six of the cowhands were charged guilty and fined $25 a head. Yet the court dismissed Derrick's case due to insufficient evidence.

The German cattlemen had grumbled at the verdict. Tensions between Anglos and Germans already ran high, since German settlers had opposed seceding from the Union during the War Between the States. Now Mason County was full of cattle ranchers who were angry that justice for cattle stealing—real and supposed—was not being fulfilled through the law. German settlers and people native to Mason County alike were troubled.

Leta suppressed the niggling worry that threatened to destroy this night of celebration. God answered her prayers. Derrick was home. She and her family—Derrick, their son, and her brother Andy—could stay put in Mason County, Texas. They wouldn't have to move every year or two the way Pa had dragged them all over the map when she was a child.

Derrick set both his elbows on the table and crossed his arms, signaling he had an important announcement to make. He winked at Leta. "Since we're celebrating tonight, it's time we told you the news. Ricky, what do you think about being a big brother sometime this winter?"

Ricky stopped pushing beans around his plate. "I'm going to have a baby brother?"

"Or a sister." Leta touched the palm of her hand against her womb. "We won't know until the baby comes."

"I don't want to wait until later." Ricky clapped his hands together. "I want it now."

"I'm afraid you'll have to wait."

"Can I at least have him for a Christmas present?"

Andy snickered.

Leta hid a smile behind her napkin. "The baby might come around your birthday. How would you like that?"

Ricky shrugged his shoulders. "I guess it's all right. Say, Davey's dog had puppies. Can I have one?" Leta admired how much his smile looked like his father's. "Since I have to wait so long to have my brother?"

"Your father and I will talk about it."

"Maybe I can have a horse of my own, since I have to wait

for my niece or nephew." Andy lifted his eyebrows and put on his most innocent expression.

"That topic is already under discussion." Derrick grinned at his brother-in-law. "Today I'd like to give all of you the world, but I'd better wait and see what happens next."

Good, sensible, steady Derrick. The best husband in the world for Leta. God was so good.

When they retired to bed later, thunder rumbled. Leta snuggled close to Derrick. The raging storms that swept across the land from time to time frightened her, and she preferred the safety of her husband's arms.

Instead of subsiding, the rumble continued—constant, moving closer and closer. More like a . . . stampede. Derrick swung his legs over the side of the bed. He grabbed his gun and headed for the main room. Leta threw on her dressing gown and followed.

Ricky sat up on his elbows in his bed in the main room, rubbing his eyes and looking scared.

Derrick ran his hand over Ricky's soft curls. "Nothing to worry about, son; you lay back down."

The boy ducked his head under the sheets as instructed, but Leta didn't for a minute think he had gone to sleep.

The rumble grew louder, the distinct sound of hooves pounding the hard earth at full speed.

Andy climbed down from the loft, rifle in his hand. "Is something after the cattle?"

That was a definite possibility. The newly reinstituted Texas Rangers tried to keep Indians and Comancheros away from American holdings. Sometimes they were successful, sometimes they weren't.

Leta didn't like her brother heading out to fight off rustlers. She didn't like her husband going into danger, for that matter—but she knew he must. Derrick handed her a loaded rifle. She grasped it with both hands and started praying. Horses neared, almost too loud to speak. She dropped to a kneeling position beneath the window.

As Derrick reached for the front door, the hooves stopped moving, snorting and neighing punctuating the abrupt silence. Leta lifted her head a few inches to see out the windowpane. Dark, shadowy figures on horseback formed a semicircle around the front door. Of the cattle in the pen, she saw and heard no sign.

"Derrick Denning. Come out and face justice."

Leta tensed and waited for Derrick's response. He half turned the doorknob, then dropped his hand.

The speaker held up both hands. "Derrick Denning. I will not ask again. You have two choices. Either you hang;" he held up a rope tied into a noose. "Or we burn down your home." A light flared in the hand of one of the other riders, and the object in the leader's right hand burst into flame—a torch. "It's your choice."

Leta gasped and the rifle trembled in her hand. Shoot the man. The thought flew in and out of her mind. They were too many, she couldn't drive them all away before someone threw the firebrand onto the dry wood of their house. She wanted to grab Ricky and run for the door. But the only exit lay through the front door—in the direction of the men threatening to burn them down.

She chanced a glance to the side. Andy stood with his rifle on his shoulder, ready to shoot. Derrick motioned for him to put the gun down.

A pale face appeared over the edge of his blanket. No! Ricky must not see this! Leta motioned for her son to sneak back under the covers.

A deep sigh drew Leta's attention to her husband. Putting down the gun, he tied a white dish towel around his arm. He turned to Leta. "Take care of Ricky." Before she could protest, he opened the door and slammed it shut behind him.

The first-quarter moon provided little light, and clouds drifted across it like wisps of smoke. Light from the torch flickered, revealing Derrick's face in sharp contrast.

"Gentlemen, whatever is troubling you, surely we can settle this like reasonable men. I come out here in peace." Derrick pointed to the white band on his arm. "Unarmed."

Rough custom said no one would shoot an unarmed man any more than they would shoot a man in the back.

The men on horseback were shadows hovering just beyond the circle of light. Leta couldn't see the faces of the men threatening her husband. "Derrick Denning, the district court of Mason County found insufficient evidence against you to convict you of the theft of cattle." Listen to the voice. Leta strained her ears. It had to be someone they knew, someone from their small community. "However, the people of Mason County witnessed your crime firsthand, and we find it necessary to pronounce a true judgment."

Derrick took a step back, then straightened his shoulders and moved forward. "Get off your horse and face me like a man."

The leader handed the torch to the man on his right and the noose to the man on his left and jumped from the horse. He stood in the shadows.

"We the people of Mason County have examined the testimony against you. We have determined that you were indeed with A. G. Roberts on the date in question. That you did aid in the illegal transportation of cattle over the Mason County line without proper inspection. That you knew that the cattle in question in fact belonged to a local rancher."

"How can you say what happened? The only people there were the folks on trial today."

"You admit to the facts then?"

Leta heard the smiling threat in his voice, although she couldn't see it. The end of the noose dangled where she could see it in the flare of the torch.

"Having examined the evidence, we have determined that you are, both legally and morally, guilty of the crime of cattle rustling. And that your punishment will be death by hanging."

The man with the noose nudged his horse forward.

A long, long five minutes later, Leta slumped to the floor. Only then did she become aware of Ricky crouching beside her, staring in horror out the window.

NEAR VICTORIA, TEXAS
SEPTEMBER 1874

Buck Morgan reined in Blaze when he approached the familiar sign suspended over the entrance to the family ranch: "Running M Ranch, est. 1834." As far as he roamed, across Texas and farther west, into New Mexico and Arizona territories, he always pictured this place as home. His father had worked hard to build the Running M Ranch into the best horse ranch in all of Texas. Buck loved the quality Morgan horses the family raised, but he loved the freedom of the open range even more. When he reached his eighteenth birthday, he kicked the dust of the ranch off his heels, coming home for only short stretches of time since.

But Ma and Pa would want to hear his current news firsthand. He owed them that much.

He spurred Blaze, and the gelding trotted forward, easing into a gallop, as if he sensed he was headed home too. His gait ate up the distance to the big house, while Buck took note of changes to the ranch. In the distance, he spotted a group of riders bringing the horses in from the pasture for the night. He turned Blaze in that direction and the horse increased his speed, giving in to the desire to reach the head of the pack.

A lanky-bodied youth on the back of a roan-colored mare turned in Buck's direction. "Pa! Bert! Buck has come home." Buck's youngest brother, Jack, edged his mare out of the band and raced across the open space.

Buck reined Blaze in to a moderate pace and met his brother. "What did you do with my brother? He wasn't any taller than a cow's tail the last time I saw him."

Jack grinned. "It's good to see you too, Buck. Come on, let's head to the house. Ma will be so happy you're home. She'll be sending messages all across town."

Oma and Opa. Granny. Aunt Marion and Uncle Peter. Tante Alvie and her husband. His married sisters. Buck could be glad his other aunts and uncles and cousins lived scattered across Texas, or else they would've rented out all the guest rooms in Victoria.

Ma was working in the garden beside the house, probably getting it ready for the winter crop, when they approached. Her back was to him. Buck put a finger to his lips and slid off the horse as quiet as a cat.

"You're home early." The faintest trace of an accent pointed to Ma's German roots. She pulled up another weed before turning around. She dropped the weeds and the spade, her hand covering her mouth.

"Hi, Ma." Buck hugged her, surprised at how small and light the woman who had always been a tower of strength felt now that he was a grown man.

"Why didn't you write to say you were coming? How long are you staying?" Her eyes searched his, and he knew she was wishing he would stay put long enough to celebrate.

"I can stay about a week." A part of him wished he could deliver his news and ride out again in the morning, but Ma would never forgive him. He sniffed the air. "Is that rabbit stew I smell cooking? I haven't had a good bowl since the last time I was home."

"And a good *Gewuerzgurken* to go with it." Ma's laughter was as light as the clouds floating overhead.

Pa, his middle brother Drew, and the ranch hands arrived, and Buck found himself the center of attention.

He didn't get any time alone with his parents until the following morning.

"Your ma tells me you're not here to stay." Pa's lips thinned. Buck's father wanted his eldest to follow in the family tradition of managing the Running M. Buck knew his reluctance still baffled his father.

"No, sir. I'm doing something I think you'll agree is important. You could say it's in my blood, since my grandpa died fighting for Texas."

"You're joining the army." Fear enlarged Ma's eyes.

"No, Ma, not since the War Between the States ended." Buck was disappointed when the war ended months before his eighteenth birthday. He had a thirst for freedom and adventure that life on the ranch couldn't satisfy. "I don't know if you heard tell that they've started up the Texas Rangers again."

Pa slowly nodded his head. "To protect the frontier and to keep law and order, the papers say."

"They need people used to Indian ways, who can ride horses as good as any Indian. All my years here on the ranch taught me that. And I even speak some Comanche." Years ago, his aunt Billie was held captive by Indians and learned the language. Buck begged Aunt Billie to speak the language to him every time he saw her, finding the strange sounds a challenge. He spoke well enough to get by.

"You're going to be a Texas Ranger." Ma looked nearly as scared as she had at the thought of him joining the army.

"Which company are you joining? One of the frontier battalions or the Special Force?"

Buck shrugged. "Major Jones isn't sure where to put me. My experience with the Comanche would come in real handy with the frontier companies. Then again, he can see someone who speaks Spanish and German being valuable in the Special Force."

"German." Ma's voice dropped. "Will they send you to the land the German Verein settled, up in the hill country? Mason County? Your uncle Georg has written of their troubles."

"I don't know." Buck wished Ma wouldn't worry so. "They might."

CHAPTER ONE

GALVESTON NEWS
January 23, 1879

But the "Hoodoos," as the gallant Hall and his rangers were called, came. They came several times, and placed themselves before the public by acts, entitling them to the gratitude of Texas.

MASON COUNTY, TEXAS
AUGUST, 1875

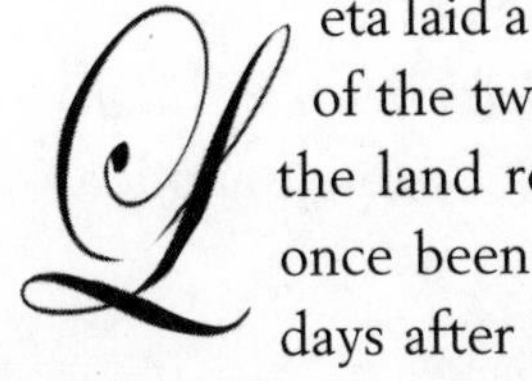

Leta laid a bouquet of sunflowers and daisies on top of the two graves in the family plot. How quickly the land revived; grass already covered what had once been two mounds of stark brown dirt. Only days after her husband's murder, their baby joined him in the ground, expelled from her womb. That second loss magnified the first. Not only had she lost her husband, but she also lost his final living legacy.

Leta let the tears fall. Andy was busy giving Ricky a lesson in roping a calf. Without her brother, she didn't know how she would've survived the past year. Poor Andy—only seventeen, too young to be the man of the house.

I'll plant a rosebush here, or maybe lilacs. Leta's dead baby girl would've loved the smell of lilacs in the spring. Her daddy promised Leta she could plant flowers on all four sides of the house, if she wanted. Cascading tears blinded her, and she crumpled on the ground, balling her apron against her eyes. If only the cotton could absorb the pain with the tears.

Her tears didn't last long. They never did. Anger and a thirst for justice followed on the heels of her tears as surely as sun followed rain. Someday, she would learn which men murdered not only her husband, but also her unborn child. They would receive justice, even if that meant returning the rough, Texas-style justice they had meted out to Derrick. She only wanted to be sure of the identity of the mob, especially the ringleader. They had killed an innocent man. She wouldn't make the same mistake.

When she wanted to run around Mason County, asking questions and demanding answers, she thought of her family. Nightmares still woke Ricky in the middle of the night, and Andy alternated between trying to take a man's place on the ranch and escaping for days at a time. If she rushed things, took unnecessary risks, she could endanger herself or worse, and then they'd be alone. She wouldn't do that, not after her own parents had died and left her and Andy alone.

The sun overhead was hot enough to dry her tears on her cheeks. It must be almost noon. Stopping by the pump long enough to wet her face, Leta headed inside to prepare the midday meal.

Buck Morgan reined in his horse, Blaze, a chestnut Morgan gelding with a white star on his nose. Below his vantage point from a hundred yards away, a woman lay prostrate on the ground inside a fenced-in burial plot. Buck considered the task Major Jones had set before him. Talk with the widow. See if she knew anything more than what was reported. Find out if she can identify the men who killed her husband. If she could, she might be too scared to say so. Buck knew she might need protection in case she found herself next in line for the mob's rough justice.

After swallowing water from his canteen, he moved Blaze forward for a better view of the tiny graveyard. Two crosses. The report he'd received only indicated one death. The woman stood up and headed for the house. She'd had her private time to grieve, and now Buck could do his job. He spurred Blaze and headed for the ranch house.

Buck scanned the landscape as he approached the house. Everywhere he saw signs of neglect. An enthusiastic bull had rammed into a fence, creating a hole wide enough for his horse to ride through. Growing up on his parents' horse ranch, he knew what it took to run a successful operation. The widow Denning wasn't managing very well on her own.

Blaze entered into the yard, and Buck slid off his back. The horse stood quietly, ground tied, like all good Morgan horses were trained to do. He heard the sound of someone chambering a round into a rifle and froze.

"Turn around real slow and keep your hands where I can see them."

The widow Denning wasn't as helpless as Buck had

assumed. He could fire the Colt pistol still in his holster before she got off a shot, but he didn't want to frighten her. He raised his hands in the air and slowly turned around. Slumping his shoulders to lessen his height, he addressed himself to a spot near her feet. "The name is Buck Morgan, ma'am. I'm one of the Texas Rangers."

Brown eyes swept over him from the top of his rolled-brim hat to the toes of his well-worn boots. He had a feeling she could identify what kind of weapons he carried, what caliber of bullets they used, and how many he had with him. Not much escaped that look.

Her rifle didn't waver. "Do you have any proof you're a Ranger?"

Proof? Most of the time the only proof a Ranger needed came at the end of a gun. But this woman was wily and smart. "I'm getting your proof." He put his palm out to advise her of the peacefulness of his gesture before reaching into the pocket of his vest and pulling out a much-creased piece of paper. "Here's the letter straight from Governor Coke, sending us out here to Mason to look into the bit of trouble you've been having lately."

"Bit of trouble? Is that what you call it?" Mrs. Denning snorted but lowered her gun. "You must be hungry and thirsty. Come on in. I'm about to fix lunch for me and the boys."

Boys? Ranch hands or children? If they were ranch hands, they were taking advantage of their employer. Buck removed his hat and ducked his head as he walked into the house. The simple cabin consisted of one large room, a stove in one corner, and blankets hiding the sleeping quarters at the back. Either Denning had been new to Mason County, or he'd been lazy, to not have built a better home for his family. With all the accusations flying about, Buck had to examine all the facts impartially.

"Do you want water or coffee?" Mrs. Denning lifted the top

off the coffee pot and wrinkled her nose. "I'll make a fresh pot."

"There's no need. I like my coffee strong." He reached for an enamel cup resting on the shelf over the sink and poured it out for himself. The kitchen was pin-neat, not a smidgen of dirt anywhere. If anyone was lazy in the Denning household, it wasn't Mrs. Denning.

Beans simmered on the stove, but she slipped outside and returned with a ham hock. Too much. He wandered next to her and took a deep breath. "Frijoles with a bit of jump to them. I haven't had a good plate of beans since the last time I was down McAllen way. I could fill up fast on a bowl or two."

She paused, knife poised over the ham hock. "Sure I can't interest you in a ham sandwich?"

"Beans will do me just fine." With a side of sauerkraut they'd be even better, but he doubted that Leta knew the German recipe.

"I bet you won't object to some fresh cornbread." She put the meat back in the corner and took out the makings for cornbread. It took her only a few minutes to whip it up and slip the pan into the oven.

Voices and a horse's snorts came from outside. "And here they come." A ghost of the warrior who had met him in the yard returned to her face. "I don't want to talk about . . . whatever you came here to discuss . . . while we're eating. My family has been through too much as it is."

Buck thought about Captain Roberts waiting back at the Ranger camp. He would prefer a complete and accurate report rather than one taken in haste. He nodded. "I can wait."

Mrs. Denning returned to the genial hostess with his nod and took bowls down from the shelf as the door swung open.

Two people entered, one a youth of seventeen or so who

was still all arms and legs. In front of him came a boy of five or six, thin with big brown eyes that stared at the stranger in the house in one wide-eyed glance. "Who are you?" He put his fists at his waist, achieving a fine stance. Buck could hardly keep his lips from twitching.

The young man behind him had a rifle held flat against his side. His hand was on the action, ready to raise it to his shoulder and fire it in one single fluid motion. This young man had all the attitude of an outlaw in the making—or a Texas Ranger. Something about the set of his eyes and his shoulders looked like Mrs. Denning. She had said "family." Her brother?

"Leta, is this fella bothering you?" His voice ground out low.

"Not at all." Her eyes flashed at Buck with a warning against what—naming his occupation? She pulled the cornbread out of the oven. "He was passing by, and I invited him in for a bite to eat. Come in and join us."

The boy dropped his arms and took a spot at the table. "I'm Ricky. Is that your horse in the yard? I like him. What's your name?"

That's what Buck thought he said, but the words all ran together as he slurped down a tall glass of water.

"Andy, put that rifle away and join us at the table."

Buck watched with amusement as the kid placed the weapon on the hearth, within easy reach. Not that he blamed him. Add the constant threat from Mexicans and Indians rustling cattle with the trouble this family had already endured, and no wonder they were jump-happy when a strange man showed up at the door.

Buck didn't say much during the meal, content to listen to the stream of questions and information pouring from the boy. He asked dozens of questions about Blaze, almost as if he knew something about horse ranching.

Buck answered the boy's questions about the horse, slipping into a role he had abandoned when he became a Texas Ranger. "Blaze is a Morgan horse." Mrs. Denning raised an eyebrow at the name but made no comment.

Mrs. Denning slipped a second bowl of beans in front of him before his spoon hit the bottom of the first. They tasted as good as they smelled. Andy said even less than Buck did over the meal.

"Can I go back out with Andy this afternoon?" Ricky's tone suggested he made the same request every day, without success.

"For today, yes, you may." Mrs. Denning flicked her glance at Buck.

Andy nodded an acknowledgment, grabbed the rifle, and closed the door behind them. Mrs. Denning busied herself fixing a fresh pot of coffee until the boys' voices faded in the distance.

"So it took the death of that German Henry Doell to get the attention of the Texas Rangers." Anger laced Mrs. Denning's words.

CHAPTER TWO

The notorious murderer Scott Cooley having at one time been a member of the [Ranger] company had many friends among the men who were in sympathy with him and his party.

Letter from Major John B. Jones
to Adjutant General William Steele,
October 23, 1875

"Although I'm a little surprised you showed up. Isn't Scott Cooley a Ranger?" As soon as Leta uttered the words, she regretted them. She didn't want to alienate this man.

"A former Ranger." The ranger's lips thinned in a straight line. The man didn't use any surplus words. "God doesn't ask a man's affiliation at the Pearly Gates. I try to do the same." He allowed a hint of a smile to lighten his face, a glimpse of life and humor reflecting an honorable man. "I can't make the clock turn back to last August. But since I'm here now, I want to bring your husband's murderers to justice." He was a dangerous man to cross—someone she wanted on her side.

"So you agree that it was murder." Leta twisted the strings of her apron, so she grabbed the shirt she was mending for Andy instead. "Some folks hereabouts say he got what he deserved after the court found him not guilty."

His blue eyes pierced her, threatening her peace. "Sit down, will you?" she said. "You make me all nervous when you tower over me like that."

Again, he showed that flash of a smile, sitting down in a chair barely big enough to hold his large frame. "Some feel that way."

"He didn't do anything wrong, you know. He was just helping out a friend and making a few dollars in the process. If he had known how things would turn out—" She stopped. Why state the obvious? Of course he wouldn't have taken the job if he'd known he'd end up dead.

"I'm more interested in what happened when they came for him. I know it was nighttime, but how late?"

"I've already told all of this so many times, I could recite it from memory. Not that Sheriff Clark has any interest in bringing the killers to justice. For all I know, he was one of the men in the mob." Once again Leta found her tongue running away with her. Accusing the sitting sheriff of involvement with the mob wasn't likely to win over a fellow lawman.

The Ranger didn't react. Instead, he asked about the time of day, the smells, sounds, sights, of the hours imprinted on her memory. He came at the question of "Did you recognize anyone?" a dozen different ways, but nothing clicked. She only remembered figures dressed like cattlemen, most of them with their faces covered, hidden by the shadows of the dark night.

"Did you recognize their voices?"

"Just the one man spoke. I didn't recognize his voice, but that's not surprising. I couldn't tell you many folks in town. The preacher, maybe."

"Was there anything distinctive about their voices?"

Like a German accent. The words hung unspoken in the air.

"I only heard the one man. He sounded . . . ordinary. Like everybody else from around here." She thought about saying "not German," but this quiet man might take that the wrong way. Besides, accents or not, the German mob had to be behind Derrick's murder. They're the ones who had gone after the rest of Roberts's men.

The man leaned forward and cupped his hands between his knees, staring at her. "There's something you're not telling me."

"I've told you everything." Even things she had forgotten. "Why would I hide anything? They killed my husband."

"Maybe it's not something you know. Maybe you suspect something." Those eyes cut through her defenses.

"If I make accusations without proof, I'm no better than they were." She'd keep her suspicions to herself. And if she ever knew for sure, she'd decide how she wanted to act. She didn't know if she wanted to depend on a company of Rangers who didn't seem all that committed to finding the real killers.

"That's a noble sentiment, Mrs. Denning." The man dusted his hat on the knees of his waist overalls and stood. "Thank you for your time. Mind if I come back if I think of any more questions?"

She nodded. "Or if you learn anything new. I'd like to know." She watched the Ranger leave the house and climb on the back of his horse. Leta surely admired the horse, and the horse tossed his neck and snorted as if he knew it.

"Ranger Morgan."

He pulled on the horse's reins to keep him from moving. "The Morgan horse—are you kin to those Morgans?"

The smile she had seen earlier came back out and played awhile. "All that matters is that I'm a Texas Ranger, ma'am." He tipped his hat, and his horse trotted across the rise in the direction of the family's burial plot.

Buck didn't head back to his uncle's farm right away, which was his headquarters as long as he was in Mason. Instead, Buck rode in the direction he had seen the boys head after dinner. He spotted the herd before he saw the boys. The little guy disappeared among the steers and cows.

From the top of a rise, he could make out the action with clarity. The boys rode among the cattle, the younger one throwing a loop in the direction of a calf, but not reaching it. Overall, the herd was small, small enough that Mrs. Denning must think a youth of seventeen and a child could manage them. Even if they sold the small herd, they wouldn't make enough money. The family couldn't manage the animals and take care of the ranch. They needed help.

Buck's anger burned against Derrick Denning. What kind of man left his wife little more than destitute? But other forces could be at work. Rustlers—be they Mexican, Indian, or someone closer to home—would find rich pickings at the defense-poor D-Bar-D Ranch. Buck was in Mason County to establish peace and find justice for the dead man if possible. Maybe he could make a difference for his family as well. God mandated taking care of widows and orphans; Buck felt obligated.

Mrs. Denning wouldn't be pleased with his interference; he might have to act in secret. For now, he'd take the long ride back to his uncle's house to think about his conversation with Mrs. Denning. Surely she wouldn't try to go after the mob herself. No one, no woman, would be that foolish.

The long August day was turning to twilight by the time he reached Onkel Georg's spread, the Lazy F Ranch. Brushing down Blaze, he admired the clean organization of the stable. Hard work, careful planning, and family effort—he had learned all of that and more from his mother's family.

In the bunkhouse next to the barn, he heard the gentle consonants and soft curses of his mother's native German, as well as a phrase or two in Spanish and Comanche. His fluency in four languages made him invaluable to the Rangers. He could blend into almost any group he joined up with; more than once, he'd fooled them by speaking their language like a native. But the only secrets he heard from the bunkhouse now were the chances of getting rain the next day—the general opinion was not good.

He stopped by the pump to wash up and smelled bratwurst and sauerkraut through the open kitchen window. Tante Ertha was fixing all his favorite German dishes. She didn't seem to think the Rangers fed him well enough.

"William! We weren't sure if you were going to make it back tonight." Onkel Georg clapped him on the back. "Any luck today?"

"It's Buck." Buck didn't like his birth name. It was given in honor of his grandfather who died in the Texas War for Independence from Mexico. He was also named after his aunt Billie, who survived years in Indian captivity. He latched onto the name Buck as soon as he broke his first bronco.

"You may be Buck to the rest of the world, but to us, you'll always be William." At least Onkel Georg didn't call him "Wilhelm," the way his opa Fleischer tended to do. "And call me George, not Georg." His uncle Americanized both his names after his move to Mason, transforming Georg into George and Fleischer into Fletcher. His pale skin, which burned before turning brown, and his graying blond hair, gave away his German roots before he spoke with his distinct German accent. "So. Today?"

Buck didn't care to reveal too much about his activities in Mason County, and not all his reasons stemmed from his taciturn nature. He shrugged his shoulders. "Not much."

"Come over here and say hello to your cousin."

Buck studied his cousin, who was his same age, same height, and of similar build. Henry Fletcher. They had spent a lot of time together when they were very young, but they had grown apart in the years since the move. He hoped they could reconnect—if it didn't interfere with the job.

"I heard you were headed over to the Denning ranch this morning. Did she have anything interesting to say?" Buck could feel both George and his cousin watching him.

"I make my reports to Captain Roberts." Buck hung his hat by the door. "You'll hear about it when the rest of the county does."

Henry opened the door, and they followed the odors of the meal simmering on the stove to the kitchen. A babble of voices greeted them. God had blessed the Fletcher family. Henry had three sisters—two married, one still at home—before he got the brother he wanted—Fred, the baby of the family. Henry had married five years ago and now with their two children, they filled every spot at the kitchen table.

Tante Ertha's face glistened where she tended the pans on the stove. Buck kissed her on the cheek. "It smells wonderful. Just like home."

A few minutes later, Onkel Georg said grace and the family tucked into the feast his wife had prepared.

"Your family is doing well." Buck played a game of peek-a-boo with Henry's youngest, a girl named Beth. "I always have more cousins to meet when I come to visit."

Henry's wife Lisel blushed at the statement, but Henry grinned. "We are expecting another baby early next year."

"Congratulations, cousin."

"The family is doing well, but the ranch has had problems. It's these rustlers."

"I thought the Indian problem had gotten better." Buck smiled to hide any of his thoughts from showing. "The Rangers have been hard at work protecting the good citizens of Texas."

"It's not the Indians who are causing the problem. It's these mavericks who steal the yearlings before they're branded, and the nonresident stockmen who don't even live here but try to run their cattle out of our county." Henry dug his fork into his plate.

Buck could see Henry looking at him from underneath his lowered eyelids, gauging his reaction. "But I thought that's how Onkel Georg built up his herd. He was a maverick too. It's not illegal." Fred scowled openly. Henry's face was impassive.

"Things were different then," Onkel Georg said. "I took some of their yearlings, they took some of mine. It all worked out."

Buck wouldn't argue the point. "The new stock law is meant to make things more fair, but it sounds like it's been impossible to keep. Even for people who have no intention of breaking any laws." He cut off a chunk of bratwurst and chewed. "People like those two men accused of cattle rustling last fall, Thomas and Roberts, from what I hear." Henry's eyes were cold. "I'd be careful who you say that to, Cousin Buck. Any impartial jury would have found those two Anglos guilty of cattle rustling last year, not to mention the people who were helping them. It is all right to say it here, among family. But some of our neighbors would disagree with you."

Buck nodded. "That's what the Rangers are here to sort out."

CHAPTER THREE

News came this morning that someone fired into a camp near Tom Gamel's and killed a Mr. Doell and wounded a young Mr. Keller in the foot.

Lucia Holmes's diary, July 21, 1875

When's Uncle Andy coming back?" Ricky pushed the beans around on his plate. "I don't want beans. I'm tired of beans."

Leta sighed. She was tired of beans too, but they filled the stomach. She stood and reached for the shelf where she kept her scant cooking supplies. A beehive on their property provided them sweet honey. She didn't use it often, but tonight was one of those times.

"Here, soak up the beans with your cornbread. And you can have a second piece of cornbread with honey."

His eyes widening, Ricky poured the honey on thick. "When is Uncle Andy coming home?" He repeated his question around a mouthful of food.

Leta was hoping he'd forget the question; she didn't know the answer. Andy disappeared from time to time. No wonder she couldn't keep up with the ranch. "He'll be back in a day or two, you'll see. He promised he'd take you fishing before you start school, didn't he?"

"Yeah, he did." Ricky wolfed down the rest of the beans, his concern about his uncle forgotten. Leta wished she could let it go as easily as her son. In spite of her desire for Andy to stay clear away from the blood feud erupting across the county, she suspected he sought out Cooley or his cronies.

The Ranger. Leta's thoughts strayed to Buck Morgan. Her heart had smiled at the sight of a man at the table, putting away a healthy portion of her special beans until he sat back, appetite satisfied. The man said he wanted to bring Derrick's killers to justice. She was inclined to believe him.

She needed to find out what had happened in town in recent days. As far as she knew, the last killing happened a little more than two weeks ago, when Henry Doell was shot. People didn't seem convinced his death had anything to do with the feud sparked by the trial for cattle rustling last fall, however. Come Saturday, she'd head to town for a few supplies and some contact with her neighbors. She hoped no gunfire would erupt while she went about her business.

Ricky didn't speak again until he finished his cornbread and took a second piece. "Do you think Mr. Morgan will come back?"

I hope so. Leta's reaction surprised her. After Derrick's death, with no one she could trust, she had stayed clear of all the men in town for fear of making new enemies. When she lost a few head of cattle, as happened from time to time, she swallowed the loss. Sheriff Clark wouldn't have acted on her complaint, even if she'd made one. She just trusted God to help them make it through another season. Sometimes it took everything she had to trust God for another day.

"I suspect he will," Leta said.

"Good." Ricky grinned. "I liked him."

His enthusiasm brought a smile to Leta's face. Ever since Derrick's death, Ricky hung back around strangers. She worried he would have trouble adjusting when he started school next month.

"He promised to give me a ride on his horse."

He had? Leta had missed that exchange. "That's good. You'll need to ride a horse when you start school."

Ricky blinked his eyes rapidly, a sure sign her words had upset him. "I don't want to go to school, Ma."

Leta suppressed a sigh. She had guessed at his hesitation before, but this was the first time he had put it into words. "You have to go to school. To learn how to read and do your sums. And so much more."

"But I already know my letters. You can teach me at home. Besides, Andy hasn't gone to school for forever. He says school is for girls."

He does, does he? For Andy, the statement represented a defense as much as a statement of opinion. Their family's frequent moves put him so far behind in school that he had to sit with the little kids when they moved to Mason County. He refused this humiliation, and Leta didn't have the heart to make him go. Instead, she tried to teach him at home, but Andy would escape outside more often than not.

But that didn't mean Ricky had to suffer the same fate. "Your daddy went to school, and he was a brave man."

Ricky pushed the now-empty plate away. Eyes fixed on the table, he said, "But what if those bad men are in town?"

"Those bad men aren't looking for boys in school who are learning their ABCs." She prayed it was so. "You did such a good job with supper. Do you want to go out and play with Big Red?"

The one living creature that could bring Ricky out of his

fear spells was Big Red—named because he was in fact so very tiny when they got him as a puppy a few weeks after Derrick's death. Still a half-gangly puppy, the dog now stood as high as Ricky's shoulders and was still growing. He had all the makings of a good watchdog.

Ricky should his head. "I want to stay inside."

Oh, dear. Leta knew they were in for a bad night. Make that a very bad night. Thunderclouds were rolling in.

Ricky lay down peaceably enough, but with the first crash of thunder, he cried out. "Mama!"

"Coming." Leta stood from the table where she was reading her Bible. Soft claws scratched at the door, and she let Big Red in. The dog was dusty but not wet, and when he dashed for Ricky's bed, she didn't stop him. She sat on Ricky's other side. Lightning zigzagged through the sky and thunder rolled. Ricky shuddered against her, and Big Red barked at the noise. She resigned herself to waiting out the storm. Words of reason and faith did little to calm Ricky at times like this.

Thunder stopped clashing for a good thirty minutes before Leta laid Ricky against the pillow, certain he had relaxed enough to sleep. Big Red scooted against his side, his gentle brown eyes promising her he would take care of her boy, no matter what.

"I know you will." She scratched his head and then put away her Bible before retiring to her own bed.

Back home in Victoria, on the flat land near the Gulf, thunder like this would send a band of Pa's prized horses into a stampede. Here in a small valley in the hill country of central Texas, the booms bounced off one hill and echoed from another, so that the first round of thunder didn't end before the next began. Thunder didn't scare Buck, but he didn't know how a deaf mule could sleep through the racket.

At least Buck wanted to blame his sleeplessness on the thunderstorm, and not on his troubling visit to the Denning ranch that afternoon. Leta Denning was some woman. It took gumption to run a ranch in the best of circumstances, let alone after a murdering mob had killed her husband in front of her entire family. And over what? A neighbor helping his friends found innocent of a confusing law?

Leta wasn't the only woman widowed by recent events. *Lord, use me and the other Rangers to restore peace and order to this troubled patch of Texas.* Thunder crashed, an exclamation point to his prayer. "Thanks for the answer." Buck's pa said he sometimes did his best praying on horseback. Buck substituted a thunderstorm for a horse. If he had to be awake, he couldn't think of any better way to pass the time.

Sometime past the dead of night the storm passed, and Buck lay on the bed his uncle provided for him, dead asleep. He woke up at the time he needed to, glad it was a Sunday morning without pressing Ranger business to take him away from worship of the Lord. Donning his cleanest clothes, he headed down to the kitchen, Bible in hand.

Tante Ertha smiled when he entered the kitchen. "Good. You are still here. Did the storm bother you last night?" Gray flecks appeared in his aunt's once-red hair, but enough original color remained to look like a cloud of fire around her round face.

Buck shook his head. Onkel Georg came in, scraping his feet at the door from the muck accumulated in morning chores. That was one aspect of ranch life Buck didn't miss at all. "I thought you might be gone this morning, but I saw Blaze in his stall. Do you have Ranger business today?" His uncle's steady blue eyes challenged him.

"No business today except the Lord's."

Tante Ertha clapped her hands. "So you are coming with us to church, then. I am so pleased." She winked. "There are several young frauleins who would love to meet you."

Buck laughed. "You sound like my mother."

"Now, Ertha. Leave him be." Onkel Georg grabbed a biscuit and popped it in his mouth. "Although by the time I was your age, I was married with three young ones already."

Later, during the service, Buck relaxed in familiar ebb and flow of the largely German congregation. The spoken Word washed over him like the refreshing rain of the night before. Reading the Bible gave a man the strength he needed day by day. But he cherished the times he got to listen to a preacher man, few and far between as they had been over the past few years. God always found a way to poke a needle in a sore spot that needed attention during the sermon.

"If you see someone in need and don't stop to help, how are you any better than the Levite who passed the man by?"

Leta Denning's image flashed behind Buck's eyelids. *God, I'm willing to help, but how?*

During prayer, the pastor led in a plea for peace and protection. The concern sounded immediate, more than the unrest hovering over the county. *It's the Lord's Day. Come back tomorrow,* he thought. But Buck's conscience wouldn't let him wait. If the pastor knew of a threat to the peace of the county, Buck had to find out. He waited until the church emptied before approaching him. "Preacher?"

The pastor stopped. "I saw you in the service today sitting with the Fletchers. Welcome to our church. My name is Johann Stricker." He extended his hand in welcome.

Buck nodded. "George Fletcher is my mother's brother. I'm Buck Morgan." He paused but he might as well say the rest. "I'm a Texas Ranger."

"Ah. A Ranger. Would your Tante Ertha be willing for us

to borrow you for the afternoon? Please say you'll join my wife and me for dinner."

After everything was settled with Buck's family, Reverend Stricker took him to the parsonage for a hearty Sunday dinner, plenteous portions of plain food. Not one word about the feud came up during the conversation around the table. Instead, the pastor prodded Buck about his journey of faith.

Touched that this man of God found the destiny of his soul more important than peace in the present, Buck slipped the Bible out of his coat and handed it over to the pastor. "My parents gave me that Bible right after I asked Jesus to be my Savior. It goes with me everywhere I go."

"The English version authorized by King James." He turned to the gospel of John and found the third chapter. "Read this verse to me, please." He pointed to verse sixteen.

Buck cleared his throat. "For God so loved the world, that He gave His only begotten Son, that whosoever believeth in Him shall not perish, but have everlasting life."

"'Also hat Gott die Welt geliebt.' God's love is beautiful, whatever language we speak it in, is it not?"

Buck chewed a chunk of bratwurst. "Sometimes hate drowns out the message of God's love for a while."

Stricker waved his hands in a circular motion that took in the children gathered around the table. "We will talk of that later. For now we will rejoice in the goodness of the Lord."

Buck nodded his acceptance.

CHAPTER FOUR

GALVESTON NEWS
August 4, 1875

Our grand jury, composed of a fine and intelligent body of men, seemed to make pretty thorough investigations of offenses against the public peace and good order, but found no more than eight or ten indictments after five days inquest.

After the meal, Stricker led him into a room with a bookcase filled floor to ceiling with well-worn books. Buck took a seat in a Biedermeier chair, sturdy workmanship he recognized as the same style favored by German furniture makers in Victoria.

"I wish we did not need to speak of this hoodoo war at all."

Stricker looked out the window at the clear summer sky. "I pray that last night's rainstorm has washed away the anger building up in our town."

"That is my prayer as well. But you don't think it has."

Stricker didn't respond directly. "Hoodoo. I should not use the word. It means bad luck, or what brings it. What is happening here is not a result of bad luck, but of willful violence, much of it among the people of my congregation." He sank into the chair behind the desk.

Probably some of the people singing so lustily in the service this morning were involved in the murder of Tim Williamson among others—perhaps even Derrick Denning. At another time, with someone else, Buck would've asked. But he wouldn't ask a pastor to betray his own people. He waited for what the pastor would say.

"I appreciate your—delicacy—in not asking to whom I refer." The man's face sagged, and he aged. "May I ask you a question?"

Buck nodded. "I'll answer, if I can."

"Do you know Scott Cooley?"

Ah. The former Ranger. "By reputation only. They say he was a fine officer; he only left the Rangers because the governor cut back on the numbers."

"I have heard the same. But sometimes the death of a friend changes a man."

A friend such as Tim Williamson. But again Buck didn't want to put words in the preacher's mouth.

"I have heard he is seeking revenge against anyone involved in the murder of Tim Williamson. That was a terrible day." He shook his head. "I thought I had seen every inhumanity possible during the War Between the States. But then Mr. Williamson was ambushed and murdered. The men tried to hide their identities by blackening their faces."

Buck cleared his throat. "That's what I heard." He waited for what else the pastor had to say. Williamson's death, as terrible as it was, was almost three months in the past.

"They say Cooley has returned to the county. I fear for our people. For the people of my congregation, yes, but also for all the people of Mason. Of what further violence might do to us."

Cooley was back in Mason County? That was troublesome news. Buck waited a bit to see if the pastor had anything further to say, but he didn't. Suppressing a sigh at the loss of a peaceful Lord's Day, he stood. "I'll inform Captain Roberts that Cooley is back in the area. We'll bring him in and warn him against taking the law into his own hands."

"Will you?" The pastor's bright eyes bore into his. "I pray it will be that easy."

So do I, Buck thought as he climbed on Blaze's back and headed for the Ranger encampment. *So do I.*

After the morning service, Henry Fletcher saw Reverend Stricker take Buck aside. How much the pastor knew, no one could tell for certain. The pastor hadn't participated in any of the revenge killings of the past few months, but he knew enough to get a lot of people into trouble.

"So that's your cousin, the Ranger." Johannes Schmidt spoke in a low voice meant for Henry's ears only.

Henry nodded.

"Is he a friend of Cooley?"

"This isn't the place to discuss that question." Lisel beckoned for Henry to join her at the waiting wagon.

"Come to my place tonight, then. Don't come alone."

"I'll do that." Henry donned the hat he had removed during the service and rode home with his family. By the time they had finished evening chores hours later, Buck still had not returned to the house. Taking care of Ranger business—but what? Unease rippled down Henry's back. So far, the Rangers hadn't demonstrated support for the Germans' cry for help when Scott Cooley set out to get justice for his dead friend. He didn't know his cousin Buck well enough to count on his help.

He saddled his horse—a Morgan mare—and caught up with his father before he went in for supper.

"You're headed out?" Concern creased his father's face. "I don't think that's wise."

"I'm taking Jeff with me. We'll be careful."

Pa's cool blue eyes settled on his eldest son. He placed his hand on his shoulder. "You must do as God leads you. Only be sure it is God's voice you are listening to."

"I will do what I must to protect this family." It was a familiar argument. "If Buck returns this evening, don't tell him where I have gone."

"How can I?" A ghost of a smile played around his father's lips. "You haven't told me."

Henry and Jeff rode hard for about forty-five minutes to reach Schmidt's ranch, in the far corner of the county. Horses crowded along the porch rail. He went to the door, ready to give the knock in the prescribed manner, but before he could, it opened. "Come in. We're nearly all here."

Henry removed his hat and followed Schmidt into the room. Members of the German community filled all the chairs and leaned against the walls. A few had taken a seat on the floor. The August heat was oppressive in the crowded room, in spite of the stone walls that usually kept the room cool in the summer and freezing in the winter. Henry wiped his bandanna across his forehead. Several men nodded a greeting.

"Don't know that it's a good idea for you to be here, Henry.

Your cousin is one of them Rangers." Adolph Hinke spoke from the chair by the fireplace.

"Henry is here at my invitation." Schmidt spoke with authority. "It might be valuable to have someone close to the Rangers in our midst. We will discuss that later."

After the remaining stragglers arrived, Schmidt called the meeting to order. "I know several of us hoped the worst was behind us when no violence marred the end of the court session last month."

Nods indicated the men's agreement.

"What about Henry Doell's death?" Hinke challenged. "He was a good man."

"That was a regrettable but unrelated incident," John answered. "But the latest news is cause for alarm. I have a confirmed sighting of Scott Cooley back in Mason County."

Around Henry, the men shifted uneasily. "Was he here when Doell was killed?"

Henry couldn't see the speaker.

Schmidt shook his head. "I don't think so. But we need to be extra careful. Some of us more than others."

Henry sent up a word of thanks that he had been absent when Williamson had met his maker. Cooley had no reason to come after him. Unless he was misinformed . . . Reason didn't make a difference with what was going on in Mason County.

"Fletcher?"

Henry blinked. "Yes?"

"Any ideas of what is happening with the Rangers?"

He shook his head. "My cousin keeps his own counsel."

"Be careful what you say to him."

"He could be a valuable resource to us. His mother is my father's sister. He understands better than you think. I don't think he'll assume Cooley is in the right just because he used to be a Ranger."

"I wouldn't count on that." Hinke scowled. "He's only half German, after all."

Henry stared down the accusatory stares. But the warning had been delivered—no doubt about it.

His only question was, should he tell his cousin?

Leta woke up earlier than usual on Monday morning and slipped out to the barn to see if Andy had bedded down with the animals rather than disturb her rest in the night. But she found no sign of his presence. Only Daisy and Elsie, the milk cows, and the two horses remaining after Andy had taken the gelding, greeted her early entrance with gentle snorts and lowing.

She looked at the rafters overhead. "Sorry I'm not doing a better job of taking care of him, Ma." She had breathed easier when the last court session came and went without Andy taking off. But now he had disappeared, again. When he did this, he claimed he was off checking on the herd. Leta didn't believe him, but aside from chaining him to the bedposts, she didn't see how she could keep him at home.

Maybe she should refuse to let him come back. If Andy thought he was old enough to wander around on his own, maybe he didn't need the security of knowing he could always come home. Showing up and taking off made a bad impression on Ricky. As it was, he didn't want to go to school, "just like Uncle Andy."

But neither could Leta shut the door on her brother, her only remaining family. She had promised her mother on her deathbed to take care of her brother. Part of Derrick's appeal lay in his stability, his ability to provide a normal home for her family. Normal, that was, until Derrick died. This local war had not only robbed her of her husband, but also of the dream she had harbored for a small place to call her own. If only she could identify the men responsible for Derrick's death.

Worrying about Andy wouldn't get the day's chores done. Grabbing the tin pail, she milked Daisy, emptied the fresh cream into a crock, and then took care of Elsie. After pouring all but a small amount for breakfast into the crock, she balanced it in her arms and carried it to the cold spring.

A yawning Ricky was pulling on his waist overalls when Leta reentered the cabin. "Where's Uncle Andy?"

"He's still gone. So it's just you and me today. It's time I get out there and count the cattle."

Ricky buried his face in the frothy cream. When he lifted his face, he had a white beard. "That's boring."

"It's important. That's where we get money for things like sugar and cakes."

Ricky giggled. "So if we have enough cows will you make me a cake?"

Leta ruffled his hair. "I'll think about it. Let's get going. We've got a long day ahead of us." Usually she assigned this duty to Andy, but too much time had passed since she had inspected the herd for herself. Soon they'd have to brand the calves. She would need to hire some extra help for that. She thought about the limited funds waiting in a jar above the stove. They went out faster than they went in. If they didn't have a successful season, she didn't know if the bank would agree to extend their loan.

Take therefore no thought for the morrow. Outside the window a sparrow hopped on the windowsill, a bite of seed in its beak. God cares more for you than for that sparrow. Don't worry. She repeated that to herself so often, sometimes she thought she worried about not worrying. Going around the corner behind the curtain that hid her bed from the rest of the cabin, she changed from her nightgown to an old pair of trousers. She wasn't going to run into anybody riding the range, and if she had to do a man's work around the ranch, she'd rather do it in the ease of men's clothes.

Ricky giggled as he always did when he saw her in trousers. "You look funny, Ma."

"It's only so I can chase after any calves that run away." She lifted a coil of rope down from the wall, suppressing the shiver that ran down her spine whenever she remembered how rope was used in Derrick's death. She packed together bread and some peach jam and filled two canteens. "You ready to go, cowboy?"

An oversized shirt dangled over Ricky's belt, and his trousers rode up on his leg. She needed to lengthen his trousers before he went off to school. "I'm wearing one of Uncle Andy's old shirts. He said I could."

"That's fine. Let's just tuck it in." She suited her action to her words. "So it doesn't get in the way." She grabbed two hats and headed out the door. The day didn't seem so bad after all. A day's ride with her son under the Texas sky. What more could she want from life?

CHAPTER FIVE

GALVESTON NEWS
September 7, 1875

Wohrle was shot six times and then scalped.

Leta bit her tongue to keep from repeating her question to Ricky. He had given her the details on the location from the hill as he remembered them. Her son was alert enough for a six-year-old, but she couldn't expect him to memorize all the particulars of the layout of the ranch.

Down in the valley where Andy had reported three dozen–plus head of cattle two weeks ago, she only counted half a dozen stragglers. Maybe the herd moved on, stampeding during the lightning storm a few nights back. Or maybe human hands caused the disappearance.

Maybe she was in the wrong place. She studied the landmarks. A grove of elms stood behind her. The rock outcropping that looked like a rooster loomed overhead. The narrow strips of land on either side of the stream disappeared into the mountains. As far as she could tell, this was it.

Ricky rode his horse around in a small circle, arching his back and calling, "yeehaw!" Leta kept an eye on him while she rode in a slightly larger circle, scanning the ground for any signs of what had happened. Large areas of grass were trampled, which could've happened while the herd foraged in the pasture. If she looked farther afield, she might spot movement in a particular direction.

But not with her son riding with her. As always, she had a gun with her, but she hadn't expected trouble when she set out from the cabin that morning. Anger soured her stomach. Anger, and tension that came with a sense of danger. Her operation was too small to warrant the attention of rustlers, and the land wasn't anything special. All the best parcels had gone to the Germans who received land grants two decades before.

Germans. Hot anger pounded through her veins, replacing the shame she used to feel for judging people on the basis of their origins. She took a deep breath to calm herself.

Ricky stopped riding in circles. "I'm hungry."

"That's good, because it's time for us to eat." They might as well enjoy the food she had packed. Then they could bring the remaining cattle back to the barnyard to protect them from whatever predator—human, animal, or otherwise—had made away with the rest of the herd. "We have peach jam sandwiches."

As Leta had expected, her son wolfed down two thick sandwiches in huge chunks. They both finished the water in their canteens and rode to the stream for a refill.

When she had descended from the horse, leaning over the stream, Leta got a prickling sensation on the back of her neck that someone was watching them.

Buck could tell when Leta sensed his presence. She had entered the glen with no more concern for stealth than a rooster greeting the morning, but she had grown more cautious as she made ever-widening circles around the pasture. Now she straightened from the stream, reaching for the rifle waiting on the saddle, and her eyes darted around her surroundings. She said something to the boy and pulled him behind her.

He decided to declare himself before she started shooting. He rode Blaze out of the elms with a bustle of noise. "Mrs. Denning. It's me, Buck Morgan, the Ranger."

She held her rifle on her shoulder, aim steady. "You shouldn't scare a body like that. You're liable to get hurt." He attributed the anger in her voice to fear. "What are you doing back on my land?"

"I didn't know this was on your ranch."

"It's a long ways from the Ranger camp." She kept the rifle trained on him.

"Would you mind putting down your weapon? It's hard to give a straight answer when you've got a bullet aimed between your eyes."

"And I won't miss, either."

"I'm sure you won't." He dismounted and raised his hands away from his own gun.

She responded by lowering her weapon. "I'm sorry for greeting you that way. I can't be too careful out here."

Buck's grandmother, Oma Nadetta, acted like the bear she was named after when someone threatened anyone in the family. Oma and Leta looked nothing alike, but they both would fight with tooth and claw to defend their own. Both of them all female in spite of the men's trousers Leta wore today. He felt heat rising in his cheeks, and he turned away.

A mistake. Wariness returned to her features. "You still haven't told me what brings you back out here."

Buck didn't have a satisfactory answer to give her. He just knew that he had to come back after the sermon on Sunday. "Let's just say I don't want to be a Pharisee." He bent over and tipped his hat to the boy. "Howdy there, Ricky."

"What's a fair-see?" The boy's face scrunched in concentration.

"A religious leader, kind of like a preacher, except he liked preaching about the rules more than showing people God's love."

"Oh."

Leta studied Buck as if weighing his motivations.

Buck gestured across the pasture. "What brings you out so far from the cabin today?"

"Checking on my cattle."

Cattle? Buck hadn't seen more than half a dozen head munching peacefully at a slight distance. "Is there anything I can do to help?"

She looked him up and down. "Since when do Texas Rangers offer to help ranchers with their work?"

"Since they have a day off now and again." He rested his hand on Blaze's saddle. "I couldn't help but notice you had a few things that need doing around the ranch. Well, I happened to grow up on a ranch, and I thought maybe I could help. That's all there is to it. And since you're short-handed since your brother's not here—"

Leta's eyes flashed. As if she was ready to tell him she had everything perfectly well under control or that Andy was somewhere else on the ranch. To her credit, she swallowed her pride. "Did you notice any sign of cattle wherever you rode from? A large herd, I mean. Not a steer here or there."

He thought about the ground he had ridden over. "Nothing obvious."

Her lips thinned. "Then there's not a lot you can do to help."

She was more stubborn than an Indian on the warpath. Buck didn't think she'd like him mentioning the problems he had noticed here and there, things a man with a hammer and some nails and muscles could fix. Maybe he should work on things away from her sight. If she knew about his efforts to help her, she'd feel obligated to refuse.

Buck decided to make one more effort. "Do you have any colts that need to be trained to the saddle?" He didn't like to brag but . . . "My family runs a horse ranch. I'm a fair hand at breaking horses." The best in the Morgan family, but she didn't need to know that.

The boy tugged at his mother's sleeve and whispered in her ear when she bent down. She straightened and studied Buck, matching him stare for stare, while silence stretched between them. He'd never known a woman who could keep so quiet. At length she nodded. "Ricky's Pa promised him a horse of his own when he started school, and we have a colt just about old enough."

Ricky's pa. Buck bet that promise had gone the way of a lot of other dreams with the death of Derrick Denning. The boy stood in front of Blaze, stroking his nose.

"Well, mister, a horse is a mighty big responsibility. Do you know how to take care of a horse?"

"I know how to ride." The boy's chest puffed out.

"That's a start." Although Buck would want to check the level of his riding before he handed over the reins to a child. "But what else?"

"Well, he's like a cow. He's got to be fed and cleaned, and of course he wants to run."

Buck laughed. "That's enough to begin with." Glancing up, he saw a gentle smile cross Leta's lips. Too bad life has handed her such a rough lot. She's not a tough-skinned rancher. She's soft and graceful . . . trying to make it on her own. "When do you want me to start?"

"Don't you have a job?" The softness around her mouth had gone. "Stopping the violence before it spreads any further?"

"It won't hurt to set a time. If I don't make it, it'll be because something has come up. And when I stop by, I can keep you informed about whatever progress we're making."

"Have you? Made any progress since first we met?" Her brown eyes challenged him.

Careful, now. "Not much." He hesitated. She should be forewarned. "But it might not stay that way. Scott Cooley is back in town."

She drew in her breath, her fingers tightening on her son's shoulders before she relaxed. "Maybe you'll catch him this time." She took the boy's hand and headed for their horses. "Come tomorrow afternoon and stay for supper if you can."

"Happy to oblige."

Henry was working in the barn when hoofbeats pounded the earth outside his barn. He grabbed his gun and went to check.

Schmidt slid down from his horse. "Have you heard the news?"

Henry shook his head. "Is it Cooley?"

"He got Wohrle earlier today."

Henry took a step back. "So he's at it again. What happened?"

"Wohrle was over to Harcourt's, helping dig a well. Cooley came up as nice as you please, and then shot Wohrle in the back of the head when he turned his back. They say he pumped him full of lead and even scalped him. And left Harcourt at the bottom of the well."

"Who's telling the tale?"

"The guy they hired to help with the well. He skedaddled when the shooting started. Cooley didn't go after him, so he must not be on his list."

Henry set the hay rake against the side of the barn and sat atop a hay bale. "He's not going to stop until he gets every last one of us."

"We should never have gone after Williamson."

"We can't change the past." Henry thought of the sermons Reverend Stricker had preached from the pulpit on more than one occasion. "There are some who would say we only are getting what we deserve, when we decided to take vengeance in our own hands."

"We did what we had to." Schmidt scowled. "I wanted to warn you and the other God-fearing Germans to be careful."

Henry closed his eyes. He wasn't a murderer. At least, he hadn't been.

CHAPTER SIX

Since I have been here, no less than ten murders have been committed, several of them right near to me. . . .The alienation between Germans and non-Germans has turned into bitter hatred.

Reverend Johann Gottloeb Stricker in
The Story of a Century: St. Paul's Lutheran Church, Mason, Texas

When Buck reached the crossroads leading either west into town or south into Gillespie County, he reined in Blaze. The receipt of a letter from Major Jones had decided his next move: south, across the Llano River over the county line to Kirschberg Ridge. The major wanted an update on what Buck had learned. He wished he had more than speculations and half-truths to present to his commanding officer.

Better speculations based on observations than hearsay, Buck decided. Jones kept a cool head on his shoulders, someone he could trust to act when necessary and not before. His slight build gave lie to the skilled soldier beneath the exterior. Buck spurred Blaze, and he galloped down the road. As long as they stayed away from Fredericksburg, in the heart of German country, Buck and Jones could meet unobserved.

Blaze welcomed the gallop necessary for Buck to reach his usual meeting place before midnight. When they rode into the crevice in the rocks, Jones was pacing up and down, his fingers tugging at the ends of a luxurious black mustache. "Morgan. Good. You made it. What do you hear of Cooley?"

Buck had organized his thoughts during his ride, and his brain scrambled for the answer. "He is definitely back in Mason County, sir, as long ago as last Saturday. I haven't discovered where he is yet."

Jones frowned. "So you didn't hear about today's developments."

Buck didn't move. "No, sir. I came as soon as I received your message."

"He went after a guy by the name of John Worley today. Worling, Wohrle, something like that. Some of the more exaggerated accounts say he scalped the man."

Wohrle—one of the men involved with lynching Williamson. Buck grimaced. "It doesn't sound like he'll stop until he's killed them all."

Jones glanced at Buck sideways. "What do you think?"

"I don't know him that well, sir."

Jones's lips curled. "I always knew you were a diplomat. What is the mood among the people?"

"What you would expect. Half of them feel like the German mob is getting what they deserve after the way they acted over the winter. The other half are scared to death and ready to fight back. It's turning into a regular Romeo and Juliet, a blood feud between two warring factions."

Jones worked his mouth. "So you don't have new leads on Cooley."

"No. The German folk don't know." And if they did, they'd go after him themselves and not tell a Texas Ranger who might warn him of the danger. "As far anybody else, either they think he's doing the Lord's work, or they just want to stay out of the middle."

"Did you learn anything from the widow Denning?"

The beautiful Leta. "Nothing substantial."

"But?"

"I'm missing something, but I can't put my finger on it. Something is off with her or more likely with her brother. I'm not sure." He cleared his throat. "I've made arrangements to spend some extra time with them over the next few weeks. I hope to get some information, and she needs help with the ranch." He braced himself for Jones's reprimand.

Jones's dark eyes stared into his. "If that was someone else talking, I would think he was interested in the widow woman. But I don't have to worry about that with you, now, do I, Morgan?"

"No, sir." Buck felt his fingers itching to cross themselves behind his back.

Jones peered at him before slapping him on the back. "Meet me again here same time next week. Use the usual method if you need to get word to me sooner. Let's both of us catch forty winks before we leave again."

Buck took care of his horse, which faced a long ride back, before lying down himself. He slept a total of three hours, opening his eyes when charcoal replaced the blackest hours of night. He grabbed the cup of cold coffee Jones had left for him and fried a bit of bacon before climbing on Blaze's back. His stomach betrayed him by reminding him of the tasty frijoles and cornbread he had enjoyed at Leta Denning's cabin.

He was a soldier, acquainted with hard food and even harder beds. He enjoyed a good meal when it came his way, but he wouldn't mistake a pretty face and a full stomach for anything more than what it was . . . a distraction.

Leta spent every cent of her hard-earned willpower keeping a smile on her face as she and Ricky spent another day looking for the missing cattle. They hadn't found a one so far. After two days of fruitless searching, perhaps she should give up the pursuit. If not for Ricky, she'd skip supper altogether. He was so tired, his horse ambled beside Leta, content to follow her mare home.

"We'll be home quicker than a rattlesnake's rattle. Some good cold milk and water to drink. No more measuring it out of the canteen." She prattled on, mentioning corn on the cob and fried okra and bread cooked in bacon grease, some of Ricky's favorite foods.

Her son managed a small smile, but his eyes brightened and his hands tightened on the reins. "I'll get there first." He grinned and kicked his horse to move faster.

Glad to see him find some energy, Leta held back a tiny bit to let him win the race.

"And Andy's home!" Ricky slid out of the saddle as slick as a sled on a snow-covered hill and ran to the barn. "Andy! It's me, Ricky! We're home."

Leta wasn't sure she recognized her brother when he came out. Grime was ground into every pore, and his waist overalls could have stood on their own if he took them off. He reeked of smoke and sweat and blood. What had he been up to?

Andy grinned at her as if he had just been gone since morning and not for several days. "I'll be in, as soon as I clean up." He headed for the pump.

Leta reheated beans from last night's supper and fried a few slabs of bacon. Ricky wolfed down a bacon sandwich and a plate of beans, but was nodding over his food before Andy came in. He had scrubbed off some of the stench and changed into the waist overalls Leta had washed on Monday. He tousled Ricky's hair and sat down before a full plate of beans. "I'm glad to have some of your good cooking."

"I've been serving regular meals." Leta bit her tongue in the effort to keep from grilling her brother about his whereabouts the last few days. "Not my fault if you've gone hungry."

"I didn't say it was." He turned his attention to Ricky. "I saw some of the most interesting things you ever did see. There was this rattlesnake sunning himself on the rock."

"That's nothing." Like any child raised on a ranch, Ricky had encountered rattlesnakes on more than one occasion.

"Oh, but this wasn't any ordinary rattler. He wasn't a proper rattlesnake at all. Just a common garter snake. He had tied a baby's rattle to his tail to scare away the rabbits."

Ricky shook his head. "You're making fun of me. A snake can't tie a string."

"This snake did." Andy winked his right eye at Leta. "He was scared of the rabbit. That rabbit had horns growing where his ears should have been."

"Andy, stop those tall tales before you scare Ricky." But Leta laughed, and so did Ricky.

"There's no such things as rabbits with horns," Ricky said.

"I'm serious. There was. Not horns exactly, but growths on top of his head that kind of looked like horns."

"Andy—" Leta said.

"I'm telling the truth. About the rabbit at least." He gave an exaggerated wink that made even Ricky laugh before he yawned.

"You'd better get on to bed, little man."

"But I want to hear more of Uncle Andy's stories." A yawn swallowed the rest of Ricky's protest.

"I'll tell you all about it tomorrow. That way I get to tell my stories twice." Andy pushed from the table. "I'll get him settled, sis, give you a break. You look tired."

Times like this, Derrick used to scoop their son into his arms and carry him to bed. Tonight Leta wouldn't even get a kiss on the forehead. Ricky must have begged for a story, because Andy began, "There once was a preacher named Jonah . . ."

Leta shook her head. Whales were as imaginary to Ricky as Andy's snake with a baby rattle and horned rabbit. Maybe she could find a copy of *Moby Dick* and introduce her son to the whales that sailors chased through the oceans. Did Jonah specify a whale or was that what her imagination conjured up? She pulled down her Bible and was reading the first chapter—a great fish, that was all Jonah said—when Andy joined her at the table.

She closed her Bible and smiled at her brother. "It wasn't a whale, you know."

"What?"

"The fish that swallowed Jonah. It only says a big fish." She closed her Bible and smiled. "But it's a grand story. A true tale of adventure."

"He asked for David and Goliath tomorrow night."

"Will you be here?" Leta said.

"I think so." He glanced away, avoiding her eyes.

"Promise me."

"I'm not a child, Leta." He slapped his hands on the table and looked at her.

Her heart twisted. He was still young in so many ways. She kept a rein on her anger—and fear. "As long as you live under my roof, you will treat me with respect, Andrew Warren.

Either you live here, or you don't. I've got to know I can depend on you or if I need to hire somebody else."

"I heard about a chance to make some cash. It kept me away for a few extra days." He dug into his pockets and slapped a few coins on the table.

"Well, why didn't you say so in the first place? Next time, let me know before you take off. You must have a way to get a message back to me."

The black look he gave her was unreadable, and she felt worried. "Don't get yourself involved in anything dangerous."

"I don't plan on it." Leta couldn't get more of a commitment from him.

Andy's whisper woke Leta in the morning. "Somebody's outside." He had a rifle in his hand. Leta peeked over the windowsill. Buck Morgan was talking to Ricky's colt Shadow in the corral. The way he was speaking to the horse, running his hands along his neck, he looked the most relaxed Leta had ever seen him.

"It's just that Ranger. Buck Morgan. He offered to break in Shadow."

"The Ranger. I thought he looked familiar." Andy drew his breath between his teeth, a hissing sound. "When did he get so friendly? Has he been back?"

If you'd been here, you would know. Leta didn't voice the thought. "He's been back once or twice. We can use his help."

"Is that Ranger Buck?" Ricky poked his head around the curtain. "He's working with Shadow!" He ran for the door.

"Clothes and breakfast first," Leta said.

Ricky gave her a mutinous look and poked his head out the door. "I'll be out soon!"

Buck waved. Ricky disappeared behind the curtain, and Leta pulled on her dressing gown before heading to the kitchen. She had nothing left from last night's supper, since

Andy had arrived unexpectedly and polished off any leftovers.

Ricky came in, his shirt buttoned in the wrong holes and hanging over the waistband of his trousers. His hair stuck out ten different ways. Leta fought the urge to laugh.

"Go get dressed proper." By the time he returned, she had rolled out biscuits. When she inspected him, he had not only buttoned his shirt, but pulled on his square-toed boots. "Well done." She handed him an apple. "I'll call you and Ranger Morgan when breakfast is ready."

"Here I am!" Ricky ran to the corral and climbed on the rails. Buck hadn't done much except start the colt trotting around the corral. Andy appeared wearing the clean trousers he had changed into last night. "I'll go watch."

By the time she got food on the table, everyone would be ready for a good-sized breakfast. She fried bacon and broke eggs into the skillet, adding fresh cow's milk, salt, and pepper. When it all finished cooking, she rang the bell before she slipped away to change into her day dress.

Andy and Ricky came inside, but she saw no sign of Buck. "Where is Mr. Morgan?"

"He said he already had breakfast."

"Nonsense." Leta went outside to the corral. "You must join us for breakfast. It's the least I can do."

Buck hid his face against Shadow's neck, rubbing it gently, and gave no indication he had heard her.

She was about to repeat her request when he turned. "He's ready for a break, so that's good. I think he knows the worst part is ahead of him." He matched his longer strides to her shorter ones. "While the boys aren't about, I wanted to warn you there's been more trouble. There was another murder yesterday."

The pleasure Leta had been taking in the morning disappeared like a smoke ring. "What? Where? Who?"

"A man by the name of Wohrle."

"One of the Germans, then."

Buck glanced at her.

"Of course that's terrible. It's just . . . When they're going after Germans, I don't worry they're after me and mine."

Buck shrugged. "Maybe so. Have you heard anything out this way? Or maybe Andy picked up something wherever he's been?"

Andy. They had arrived back at the cabin. "I haven't heard anything. It's good to have Andy home again. . . . I hope you like biscuits and bacon gravy, because we have plenty." Buck didn't say much, but ate steadily, polishing off as much as Andy and Ricky put together. Cooking for a grown man again did Leta's heart good. Ricky was too excited to eat much. He rushed through a single plate of eggs and bacon and then sat, drumming his fingers on the table, watching every mouthful that went into Buck's mouth.

Buck took his time eating the food, and drank the coffee in small sips. At last he stood and carried the dishes to the sink. "I expect Shadow is ready for us now."

CHAPTER SEVEN

SAN ANTONIO DAILY HERALD
October 11, 1875

[He] says he has a list showing the names of the men he intends to kill.

As Ricky followed Buck out the door, Andy made to follow.

"Hold on a minute, Andy." Leta poured fresh coffee into his cup and gave him the last biscuit. "While Buck's breaking that colt with Ricky, I have some things I want to talk about with you."

Andy sat, his expression guarded. Leta thought of the information she wanted to demand from her brother, but knew he wouldn't tell her. She considered the benefits of an ultimatum: act right or get out. But she couldn't do that, not after she promised Ma and Pa that Andy would always have a home with her.

Andy paused, probably waiting for a lecture, then shrugged and ate the biscuit and drank the coffee.

By the time he finished, she had gathered her thoughts. "When was the last time you checked the herd?"

"When I went out looking with Ricky. Last Saturday." Instead of looking at her, he glanced to the side.

"Did you get a count?"

He squirmed a bit. "We saw them off in the distance. We didn't get close enough to count 'em."

As she had suspected, he had left the job half-finished. "So when was the last time you rode through the herd and counted?" She added more coffee to both their cups. "You're not in trouble." Not yet, anyhow. "But I need to know."

At length, he raised his eyes to meet hers. "It's been a couple of weeks."

She held her breath for a moment. "None were missing?"

"I would've told you." His voice skipped an octave. "Someone stole the cattle?"

"Stolen or lost. They're missing. And not just the yearlings. I expect some of that. I've gone out with Ricky these last two days, and we've only found a half dozen."

Andy looked pale under the summer bronze of his skin. "It's my fault. I should've kept a closer eye on them."

Leta shook her head. "I don't blame you. You couldn't confront rustlers by yourself. I just wish I knew when it happened." She chuckled ruefully. "I don't know if that would help."

"Have you told the sheriff?" He stopped. "Of course not. Sheriff Clark wouldn't do nothing."

Leta didn't bother denying his statement. They both knew

Clark sided with the German mob that started the violence last year. She shook herself. "We'll worry about that later. Let's go watch this Ranger break Shadow."

Buck slipped the halter over Shadow's head and paced the corral, holding the lead with his right hand. But the colt wasn't cooperating.

He looked over the horse's neck at Leta but spoke to Shadow as if she was invisible. "So you don't want to go where you're led. I can't say that I blame you, pal, but that's life for a horse." He slowed and circled to his left, holding on to the lead. The colt snorted but turned as the lead forced his head in Buck's direction. Buck continued his slow turn, until they had completed a tight circle in the center of the corral.

"What's he doing, Ma?" Ricky shaded his eyes against the sun.

"I suppose he's getting Shadow used to going where he tells him to go."

"Oh."

Buck repeated the process, turning right this time. Then he stopped and petted the colt. "Good job." He turned Shadow a final time, nearing the spot where the Dennings waited. He stopped, and the colt stood still, his body inches away from the fence posts.

"Are you done?" Disappointment raced across Leta's face. Buck was glad she had come out in time to see what he was doing with Shadow.

"For today." Buck smiled and tipped his hat. He removed Shadow's halter. Free of the restraint, the colt raced to the far end of the enclosure.

"Can I ride him now?" Ricky was already sliding off the railing.

"Not yet. But soon."

The woebegone expression on Ricky's face made Buck want to laugh. He tried to remember how old he was when he first had a horse to call his own. Younger than Ricky. Pa picked out a filly for his son the year he was born, so that she'd be saddle-broken by the time Buck was old enough to ride. He'd mourned Wind Spirit when she died, and even Blaze was getting up in years. Soon he'd have to get himself another Morgan horse. He wouldn't have any other breed.

Ricky's colt wasn't as good as the purebred Morgans his family raised, but he was a good animal. "You've got a good horse. He's got plenty of spirit, and he'll do you proud. But first he has to go to school, learn how to be a good work horse."

"Horses go to school?" Ricky scratched his head.

"A different kind of school." Leta smiled. "And now we must let Ranger Morgan go about his business."

Business. She would have to remind him of his real reason for being in Mason County at all. He turned to Andy. "I'd like to chat with you for a few minutes."

The kid's eyes slanted toward his sister, and she jumped to his defense. "Andy doesn't know anything more than what I already told you."

"I want to hear the man's version of recent events." A subtle challenge to the boy's burgeoning manhood might encourage when a direct threat might not.

Sure enough, the boy's shoulders lifted. "I'll help any way I can."

Buck nodded with his chin toward the barn. "Help me get Shadow settled while we talk." While they headed into the darkness of the barn, Buck debated the best course of action to take with the kid. Seen through the lens of the violence sweeping the county, the boy's disappearance ranged between foolhardy and suspicious. Seen through the lens of a boy growing into his manhood, maybe a different story would emerge.

"How old are you, son?"

"Seventeen." He cleared his throat. "I'll be eighteen come January."

Seventeen going on eighteen. The War Between the States was raging when Buck was that age. He wanted to leave the dust of the Running M behind him and join the nearest cavalry company he could find, maybe join up with his cousin Riley. He felt chained to the ranch, every day a servitude designed to feel like a year. By the time he reached eighteen, the war ended, the Confederate soldiers streaming home in defeat.

Andy was staring at Buck, probably wondering why he hadn't said anything. He had learned that silence could sometimes provoke more information than a threat.

"I don't know any more than Leta already told you."

"I'd like to hear it in your own words."

The boy sat down on a hay bale. "We don't . . . talk about that night."

"Anything you remember would be helpful."

"It was them Dutch. Everybody knows that."

Buck had heard too many slurs cast against "the Dutch," the word for German, "Deutsch," to let his words bother him. "Suppose it was. Could you name any individuals?"

The kid ran a hand through his hair. "Might have been Henry Doell. Maybe August Keller. John Wohrle for sure."

The kid was smart. Everyone he named was dead. "Sounds like the same people who went after Tim Williamson."

Andy lifted two brown eyes, darkened as if by hidden secrets. "It stands to reason."

The kid probably thought Scott Cooley was a hero. Buck scratched his chin, wondering how this kid's path might have crossed with the ex-Ranger's. Nothing came to mind, but anything was possible.

"You're sure it was Germans who killed your sister's husband?" Buck asked again, studying the boy's face as he answered.

"Who else would it be?"

Buck dropped that line of questioning. Interrogations that led someone to dig in his heels only led away from the truth. The boy's whereabouts the past few days was of greater concern. Whether the boy was innocent of wrongdoing or not, Buck hated the way his absence had worried his sister. It went against the natural order of things, for a fine woman like Leta Denning to be running a ranch and caring for a half-grown man.

"I haven't done anything wrong," Andy said. "If you want to help my sister, hunt down whoever it is that stole her cattle. That'd be more help than asking me a bunch of questions."

So Leta's cattle had been stolen. Why hadn't she told him when he came by the last time? But that wasn't this kid's business. Ire against his irresponsible actions prodded Buck into speech. "You're right—you haven't done anything. Everything on this ranch could use a little elbow grease." Buck speared the kid with his gaze. "Acting like a man means more than taking off whenever you please. It means taking care of what's yours. Like your family, and this ranch."

The kid's shoulders drooped, and he hung his head. "Used to be okay, when Derrick was alive."

"Well, he's not." Buck thought of his own family. He knew he was blessed to have both his pa and his ma alive. "And nobody expects you to fill his shoes, but you can do more than you have been doing."

Maybe a challenge would do the kid good. He thought of the myriad signs of neglect he had seen around the place. "I'll be back here every morning until that colt is broke for Ricky. That barn better be cleaner than a house ready for company, and the animals treated just as good. Plenty of clean hay and food. Every day."

"Is that all?" The boy half sneered.

"That'll do to start. Every morning. Stand up like a man."

"Yes, sir. I'll do it."

At least the kid looked him in the eye. That was a beginning.

CHAPTER EIGHT

SAN ANTONIO DAILY HERALD
September 14, 1875

We fear this is but the beginning of a bloody solution of the difficulties about stock, that have become so serious of late.

"Your punishment will be death by hanging." Before the words stopped echoing around the yard, the horse whinnied and ran away. The rope stretched and snapped . . .

Leta sat up in her bed, cold sweat dotting her eyebrow. She lit the lantern and reached for the journal by her bedside. In it she wrote snatches of thoughts, drew pictures of things that drew her attention, put her most pressing prayers on paper. Lately she'd been recording her dreams ever since the

Ranger had showed up at her doorstep, dreams had troubled her in the dead of the night. Dreams of that terrible night. Before, when they haunted her sleep, she had prayed for God to remove the memories. And they had stopped—until the Ranger came and stirred everything up.

When the dreams came back, she fought past the fear for whispers of memory her waking mind shut out. For a few minutes, she retained scraps of memory, and she dashed the words on paper in an effort to capture them all. So far, she had cobbled together enough details to identify five of the men who took part in her husband's murder.

But should she show the list to the Ranger? Turn justice over to a representative of an organization that seemed intent on doing nothing? *God, give me wisdom.*

She shut out the voice that reminded her, Vengeance is mine; I will repay, saith the Lord. God might work through human agents to bring about that vengeance. From the look of the night sky, morning wasn't too far off. Leta decided to get dressed.

Buck had come by the last two mornings, continuing his slow courtship of the colt. Courtship described the process better than "breaking." Buck didn't jump on Shadow's back or ride him until the colt was too tired to fight back anymore.

Since Buck would return today for the third morning in a row, Leta wanted to serve him something special to thank him for all his time with Shadow. She had a few fresh blueberries set aside, and they'd make dandy flapjacks. Add eggs scrambled with all kinds of meat for a breakfast a man could sink his teeth into.

She wanted to hum, but that would wake up the boys and she treasured the time alone. She settled for singing in her heart with a smile on her face. She hadn't felt this way about breakfast since . . . that last day with Derrick.

She refused to believe she was this excited because a man made her cabin a daily stop. God was using him to provide for her needs, like He promised, that was all.

Lured by the kitchen aromas, Andy and Ricky woke up early. Andy disappeared in the direction of the barn, as he had yesterday.

Movement outside the window caught her attention, and she poured a cup of coffee, adding two sugars. She handed it to Buck when he walked through the door. "Take a seat. Breakfast will be ready in just a minute."

Ricky tugged at his sleeve. "Can I ride Shadow today?"

Buck laughed. "Soon."

Selecting the only plate without a chip in it, she piled it high with eggs and pancakes. He raised his eyebrows. "This is a feast."

"I wanted to thank you for all your hard work with the colt."

"It's been my pleasure." He kept his eyes steady on hers, and heat crept into her cheeks.

"Riding the colt is all Ricky's talked about. I tell him he has to wait until you say he's ready."

"After I get the colt broke, I'll stop by and teach Ricky some tricks for riding him. It'll take a big boy to handle that horse, but I think he's up to it." Buck winked. He reached for the honey and paper crinkled.

My list. Leta reached for it, but he didn't let it go. "Sorry, I forgot I left my recipe on the table."

He frowned. "You need one Ernst Jordan to mix flapjacks?" His raised eyebrows demanded an answer.

Leta set down the plate she was fixing for her son. "Ricky, go on out to the barn and see if Andy needs any help."

"Ma! I'm hungry."

She wrapped a flapjack around a spoonful of eggs. "That should hold you over."

Stuffing the flapjack in his mouth, Ricky banged out the door.

"I'll ring the bell when I'm ready," Leta called after him, but she doubted he heard.

Buck studied the paper he held in his hands. She wanted to grab it back, but she couldn't call back the names. They were branded in her mind. Ernst Jordan. Peter Jordan. Henry Fletcher. Adolph Hinke. John Schmidt.

Buck studied the list for a few minutes, then turned it over. She suspected he could recite all five names, back to front if need be, as well as she could. He didn't speak, but she matched him, silence for silence.

"Are you sure?" He tapped the paper with his forefinger.

She could lie, say she was uncertain when her mind had settled the matter. But under the icy calmness of those blue eyes, she could only nod.

"So . . . the sheriff and his deputy aren't here, Clark and Wohrle."

She wished she could say they were there. They were linchpins of the Hoodoo bunch, and she laid much of the blame for what had happened in the county at their feet. And Wohrle was dead. Again she felt compelled to speak the truth. "No. I'd recognize them for sure, and they weren't there."

"How do you know Ernst Jordan was there?"

"I saw his beard underneath the hat. Pure white, it was."

"Blond hair can look white in the moonlight."

She shook her head. "He was the right height. I'm sure of it."

"Peter Jordan?"

"His hair sticks up all over the place. His hat never sits straight on his head."

"Henry Fletcher?"

"He was one of the youngest men there, away at the edge.

His horse shifted into the light long enough for me to see his face. The same thing with Adolph Hinke."

"And John Schmidt?"

"I'll never forget him." Her voice trembled. "He's the one who put the noose around Derrick's neck."

Buck took her over the same material three times, asking his questions in different ways. Her answers remained consistent. "How many more do you think were there?"

"At least three more, maybe as many as five." Her mouth twisted. "They talked about meting out justice, as if they had assembled a jury of twelve men, but there weren't that many." She had turned a shade of gray.

Buck regretted the necessity of asking her to relive those awful minutes, but she had displayed a strength that reminded him of his mother. "I'm surprised you didn't pull up stakes after what happened. Move closer to your family." He paused. "You don't have family about these parts, do you?"

If possible, she lost a bit more color. "Andy's all the family I've got left. Our ma and pa died a short while before I met up with Derrick."

For a moment, Buck felt a pang of jealousy for the man who had rescued Leta in her time of grief. Had theirs been a marriage of true love, gratitude, or convenience? He had no business asking the question, even if only in his mind. "You've seen hard times."

Her chin went up with that. This one had spunk and pride, and he'd better remember that.

"No one's life is free from pain. Even the Lord said, 'In the world ye shall have tribulation.' There been good times as well. I have no complaints overall." She flashed a smile and a small bit of color crept back into her cheeks.

He nodded, letting his smile express his approval. Maybe someday she'd trust him enough to tell him the secrets behind the dark pools that crept into her eyes from time to time.

But not now. "Call the boys. The food is getting cold."

"I've had it in the oven." When she rang the bell, the boys came running, and the food disappeared quicker than ice on the 4th of July. After they ate, Leta came outside to watch Buck work with the horse. Her daily presence pleased him.

Ricky ran to the barn and returned with the saddle. "You said you're going to ride him today." The boy squirmed like a worm inching its way across topsoil.

"No. I said we would start training him to the saddle today."

"That's the same thing."

Buck grabbed a fair-sized rock from the ground. It dragged on his arms, a good weight. "What do you think weighs more? You or this rock?"

Ricky's face scrunched in concentration. "Me, I suppose."

"Yup." Buck nodded. "I bet that saddle is heavy."

Ricky's shoulders went back. "I can carry it. I'm strong."

"I know. Just like Shadow is strong." He pointed to the colt's back.

Ricky's face mirrored Leta's enthusiasm and confusion mixed in equal measure. Buck winked at her before turning back to the boy. "I bet you're strong enough to carry this rock as well as the saddle." Without warning, he dumped the rock on top of the saddle.

Ricky lunged forward, thrown off balance. "What did you do that for?"

"An object lesson." Buck grabbed the stone and tossed it aside. "You weren't expecting the weight of the stone, and you didn't like it when I added it to your pile."

Ricky's mouth flapped open, but Buck didn't allow an interruption. "I know you're strong enough to carry the extra weight. But you didn't like it, and that colt won't like it either. We have to get him used to the idea."

Ricky nodded, and Buck took the saddle. He draped all but the blanket over the fence. "We start with this." He shook out the blanket.

Andy swung up next to the saddle. "Never heard it took so long to break a horse."

Buck knew the look. He had seen it—felt it—on plenty of boys' faces, including his own. The need to prove himself, to be strong and brave—women might call it recklessness.

Buck turned the horse rug over, running his hands over the surface, checking for burs and anything that might irritate the colt's skin. "This is good." He approached Shadow with a chunk of carrot in his palm. He took it, his lips snuffling over Buck's skin, and followed him around the corral. A few feet away from Andy, he stopped and stroked the colt's nose. "A man depends on his horse out here. You treat a horse right, he'll give you everything he's got."

Andy snorted. "I figure he'll do that for anyone who shows him who's boss."

"You listen to Mr. Morgan," Leta said. "He's right." Her sleeve brushed his hand as she reached out to pet the colt's neck.

Ricky scrambled up the fence. "I'll be in school before I get to ride him." His lips turned down.

Buck had enough of explanations. He returned his attention to the colt, rubbing his nose, speaking softly. He moved down his neck, along his withers before coming to rest on his back. Still whispering in the colt's ear, he laid the rug on his back so quickly that he might have been a hummingbird flapping his wings. Shadow quivered and flicked his tail but didn't bolt. "Good boy."

Fifteen minutes later, Buck removed the blanket and stepped out of the corral.

"Is that all you're doing today?" Dirt would jump into Ricky's mouth if his jaw dropped any lower.

"That's it." Buck lifted the saddle but looked at Ricky. "You know where this goes?"

Ricky accepted the equipment and lumbered to the barn. Andy jumped from the fence. He stared at Buck. "I figure you didn't get your name by whispering to a horse."

Laughter tickled Buck's throat, and he let it go. Andy scowled. "I'll check on Ricky."

Humor glinted in Leta's eyes like the sun poking fingers at the sky before dawn. "After that, you'll have to tell the story."

He smiled, twirling his hat on his hand. "Another time." But Buck had never wanted to tell the story of how he came by his nickname, not until now. Not until he knew he wanted to make Leta smile like that as often as possible.

The names on her list leapt to mind. Jordan and Jordan. Hinke and Schmidt. Fletcher.

How could they have peace when Buck's cousin was involved in the murder of her husband?

CHAPTER NINE

"[To] every man who is in sympathy with Scott Cooley . . . and who does not wish to pursue him . . . I will issue him an honorable discharge . . ." The major paused and about fifteen men stepped to the front.

James B. Gillett in *Six Years with the Texas Rangers: 1875–1881*

Leta watched Buck's departing back for a fraction too long. How good he looked on that horse, a man who promised to hunt down the men who murdered her husband. If he managed to corner them, she'd grab his Winchester and shoot them herself. Of all the men involved, she most wanted the head of the man who had tightened the noose and kicked the horse out from under Derrick.

John Schmidt. The man was too young to have such a blot on his soul.

Buck disappeared in the trees. The sun was high overhead;

she had wasted the coolest hours of the day, hankering after a lawman, a Ranger at that, who would ride away someday and never come back. If she ever married again, she wanted someone settled—a rancher, or maybe a farmer; even a storekeeper.

Shaking the woolies from her brain, Leta headed for the barn. If she didn't give Andy direction, he'd loll about all day.

The door hung open, and Leta entered the dusty darkness. Her ears found the boys before her eyes did, soft voices drifting down from the hayloft.

"I never saw so many bullets in my life." Ricky's voice arched higher when excited.

"Guess he has to be ready to shoot Indians."

"Have the Indians come back?"

Leta swallowed. It had been impossible to shield her son from the recent raids in Loyal Valley in the southern part of Mason County. People would talk, and he caught every word like a leaf seeking water.

Leta arched her hand over her eyes to focus her vision and saw blue flannel shirtsleeves sticking out from the hay. "It's time to get to work."

Scampering feet followed a grunt, and the boys landed at her feet, brushing straw from their hair.

"Andy, I want you to fix that fence in the far pasture. Don't want to lose more cattle because they knock down a few boards to reach the greener grass on the other side."

"Me too, Ma." Ricky bounced up and down.

Leta hesitated. Andy didn't accomplish as much when he brought Ricky along, but she could use some peace and quiet. Maybe she'd grab some rest; she hadn't slept well for several nights. "All right."

Leta hummed as they rode away. Today had turned into a perfect day, from the pleasure of Buck's company to some treasured time alone. Cooler than usual for August, a thin cloud hinted at refreshing afternoon rains, but for now the air remained dry. She'd bring her rocker outside, read her Bible, and commune with God in the church of nature before starting housework.

She opened to Psalms, expecting David's poetry to lift her in worship. Instead, in Psalm 58, she found an imprecation that resurrected her feelings of the morning. "Do ye indeed speak righteousness, O congregation? do ye judge uprightly, O ye sons of men? Yea, in heart ye work wickedness; ye weigh the violence of your hands in the earth." David could have been talking about Mason County. She scanned the reprisals David demanded of God: Break their teeth! Let them melt away like a snail left in the sun! Let them never be born! David put her feelings into words.

Leta wrenched her mind away from the dark thoughts and turned the pages, looking for something to lift her spirits. She didn't read Psalm 59, written when Saul sent men to kill David. Psalm 60 began "O God, thou hast cast us off, thou hast scattered us, thou hast been displeased." Keep reading.

In Psalm 63 she found respite, words precious to anyone who lived through a Texas summer. "My soul thirsteth for thee, my flesh longeth for thee in a dry and thirsty land, where no water is."

Something brushed her arm, a fly maybe, and she batted at it with her hand. The feather-light touch returned. "Ma, are you awake?" Ricky's voice was as light as his touch had been.

Leta bolted awake and almost fell out as the rocker slid forward. She couldn't have slept away the day. No. The sun was directly overhead, high noon. "What are you doing back so soon?" Her voice sounded sharp, sharper than it needed to.

"I checked the fence all the way there and back," Andy said. "There's not a break to be seen. Some of it looks like fresh wood."

"Ranger Buck must have fixed it." Ricky didn't find anything strange about it.

The glare in Andy's eyes matched Leta's mood. That man was becoming too much a part of their lives for her peace of mind.

Lightning split the sky, roaring like it wanted to tear into the earth as well. Buck as well as the other Rangers in Company D had given up on tents or any kind of sleep. The wind picked up everything not nailed to the ground and tossed it a mile away like a tornado. Trapped by walls of water, they couldn't escape the rain.

Buck hadn't seen rain like this since he had left the family ranch near the Gulf Coast. Rain fell in sheets, as if someone had turned the Llano River on its head, causing it to flow from heaven to earth instead of west to east. As big as he was, he didn't want to risk standing. If he so much as unbent an inch, the wind might pick him up and drag him across the ground.

Instead, he curled his body and huddled between Steve Sampson and Jim Austin. "I never seen weather like this in summertime," Steve said. "Winter either, except last January, when we hunted the Comanche up in the Panhandle."

A shiver swept across Buck's nerves at the memory. Ten days hunting Indians in the winter desert, days as dry as a creek bed in summer and nights as cold as an angry woman. Not to mention one cold winter he spent holed up in a Colorado mountain town a few years back.

Jim grunted. "I don't think I've ever been so cold and so thirsty at the same time."

"And when we found water, we had to break the ice." A smile tried to break through onto Buck's face, but with rain driving through his clothes, he didn't have the energy to smile.

"Too bad we can't bottle up this rain and carry it around for when we need it."

"It'd fill a well as big as the Rio Grande." Steve drew the lapels of his jacket together. "Wish we had drawn guard duty with the horses before this storm started."

"I hope they found a good spot to settle for the night," Jim said. "I wouldn't mind curling up against my old pony. That, or a good woman." He laughed.

Buck had to agree. Times like this he could almost envy married men who had the company of a good woman. His thoughts drifted to Leta Denning. There was a woman to tempt a man to settle down. How was this plague of wind and rain damaging the small repairs he had made here and there around the ranch? The best workmanship couldn't withstand much of this weather.

The sky edged a shade darker, and after a meal of cold beans, Buck spared a thought for the horses. They'd be standing, huddled together, forming a natural barrier against the relentless weather. He edged his Stetson over his forehead to lessen the damage to his face, leaned against Jim's back, wrapped his arms around his chest, and closed his eyes. The wind blew from the southeast, drawing Buck's thoughts to his parents' ranch on the Gulf Coast.

Rain pounded them for a night and a day. The hours dragged without a card game or a good book or pranks to pass the time. When at last it lessened, he approached Captain Roberts. "I'll be gone awhile."

Roberts nodded. "You don't report to me. Do what you need to."

Buck stopped by Major Jones's camp and spoke with the commanding officer. "I see you survived the hurricane. Or did it miss you fellas up there in Mason?" Jones glanced at Buck's still-soaked jacket. "I guess not. Take off the coat and take a seat by the fire. I know you won't stay put long enough to dry out. Tell me how things are in Mason."

Buck scooted closer to the flames and tossed another log on the fire. "It's been a quiet month." Buck looked at the major. "Roberts says the Rangers are keeping the peace."

"What do you think?"

"Until Cooley is accounted for—" Buck chafed his hands in front of the fire and spread them apart. "There's a lot of support for him among the ranks, since he used to be a Ranger."

"I received a report that Captain Roberts dealt with that problem. That he asked the men who felt they couldn't discharge their duty to step forward and they would receive an honorable discharge. And that fifteen men took him up on it." Jones looked sideways at Buck.

Buck coughed. "I was there. It was more like three men." Should he say anything more? "Most of the men take great pride in being Rangers, sir."

"And they didn't quit." Jones ruminated. "Keep me informed." He stood, the interview at an end. "Papers say the hurricane hit Victoria hard. I'm sure you're worried about your family. Take a few days—a week if you need to—and check on your family."

"Thank you, sir. I appreciate that." Buck shrugged back into his jacket—now only slightly damp. He left before the major could ask if there was any progress on the Leta Denning case.

Buck didn't know how he would have answered that question.

CHAPTER TEN

VICTORIA ADVOCATE
May 26, 2010

The National Weather Service began keeping records in 1851 . . . Notable storms that struck the Texas coast include: The Category 4 1875 storm that struck Indianola, killing 176 people. The Weather Research Center reports that three-fourths of the town was swept away by the storm surge.

The trip home took longer than Buck had anticipated. With roads destroyed and the countryside mired in mud, even Blaze found it slow going. Buck could have bypassed the town of Victoria to get to the ranch, but he wanted to see what damage the hurricane had done to his hometown. If anything, the newspaper reports hadn't touched the full extent of the damage. Some sections of town were almost literally swept from the face of the earth; he estimated the number of buildings destroyed numbered closer to two hundred than the hundred suggested. The destruction down in Indianola would be much worse.

Sunshine struggled to dry the land, but water still stood an inch deep in some places. Malodorous fumes announced the death left in the wake of the storm.

One steeple remained a beacon of hope, and he turned in the direction of St. John's Lutheran Church. The church had lost shingles, and a three-foot portion of the half-timbered wall had been shattered, but it remained standing.

All manner of things hung from branches to dry in the sunshine. Smoke drifted from a fire, and the tempting aroma of beans drifted through the air. At least a dozen children, German, Mexican, and American, dashed across the lawn. The church must have opened its doors to all who had lost their homes. He expected nothing less from Tante Marion and Onkel Peter.

One of the older boys waved and ran to meet Buck. His cousin Karl had grown half a foot since Buck's last trip home. He had his father's good looks and his mother's sweet nature; the family suspected he might follow his father into the ministry some day.

"What are they feeding you? Growth tonic?" Buck jumped down from Blaze's back and hugged his cousin.

The boy ducked his head, and Buck grinned, remembering the embarrassment of sudden growth. He changed the subject. "It's good to see you. I see the church survived."

"William Meino Morgan, as I live and breathe." Tante Marion bustled out of the church, followed by her husband. "I thought you were off fighting Indians with the Rangers." She flung her arms around him and looked into his face. "I declare, you look more like my brother every time I see you."

Buck grimaced at the use of his birth name. "It's good to see you. How are my folks? Are they here?"

Uncle Peter shook his head. "Both the Fleischers and the Morgans waited out the hurricane at the farm. Since the Fleischers' farmhouse is half-timber, it withstood the winds fairly well. But . . ." His voice trailed off. "They had not yet determined the extent of the damage when we saw them last. This storm has been hard on my parish."

A question trembled on Buck's lips, one he hesitated to ask. "Did everyone—survive?"

Onkel Peter clamped his hand on Buck's shoulder. "Your sister-in-law went into labor. It's touch-and-go for both her and the baby."

Buck's brother had been ecstatic about the coming child after five long years of a childless marriage. The family was hoping for a boy to take over the Running M some day. His throat went dry. He thought of the tiny mound back at Leta's ranch, a loss she had never shared with him, and marveled again at her strength. He drew in his breath. "Are they still out at Opa's farm?"

"Yes."

Buck turned to leave, but his uncle tightened his grip on his shoulder. "Be prepared. The winds did great damage."

Buck looked into his uncle's clear blue eyes. "I'm here to help. I have leave to stay for a few days."

"God go with you all. You remain in my prayers."

Nodding, Buck mounted Blaze and headed for the ranch.

Leta glanced out the window as orange streaked the sky. Buck hadn't come to the ranch ever since before the bad rain. She told herself it didn't matter. He hadn't promised anything, and she hadn't expected him to stick around.

Except she had begun to think this Ranger might be different. That he might be steady, reliable—dependable. She shook her head to clear away the thoughts. If wishes were horses, Ma used to say. Whatever happened, Leta would have to accomplish on her own. With God's help, of course.

Except for the few years God loaned Derrick to Leta, she had been on her own. She wished Buck had been able to finish breaking Shadow. He was almost ready, Buck had said. If he didn't come back—since he hadn't come back—she'd have to figure out something else. Soon. Ricky was ready to climb on his colt's back, with or without Buck. She'd ask the livery owner about what to do next; he should know. She could convince Ricky to wait a little longer. Waiting for Buck to come back? Her traitor heart hoped he would.

While she was in town she'd talk with Lucia Holmes, if she was still in Mason. She had heard rumors that she might leave the county. She almost wished she could do the same. All she wanted was a quiet spot to call home. Instead, she had ended up in Mason, the most dangerous county in all Texas, at least for the past year.

So, she'd talk with . . . somebody . . . maybe the pastor . . . and get a sense of the mood in town. With Buck out of the picture, she wanted to lodge a complaint with someone about the missing cattle. Maybe she could ride out in the direction of the Ranger camp. Report the cattle theft and find out what had happened to Buck. In spite of her initial reaction to let the loss go, she had changed her mind.

She busied herself getting the cabin in order so she could take a midweek trip to town tomorrow. Feeling better for having made a decision, she swept through cleaning and baking and made cookies. Andy and Ricky wandered home in the late daylight hours, chattering. Ricky sat in front of Andy on his horse, but he didn't seem to mind, if his laughter was anything to go by.

Andy's eyebrows raised as he walked past the rugs hanging on the fence, where she had beaten out the dust. "You've been busy today."

"I hope you have too." She kissed his cheek. "We're going to town tomorrow."

"Can I get some lemon drops?" Ricky said.

How many pennies could she squeeze out of a dime? Leta shook her head. She could spare a penny or two for candy. "Ask me tomorrow." If she said yes tonight, he would ask for more and more until they stopped at the store.

"He deserves a reward. He worked hard today." Andy winked. "I did too." A mischievous gleam in his eye suggested he'd like a reward too, only he wouldn't be satisfied with a bag of lemon drops. "We got to all the fenced-in pasture. The fence held up well under the winds—there's a couple of sections that need fixing, but it's not bad." He shook his head. "That Ranger did a good job, I have to say."

"When is Ranger Buck coming back?" Ricky asked. He did every time one of them mentioned Buck.

"Rangers go all over Texas, Ricky. He's probably off scouting Indians someplace."

"He's a good scout. He's brave."

"Yes, he is." She could list Buck's good qualities from now until the cows came home. If the cows came home. If she waited for him to return until the cows came home, she'd never see any of them again.

"While we're in town tomorrow, I'm going to talk with Miss Moneypenny about you starting school."

"Miss Moneypenny?" Andy had had Felicia Jones for his teacher.

"She's new to town." She smiled at her brother. "I hear she's pretty."

Andy's grin matched his sister's. "If she's pretty, I might go back to school."

"Oh, you. Go ahead and wash up, and we'll have supper."

The weather held clear in the morning. Leta let the strings of her sunbonnet flutter in the light breeze. The sun dried the water on the fields, and the grass rippled green in the breeze. Their first stop was the mercantile.

"Can I have a lemon drop? You promised." Ricky stared at the jar on the counter.

"I promised to think about it. But yes." She handed Mrs. Zeller a penny. "I'll be back for supplies later."

"I'm sure you have business in town. Why don't you leave Ricky with me? He can help me, umm, count lemon drops." Mrs. Zeller winked at Ricky. "Would you like that?"

Ricky's eyes widened. "Can I, Ma?"

Leta hesitated. But there were things easier to discuss without Ricky's presence. "Maybe for a short time. Andy, I want you to come with me."

The door closed behind her, and she relaxed. She loved her son, but he wore her out. She paused at the bottom of the steps, debating about where to go first: the livery or the church. The church, she decided. She turned in the direction of the parsonage.

Something seemed different about town today, emptier than market days. Of course, few people ventured out unless necessary ever since the violence had started. She shivered, glad she had a strong male escort with her. Then again, maybe it didn't matter. No one had harmed any women or children to her knowledge, not unless she counted the babies born early, her own tiny girl as well as Helena Wohrle's loss in February.

"It sure is quiet here today." Andy gestured to the empty street. "Where are the children playing? All I can hear are those cattle."

Leta associated the familiar sound of cattle lowing with the ranch and not with town. Cattle drives usually skirted the town. Curiosity drove her to locate the herd, and Andy followed.

Horns and shaggy brown hides appeared in a pen near the jail. They looked like Angus cattle, the same breed she raised. The nice-sized herd consisted of a couple dozen head like the ones she hoped to bring to market before her cattle disappeared. She wondered who they belonged to. Drawn by jealousy or curiosity, she couldn't tell, she moved closer.

Something elemental about the animals appealed to her. Spend any time with them, their personalities distinguished one from another. Like that steer over there, with a nick on his ear and a tiny white spot on his nose. He was a ringer for one of her missing cattle, a sweetheart named simply Boy.

The steer approached her, and she stared past his milky brown eyes to the brand on his back. A B-Bar-B looked suspiciously like a D-Bar-D with a line slashed through the middle.

She shivered.

This steer didn't only look like the one she owned.

He was Boy. They were her cattle—all of them, changed to a B-Bar-B brand.

CHAPTER ELEVEN

Mr. Doell [Heinrich] found the cow with the blotted brand and said, "I'm going to keep this cow, but there won't be any trouble." . . . Gamel had the nerve to make Henry swear the Indians did the job.

Interview of Henry Doell

Buck found the old Victoria-Indianola road a slight improvement over the open pastureland on either side. Everywhere he saw signs of devastation. Entire farms had disappeared, leaving only sticks and stones and flattened fields as evidence of human dwelling. He sent up a prayer for his parents' neighbors, people he knew and respected, for their well-being and recovery. The people of Victoria were a resilient group; they would rebuild.

He told himself that people mattered more than things, but his heart still crushed in his chest when he turned onto the road that would take him home. The sign that read "Running M Ranch Est. 1834" had served as a signpost for his entire life.

Buck remembered that his grandfather hung the sign with the help of his two sons when Aunt Billie was just a baby. His grandfather had died a short time later, fighting for Texas's independence from Mexico. The sign not only told the story of his family, but of Texas itself.

The sign was gone. He nudged Blaze toward broken timbers scattered across the ground, chain links broken apart as if by Thor's hammer. In the distance, he saw a few beams standing where once the Running M had thrived. The grove of acacia trees that supplied the family's Christmas trees was decimated, only a handful of limbless trunks remaining.

Noah's world after the flood couldn't have looked much worse than this. Buck shook his head. Of course it had. Still, he had never seen such damage except for the time a tornado had swept through the town where he was working.

His mother's people had fared better; they found a place of safety while the wind and rain tore apart their home. Instead of continuing down the road, he decided to go cross-country and see what had happened to the land. He turned Blaze to the left and headed north, to the creek that separated the two properties.

The paddocks, the pride of the Running M, lay tossed about like a giant's toys. When Onkel Peter said everyone had survived the storm, Buck hadn't asked about the horses. They couldn't all crowd into the farmhouse. He pressed forward to the fenced-in pasture beyond the yard. Blaze's ears pitched forward, and he pranced. "You recognize this place, fella? That's good."

Overhead a bird flew past and broke the eerie stillness of the day. God counted the sparrows. He cared about every life lost to the storm. He was always there, through bad times and good. That's what his parents had taught him, and they'd had plenty of experience with both.

The creek had flooded, the water spread out far on either side of the banks. Buck found the spot where they used to ford the river. "Let's try it."

Blaze whinnied and stepped into the standing water. Buck draped his firearms and ammunition around his neck and guided the gelding's steps to solid footing on the other bank. By the time they scrambled out, Buck felt like he had endured a night's campaign.

Straight ahead and to the left lay Oma and Opa's house. He urged Blaze to a gallop.

Leta studied the small herd in front of her. She couldn't see the brand on every steer in the pen, not without going among them, but she'd bet they were all hers. As far as she could count from where she could see, there were two dozen steer in the pen. Pretty near the same number that were missing from her herd.

Boy knocked his head against her arm.

"You know me, don't you, Boy? Sorry I don't have anything for you."

"Leta?" Andy loped across the street to join her. "I thought you were heading—" When he saw the steer his sister was petting, he stopped speaking. "That sure looks like Boy."

"It *is* Boy. Look at the brand."

He leaned forward and gave a low whistle. "Are they all yours?"

"You're taller than I am. What do you see? How many head?"

He hooked his foot to the bottom railing surrounding the pen and leaned over, counting under his breath. "Twenty-five."

Her lips formed a straight line. "That's what I thought. I'll have to chance talking to the sheriff. I have to tell somebody about this before they ship the cattle off somewhere else." She whirled on one foot and headed for the jail.

Approaching the structure, her steps slowed. Too many men had been dragged to their deaths from its cells over the last year. Was she making a mistake? Squaring her shoulders, she took a step toward the door.

"Leta, are you sure? We don't know who did this." Andy's voice reflected some of the same worries that had bounced through her mind.

"How many B-Bar-Bs are there in Mason County? We can figure out the brand."

Andy shrugged and followed her. Last summer, she was helpless to protect Derrick, not against ten armed men, not with the life of their son in her hands. But today, on a sunny day, on a street so quiet a stranger couldn't guess anything bad had ever happened in this town, she felt she could talk to the law.

All her courage came to nothing. No one was at the jail. She walked around the small room and called to the back. "Is anyone here?" No one answered.

She crossed her arms and debated what to do next. The problem was, she couldn't trust anyone to be impartial in the affair. No matter whom she went to, she might stir up more violence.

Hooves pounded on the street. A small group of men rode on horseback with ammunition strung across their chests, Winchesters hanging by their saddles, and a confident air that shouted "Rangers!" She stifled her disappointment that Buck wasn't with them. Perhaps this was her answer. She took a step forward and waved.

The first rider halted. "Can I help you, ma'am?"

She straightened her lips and threw her shoulders back. "Yes. I'd like to report a cattle theft."

The man glanced at the others and brought his horse to a stop. He was a few years younger than Buck, she decided, darker and more wiry where Buck was tall and broad.

"You are Rangers, aren't you?" What if she had just stopped Scott Cooley or one of his gang? No, that wasn't possible.

"Yes, ma'am. But let's find a place to talk in private. Whispers in these parts turn into shouts."

Andy stepped forward. "We don't want to leave town, because someone has our cattle right over, in that pen." He pointed to where the Angus cattle lowed and bumped against the fence.

"Is that so?" He dismounted and tied his horse to the top rail. "I'll catch up with you later," he said, and the other Rangers rode down the street. "What makes you think these are your cattle?"

Boy nudged Leta as soon as she came near the fence again. "I'd know this fella here anywhere. It was his mother's first birth and it took a lot of hard work to get him born. I wished I could keep him for stud but . . . that's not the life of most of our bulls."

The man bent forward. "Any identifying marks?"

Leta listed them—from the spot by his feet where his hair swirled in a different direction to the white mole behind his left ear. The Ranger checked each mark she mentioned and nodded. "He does seem to be the one. My name is Steve Sampson, by the way."

"I'm Leta Denning. This is my brother, Andy Warren."

"Any relation to Derrick Denning?"

"His widow." Even after a year, the words stuck in her throat.

"I'm sorry for your loss, ma'am." He stared at the brand. "It looks like the brand has been tampered with."

"Changed from D-Bar-D to B-Bar-B." Andy snorted.

The door to the saloon opened and men streamed out. Leta recognized Barnabas Benton.

"B-Bar-B," Andy said.

Danger surged through the street that seemed so peaceful only moments before.

"He's the one responsible for the theft?" Steve asked.

"It's a good bet," Leta said. "His initials are BB—Barnabas Benton."

He slung the rifle between his hands and walked to the men. Leta breathed a sigh of relief when the other Rangers rejoined him.

The two groups of men stopped with only a yard separating them. Steve put his hand on the butt of his Winchester. "Do any of you gentlemen know anything about those cattle waiting in the pen?"

Benton stepped forward. He glanced at Leta, and his lips lifted in a sneer. "Yes. I just sold them to Mr. Barler here."

Leta took in the identities of the men with Benton. Barler . . . Jordan, both Ernest and Peter . . . her mouth went dry.

"I am placing you under arrest for cattle theft." The Rangers made quick work of securing Benton's hands. "The rest of you, go on about your business. You won't be going home with any cattle today."

Leta looked for a door to slip into, but the street was as bare as a field after harvest. Barler and his group passed by. "Good day, Mrs. Denning."

Fear galloped down Leta's spine. "Good day, Mr. Barler." She kept a pleasant expression on her face until the group passed them by, a few on each side, parting like a wave around an obstacle, threatening to engulf her.

As soon as they were out of sight, Leta shook herself. "Let's get Ricky and go home."

Andy looked at her sideways. "We haven't done half the things you wanted to."

"But we found our cattle, didn't we?" She heard the high note in her voice. "I'm sure the Ranger will be able to find us."

CHAPTER TWELVE

They carried their stolen stock to the head of the Llano where it was kept for some time, the brand and other marks by which they could be identified changed, and then sent off to different places.

Letter from Major John B. Jones
to Adjutant General William Steele,
July 1, 1875

The scene at Opa's farm looked deceptively quiet. Rain shimmered on the grass, a cruel parody of fresh air and sunshine. Tree limbs and broken boards stacked by the remaining wall of the barn testified to clean up after the storm. In the field, the crops lay flat, but the rock wall stood tall. Buck spotted a familiar sight. The Morgan horses. Blaze neighed and tossed his head.

"Do you want to say hello?" He led the horse to the field, removed his saddle, and let him loose with the pack.

A willowy young woman left the half-covered barn, carrying two buckets of milk. He trotted in her direction. "Stella?"

She nearly dropped the buckets, but managed to lower them to the ground. "Buck!" His sister threw her arms around him and held him tight before stepping back. "What are you doing here?"

"Major Jones gave me leave to come home." He bent down and picked up the pails of milk. "I see the cows are okay."

"Poor things, what a time they had of it when we couldn't get to them during the storm." She smiled. "Oh, it's so wonderful that you are here."

They approached the house, and Buck slowed down. "How is Faith?"

Stella sighed. "I supposed you talked with Onkel Peter."

He nodded.

"She's holding her own." She paused. "The baby died last night."

Buck felt a pang as if the child had been his own.

"And how's Drew?"

"Staying too busy cleaning up the farm to take the time to cry. Staying away from Faith as if this was her fault. Men."

Buck shook his head. Some things never changed. Stella was sharp of tongue and kind of heart. He was glad to be home, even in the circumstances. The Morgan family came from strong stock. He'd find peace for his soul no matter what happened in their world.

All too soon, his visit home came to an end. Buck stared at the wagon, half filled with travel trunks. After a long talk, Stella decided she would travel with Faith as far as her family's home in Austin, and then continue on to Mason to visit with their cousins. Women sure needed a lot of possessions to go anywhere. A Ranger traveled light, carrying basic necessities and maybe a pack of cards or a Bible and not much else. Stella caught him studying the baggage. "Be glad we packed for a short trip." She winked. "We're traveling light."

He tried to smile—and failed.

"Is it that bad? Do you need me to unpack something?"

That did bring a smile to his face, and he shook his head.

Oma came to the porch. "You must eat before you leave." She had scraped together a feast from the ruins of the hurricane.

He wouldn't deprive her of the pleasure of feeding him. "I'm looking forward to it."

He marveled at the resilience of his grandparents. Fire once consumed their first home, and on that night Pa had rescued Ma from the flames. Now, Oma and Opa had to rebuild their lives for the second time since moving to the farm.

Things were even worse at the Running M Ranch. That long ago fire had bypassed the ranch, but the hurricane had not. They would have to rebuild, along with all of Victoria.

Drew hovered in the doorway, and Buck motioned him aside. "Are you sure this is what you want to do?"

His brother clenched his teeth. "Faith needs more care than we can give her here. At least now." He turned haunted eyes to his brother. "I don't understand how God works." Faith, as pretty and as fragile as a bluebonnet, was more suited to life as a plantation belle than a rancher's wife. But Drew fell hard when he met her on one of his rare trips to Austin, and the entire family now treasured her as much as he did.

"Me neither." Buck wouldn't offer platitudes. He had seen too many things he didn't understand to quote simple answers. "It just seems like you need to be together at a time like this. You can't simply run away from the pain by avoiding her."

Drew nodded. "You're right. It's just so hard."

"Most of the time, the hard thing is the right thing. Running away isn't what a man's job is."

"Buck, Drew!" Ma stood at the kitchen door, hands on her hips. The two men went over to her. She fussed over Buck's shirt, fiddling with the studs. "It seems like only yesterday when I sent you off to school." She dropped her hands. "But I know you do not like me to reminisce. You are a grown man." She stood on tiptoes. "Don't wait so long to come home the next time." She patted his shirt and stepped back.

"Let the man go." Pa's once-blond hair was now mostly gray, but he still stood tall, his back as straight as it was years ago when he had first put Buck on a horse and taught him the Word of God. "We're sending two of our most precious possessions with you, so take care of them."

Buck's mouth went dry. So many things could happen on the road. "I will do my best."

His parents exchanged a look. Ma lowered her voice. "We're letting Stella go free like a bird, but we hope she will choose to fly home. She has a wandering spirit, that one. We'd rather she go with you than to take off to pan for gold on her own."

"You're saying she's too much like me." Buck chuckled, then turned serious. "She might be safer in Alaska than in Mason. Things there are still unsettled."

"But she'll be with family. A girl shouldn't go on a trip alone." Ma shook her head. After Ma's family had made the long trip from Germany to Texas, she settled in Victoria. She only ventured out of south Texas one time, to visit Onkel Georg and Tante Ertha. She was a homebody.

Stella chose that moment to descend on them. "Are you going to stand there jabbering all day or are we going to get going?"

Buck clamped his hat on his head. "Let's head out."

⟵ ★ ⟶

Leta sat in front of the cabin, churning butter. Boyish laughter tickled her ears and she glanced at the sky. The sun hadn't yet reached its zenith; it lacked at least an hour until noon. Andy was taking his break early again. After Ricky started school, maybe he would settle down.

School. Buck had used that word to describe training Shadow. They had to finish the job soon. Ricky would need the mount when he started school. The livery owner had agreed to spend some time with boy and horse on Saturday, for a price.

At least they had their cattle back. For now, she kept them in pens close to the house. Until she had people to stay with the herd day and night, she wouldn't leave them in the open.

Leta had to find a way to hire extra hands, although she didn't see how. Where was God's promise to provide all her needs? *He sent me rain when I needed it,* she thought suddenly. Too little, too late. She suppressed the ungrateful response. The rain had done the garden good. Maybe she'd grow enough to sell at the town market. Next year, after this year's heifers birthed their first calves, she'd have extra milk and butter.

Next year . . . if they survived until then.

The boys' laughter grew loud, and she smiled—until she heard a sound that chilled her under the sunbonnet.

A horse's cry.

She jumped up and raced to the corral. Shadow ran in circles, Ricky on his back.

"Look, Ma, I'm riding!" he shouted.

Shadow snorted at the noise and kicked up his back legs.

Ricky grabbed the saddle horn, but his right leg fell out of the stirrup and slipped toward the ground. His left leg followed. He fell in a heap on the ground. The colt's hooves crashed into Ricky's soft body before he ran off.

"Ricky!"

Andy ducked under the fence and grabbed Ricky by the shoulders. One of Shadow's hooves clipped her brother's side. He stumbled, but he got Ricky to safety.

Leta bent over her son, who lay still, eyes closed. When she took him in her arms, her hands came away bloody. She shot a prayer to heaven. *Forget all my other complaints. Just spare my son. I can't lose him too.* Tears streamed down her face, but she swallowed them. "Ricky, Ricky." She spoke in loud, clear tones, willing him to wake up. His eyes remained closed.

Andy came out of the barn leading her mare—their fastest horse. "I'm going for the doctor."

She tried to stand with Ricky in her arms, but fell back to one knee. When had he grown so heavy? "Help me get him inside before you go."

Moments later, she was alone with a son who wouldn't wake up. She made him comfortable on the bed and checked his back. She bit her lower lip. Parallel gashes split his skin. She sponged away the blood and discovered the cuts were thin but not deep. She probed around the hoof print with gentle fingers, breathing a sigh of relief when she didn't discover any broken bones. Time would show how badly his back was bruised. Ricky stayed deathly still. She leaned over and felt his precious breath on her cheek.

She put ointment on the cuts and strapped rags around his chest. His ribs would be sore, if not broken. She didn't think they were broken, but she couldn't be sure. The immediate problems solved, she once again said, "Ricky? Ricky?"

He didn't respond. She hadn't expected him to. If his mind was awake at all, he would have screamed at her to stop poking his ribs. She lifted his head enough to slip her fingers underneath. She felt hair and grit, but no blood. There was a bump the size of a walnut at the nape of the neck, probably caused when he hit the ground after falling off Shadow's back.

That might be what made him unconscious. She went for her medical guide and read the passages on head and chest injuries. She read no guarantees that he would wake up, nor did it offer a prescribed treatment. She blinked back tears. Hadn't she lost enough already?

It did say to keep his feet elevated. She tugged off his boots. She didn't want to take the pillow from under his head, so she grabbed the pillows from her bed and plumped them under his feet.

Keep him warm. The August sun heated the inside of the cabin to oven-hot temperatures, and they slept with as few covers as possible. But . . . just in case . . . she tucked an extra quilt around him.

She checked his forehead—slightly warm. The cuts posed a danger for infection, or perhaps being knocked unconscious brought on a fever. She dipped a cloth in cool water and wiped it across his forehead. She took his hand and kissed it. "Your pa and I were so happy the day you were born. He took you in his arms and announced, 'Now he looks like a junior!' So you became Derrick Denning Jr." She wiped at her eyes. "He loved you so much."

She stopped speaking, unable to continue. Her thoughts became a tumbled prayer. Derrick used to say everyone prayed on the battlefield; he had joined the Confederate Army a year before the war ended. He had said God was more real to him during those awful months than at any other time in his life.

Like those soldiers on the battlefield, Leta cried out. "God, help. Don't punish my son for things I did. Let Andy find the doctor quickly." The town of Mason was so far away, and the doctor could be anywhere. Alone, without anyone to assume strength for, she allowed the tears to fall.

Horse hooves hit the ground outside, and she stood. God had answered her prayer speedily. *Thank You, God.* Surely the doctor had a better idea of how to help Ricky.

"Help is here, Ricky. I'll be right back."

She rushed to the door and flung it open.

Tears jumped into her eyes again. God hadn't sent her help in the form of a doctor.

He had sent her Ranger Buck instead.

CHAPTER THIRTEEN

SAN ANTONIO DAILY HERALD
May 25, 1875

Indians and Mexicans are making a fearful raid in our part of the country, just at this time, stealing our property and killing our citizens.

Buck's lips lifted in a smile as he approached Leta's cabin with his sister. Unease quickly replaced the smile. Aside from the animals, he saw no evidence of life.

A saddle straddled the fence, untended. Buck shook his head. Leta knew better. Maybe Andy had left it out, but still . . . Shadow scampered across the corral toward him and snorted in greeting. Buck could guess his thoughts—I've missed you.

"Is she the reason you've been sighing ever since we left Faith with her family?" Stella nodded in the direction of the cabin.

Buck ignored her question. Arms crossed and face flat, Leta looked as forbidding as she did the day they had met. He strode across the yard and stopped a few feet away from her. "Leta—Mrs. Denning—are you all right?"

She clamped her mouth shut and then opened it. "I didn't think we'd see you again." She made the words sound like an accusation. "I see you have company."

Could Leta be jealous? Pleasure tickled Buck at the thought. "That's my sister, Stella. She's come up to—" He stopped in midsentence. As far as he knew, Leta didn't know of his kinship with the Fletchers, and he wanted to keep it that way as long as possible. "She's staying with friends for a short time."

"She picked a strange time to visit Mason County." Leta tapped her fingers on the sleeve of her dress. "Maybe this is best after all. Come inside." Without further explanation, she whirled around and went inside.

"Leta, huh?" Stella leaned over the side of the wagon. "Sounds mighty friendly."

"She invited us inside." Buck ignored her friendly jab. "Something's wrong." Wind whispered across his neck, stirring his hair, as if someone was watching. He surveyed their surroundings, but saw no one.

"If you keep this up, you'll be scaring me," Stella said as he lifted her to the ground.

He continued sweeping the horizon and noticed the full pen of cattle. He nodded in their direction. "That must have been what I heard." So Leta had recovered her stolen cattle. He was glad for her sake—and a little sad he hadn't done it for her. He escorted Stella to the door, knocked, and entered.

"In here." Leta's voice sounded muffled. Stella looked at Buck with a question in her eyes, but he just shrugged and walked behind the curtain.

Little Ricky Denning lay on the bed, as still as the dead. Buck took a step back, and Stella squeezed past him. She stopped as soon as she saw the boy.

The quilt covering the boy rose a fraction of an inch, and Buck relaxed. Ricky was still alive. "What's happened?"

"Shadow." The colt's name came out raspy, and Leta cleared her throat. "Ricky tried to ride him today."

Guilt struggled to the surface. "It's my fault," said Buck.

The look she shot his way screamed her agreement, but she didn't say anything. "Andy's gone to town for the doctor. Do either one of you know any doctoring?" She realized Stella stood there, and she pasted a smile on her face. "I apologize for my manners. I am Leta Denning."

"And I'm Stella Morgan. Buck's sister." She moved forward and took a seat opposite Leta.

Leta arched her eyebrows, and a green glint flashed in her eyes, but she didn't ask any more questions.

"I see you've already consulted the book. My grannie swears by it. And I've learned a thing or two from my ma." Stella pulled back Ricky's eyelids and stared at his eyes, then clapped a single time and checked his forehead. "He's not responding to stimuli, but he doesn't have a fever, either."

"What do you think, Buck? Have you seen injuries like this with the Rangers?"

Buck looked at the still form of the child who couldn't stop moving when awake. "Closest thing to it was the time Drew conked out once when he fell off the barn roof. Scared Ma half to death." He smiled. "He woke up about fifteen minutes later."

"It's been two hours," Leta said.

He didn't have an answer for that.

Leta stood. "Don't let me keep you any longer. I'm sure you want to get settled before night falls. The doctor will come when he can."

"Nonsense." Stella shook her head. "We're not going to leave you here, alone." She glanced at Buck. "Do you need to report to your company?"

Buck shook his head. "Not yet."

"Take my seat." Stella stood. "Mrs. Denning, have you had dinner?"

Leta shook her head.

"I didn't think so. I'll go rustle up something to eat. You stay here and keep Mrs. Denning company." Stella disappeared behind the curtain and soon they heard pans rattling.

"Why did you bring your sister here to Mason County?"

"She wanted to see the world. A true Morgan, Pa says."

A sad smile passed over Leta's face. "Your family sounds nice."

Buck grunted. "I consider myself blessed. It must be hard for you, without family."

Tears sprang to her eyes. "I'm used to it."

Buck shot a sharp glance at her, but she had bowed her head. Sometimes his family stifled him, but they were his foundation. He didn't know how he'd feel without them. "I'm sorry."

She lifted her head and bared her teeth in a forced smile. "But God is always with me, so I'm never alone. Isn't that what the Bible says?" A single tear slid down her cheek.

Buck's hand moved without volition and caught the tear with his finger. "You're not alone now."

"But I will be again. The next time you go away. God takes away everyone I care about." She sobbed without making a sound.

"Food's ready." Stella's cheerful voice interrupted. "I'll bring you a plate."

Leta shook her head from side to side. "I'm not hungry."

She spoke too softly for Stella to hear, and his sister pulled back the curtain with her free hand. As soon as she spotted Leta's distress, she set the plate on the nightstand and knelt beside Leta. "Oh, honey, go ahead and cry." That sounded like something their grannie would say.

Leta buried her face on Stella's shoulder. Stella shooed away Buck with her hand. Nodding, he retired to the main room and fixed himself a plate.

He forced the food down while he added his silent prayers to Leta's cries. *Comfort her, God. And heal Ricky.*

Stella joined Buck at the table. "She's resting. I convinced her to lie down next to Ricky on the bed. Poor thing." She poured herself a cup of coffee and stirred in a spoonful of sugar. "Does she live here all alone?"

"She has Ricky, and her brother Andy lives with her here."

"Hard to imagine, isn't it?" Two cabins this size could fit on the first floor of her family's house. It was one big room, with sleeping quarters curtained off. To think she'd complained about sharing a bedroom with her two sisters until they got married.

Stella inspected the interior, imaging life in the small space. Red-checked gingham curtains hung on the small window in the kitchen and a larger one looking out on the front yard. The quilts used for room curtains featured the Lone Star pattern, meticulously sewn in a hodgepodge of fabrics and colors that spoke to a cheerful spirit. A table with a kerosene lantern also held a couple of books, including what looked like a well-worn Bible. Pegs by the door held coats and hats. Not a speck of dirt rested on any surface, which was amazing given the constant traffic and wind. The kitchen pantry, though small, was well planned. Stella's glance landed on a slim volume on the shelf behind Buck's chair. "I bet she keeps household accounts in that."

Buck glanced behind him. "Maybe. She's having a hard time of it."

"You care for her, don't you?"

His head snapped back, and he glanced at the curtain that hid Leta. Not seeing any movement, he relaxed. "Yes." He spoke so low Stella could barely make out the words. "You wouldn't dare tell Ma."

"Don't worry." Stella smiled. In spite of the difference in their ages, they had always been close. As a child, she had followed him around in trousers and did everything he did. Now they fell back into that easy camaraderie. "I want to keep you on my side. You're the only member of the family who recognizes I've grown up."

Buck laughed. "I felt the same way, and I was the oldest. Ma says I'll always be her baby boy. It's just her way."

"Hah." But Stella smiled. "Do you think Mrs. Denning will let us stay here? Tante Ertha will mother me just like Ma."

Buck shook his head. "Leta doesn't need another person to look after."

As his sister began to protest, horse hooves clattered outside and Buck rushed to the window. "It's Leta's brother, Andy."

Stella peeked over his shoulder, and saw a gangly youth ride around the wagon, staring into the bed, his face a study in concentration. He placed his hand on his rifle.

Buck opened the door. "Andy, it's Buck Morgan."

The boy whirled around. A mixture of relief and disappointment ran across his face. "I wondered if maybe someone else got word to the doctor."

"Unfortunately, no. You didn't find him?"

"There was an accident down in Loyal Valley. The doctor has been gone since last night." The kid swallowed, his Adam's apple bobbing up and down. "Is Ricky any better?"

"He hasn't regained consciousness." Buck glanced at the corral. "I'm sorry I didn't make it back sooner. Ricky might not have been hurt if I'd had a chance to finish training that colt."

Andy scowled. "Leta didn't think you were coming back."

The tightening of the lines around Buck's eyes told Stella those words stung. "I went home to help my family after the hurricane. They live down near the part of the coast that got the worst of it. I'm sorry for the delay, but I promised I'd be back."

"I guess Leta has learned she can't believe every promise made to her."

Buck straightened, pulling himself to his full height of six feet three inches. They reminded Stella of two stallions challenging each other for control of the herd. If they were horses, she'd let them fight it out. But they were men—at least a man and a boy on the brink of manhood—who should know better.

"Buck, where's your manners?" Stella stepped between them. "I'm Buck's sister Stella. And you must be Mrs. Denning's brother. I bet you're hungry after all that riding. Come on in and eat."

Andy relented, and he turned from man back to boy before her eyes. "I'd like that. Glad to meet you, ma'am." He lavished a smile on her that made her feel all grown, and she decided Andy might not be so bad after all.

Day blended into night. Leta stirred and reached for Ricky. His chest still rose and fell, but his eyes remained stubbornly closed. The murmur of deep voices reached her, and memory returned. Buck came back. Andy didn't find the doctor. Her heart offered a wordless prayer to God.

There was a woman. Buck's sister. Leta struggled to rise.

"I've got everything under control. Go on back to sleep."

At the quiet reassurance, Leta sunk back against the pillow and fell asleep. She didn't wake again until the predawn hours. Her eyes slowly adjusted to the dark, and she could see Buck's silhouette on the chair at the end of the bed. His hands were folded, and she heard soft sounds, quiet whispers she couldn't understand. He was keeping watch over them in prayer. Her heart warmed to the thought. Ricky's chest continued to rise and fall. He looked as though he had fallen asleep the night before, ready to wake up in time for breakfast. He looked so small, so vulnerable in the big bed. She touched his blond curls with her hand, something he ducked away from when awake.

Ricky stirred, squirming away from the light touch of her hand. She inhaled and breathed his name. "Ricky."

He opened his eyes, black in the darkness. "My head hurts."

CHAPTER FOURTEEN

Quiet can hardly be restored until some steps are taken to bring the perpetrators of the late murders . . . to justice and this cannot be done in this county by any jury grand or petit summoned from the vicinity.

Correspondence between
John Holmes and Governor Coke
September 8, 1875

I'm sure your head does hurt. You got a bad bump." Leta cried tears of joy.

Ricky lifted up on his elbows. "Ranger Buck, when did you get back?"

"Last night." The smile on Buck's face mirrored Leta's joy.

Yawning, Ricky's eyes drifted closed. "I wanna go back to sleep."

"That's not a good idea." Leta panicked. She feared if he closed his eyes again, he wouldn't wake up a second time.

Buck looked at her and nodded in understanding.

"Before you fall asleep, I want to hear about everything that's happened around here." Buck kept his voice calm. "Did it rain a bunch?"

Ricky nodded. "I had to stay inside forever."

Leta relaxed a fraction. Buck would keep her son awake. "I'll go fix us breakfast."

In the main room, Andy was snoring in the rocking chair, a quilt wrapped around him. He'd had a rough day and night. She was proud of him, for everything he had done during the long difficult day, for his good sense in letting Stella have the only other bed in the house.

Buck hadn't slept at all, as far as she knew.

Thank You, God, that Ricky is okay. Her heart lighter than it had been for weeks, Leta went to the henhouse to collect eggs: an even dozen, plenty for a feast. Cutting twelve slices of bread, she used a glass to make circles in each of them. Butter from yesterday's churning sizzled in the fry pan. She dropped the bread in the butter and started cooking her son's favorite breakfast.

A scuffling sound alerted Leta to someone's approach. Maybe Ricky had gone ahead and gotten out of bed. When she turned around, smiling widely, she encountered Buck's sister.

"Mmm, sunshine eggs. Do you mind if I fry up the holes?" Without waiting for an answer, Stella found a knife and slathered the round slabs with butter. "What's the news on your boy?"

Leta's wide smile returned. "He woke up." She nodded in the direction of the curtain. "Buck is talking with him to keep him awake."

"God is good." Stella located the flat griddle on the shelf and placed it over an open flame. "So this is a celebration breakfast." While the griddle heated, she poked through the jars on the shelf. They worked side by side, the other woman fitting in with ease around the small space.

"Where'd you get this?" Stella peered at a calendar tacked to the wall near the stove.

"The general store gave them away last Christmas." Leta liked the painting of a cardinal sitting on the branches of a sumac tree; she might keep it next year, at least the picture.

"Today's date is circled. Is it somebody's birthday?"

"Today?" Leta dropped the last egg in the skillet. "Today is Thursday . . . is it the ninth?"

Stella nodded, and Leta froze. "The court is holding session today. They're bringing in the men who stole my cattle. I have to be there." Butter spit from the skillet and landed on her hand. She brought it to her mouth and sucked the hot spot.

"I'll finish up here. You go get ready."

Bless this young woman. She seemed to be as steady as her brother—as dependable as Andy was unpredictable. "Thanks." She had to get ready quickly; after sleeping in her clothes all night, she had to change. She tiptoed behind her curtain. Pouring water from the ewer into a basin, she began the process of preparing for the day.

A few minutes later, Stella poked her head around the curtain where Buck sat with Ricky. "Good morning, Ricky! Your mother told me you were awake and ready for some eggs in a hole."

"Who's that?"

"She's my sister." Buck swept the boy up in his arms.

"I can walk!" Ricky squirmed, and Buck set him down.

"Where is Leta?" Andy asked, waking up with a yawn.

"Right here." Leta came in, wearing a pretty blue dress with red flowers printed on it. She made a beeline for Ricky and hugged him. With his face between her hands, she kissed his forehead. "I love you."

"Ma." Ricky's voice held the embarrassment of all boys everywhere.

"You're awake!" Andy didn't repeat his sister's embrace, but he clapped Ricky on his shoulder. "You had me scared."

"Can I ride Shadow today?" Ricky asked.

The four adults looked at each other. Stella could tell Buck wanted to laugh. He probably would have asked the same thing at Ricky's age. "Let make sure the colt wasn't hurt yesterday." He looked at Leta and winked. "I understand you have court today."

Leta frowned. "I don't want to rustlers get away with it." She laughed, a hollow sound as brittle as a dried leaf. "Not that it will make any difference. I don't know if the judge is afraid a guilty verdict will stir up more violence or what, but prisoners from both sides of the feud get little more than a small fine. If that." A haunted look darted into her eyes.

"I'm coming with you."

Stella sat down, watching the exchange between the two of them. Buck seemed to have met his match in the widow.

Leta blinked and shook her head. "That's not necessary. You must need to get back to the Ranger camp. You don't have to hold my hand." Her shoulders sagged and she grabbed the edge of the table as she sat down.

Stella sent a worried look in Buck's direction. In spite of Leta's protests, she needed protection today.

"The Rangers are here to reestablish peace," said Buck. "Showing up at these trials is part of the job." He took a seat next to Ricky, opposite Leta at the table. "Now how about some of these eggs?"

Leta had a hard time convincing anyone to stay home. Andy had wanted to come, and of course, Ricky thought he should tag along.

"Andy, you have to stay home," Leta said. "If the doctor comes out, I want you to tell him just what happened yesterday."

"And I can tell him what I observed after I arrived. Between us, he'll have a full report." Stella smiled at Andy. "And I might need your help to keep Ricky corralled."

Leta doubted that, but Andy reluctantly agreed to stay behind. She should feel glad Stella offered to stay with Ricky for the day. Glad to have Buck's support. With the Ranger's presence, the likelihood for violence went down.

Knowing how she should feel didn't change a thing. Her insides boiled hotter than bacon grease. Buck walked back into her life as if he had never left, but she couldn't afford to depend on him again. Not for her safety or her happiness or—anything. Her and God—that was all she wanted or needed. All she ever had.

Horses and wagons lined the street near the courthouse by the time they arrived. Many of the people milling around were locals, but among them she saw gentlemen dressed in suits and holding notepads in their hands. "Reporters." She glanced at Buck. "What if they connect my case with Derrick's murder?"

Silent thunder filled Buck's face. He took her elbow. "I'll escort you inside." Without waiting for her permission, he propelled her forward. "Coming through."

The crowd parted, but she heard whispers. One man, dressed in a gray wool suit, out of place on this late summer day, blocked their path. "Mrs. Denning, what do you think will happen today?"

Leta ducked her head, wishing she had worn her sunbonnet to hide her face. Buck pressed past the reporters who jumped in with more questions. He opened the door and she scooted inside, drawing her first real breath since they had dismounted. How she would have handled the gamut without his quiet presence, she shuddered to think. But she couldn't depend on him. Reason fought with feeling.

"Where do you want to sit?"

Leta looked around. A lot of people had already found seats, women as well as men. She spotted a couple of women from her church and pointed, relieved to see familiar faces.

He escorted her to the seat, but didn't join her. "I'll be by the back door."

"Thanks." When the judge called the court to order, she glanced back at him. No one could get past him to harm her, and she relaxed.

The day dragged on. A couple of cases were heard before hers—one bound over for trial, one dismissal of charges. Her stomach churned at the thought of testifying at trial, with everyone watching.

Once again she glanced back at Buck and allowed his solid presence to give her courage. He might not smile—he seldom did—but she felt better knowing he was there.

After the noon recess, the judge called for her case. Steve Sampson joined Buck at the back of the courtroom. She kept her face turned forward, waiting for the defendant to appear.

The clerk repeated the call. The defendant—Barnabas Benton—didn't come in. The judge frowned. "Sheriff Clark, where is the defendant?"

Clark squirmed under the judge's glare. "He knew the hearing was today, your honor."

"Hmph. I'll issue a bench warrant, then. This time, keep him in jail until the next session."

Leta shrank back. The prison in the past year had proven as full of holes as a fishing net. They could be anywhere in

Mason County or even beyond, with a thousand places to hide.

Buck made his way to her side as soon as the gavel came down. "I'm taking you home. Steve will stay for the rest of the afternoon."

The same reporter jumped in their path when she left. "You will leave the lady be." Buck shouldered past him.

She couldn't have put two words together. Frustration tied her tongue in knots. Anything she tried to say now would come out backward. Sheriff Clark tipped his hat to her as she walked out of the courthouse. She wanted to spit in his face. If he didn't keep those thieves in jail, they'd never pay for stealing her cattle.

A cadre of Rangers waited across from the courthouse, presumably to keep the peace. Their heads swung in their direction when they came out the door, and one of the men nudged his mount forward. "Morgan, I thought you were gone down south."

A shrug rippled down Buck's arms where he held her elbow. "I got back early."

The Ranger—tall and lanky, like Buck, but with dark curly hair and a beard that refused to submit to a razor—dismounted. Buck introduced her to his friend Jim Austin.

"We were right sorry to hear about your husband's murder, Mrs. Denning. We're going to bring a stop to this violence."

Leta nodded. "I hope so." Her voice didn't carry much conviction, but she didn't care.

Shuffling his feet, Austin shrugged before he led Morgan aside. They stood about three yards away and spoke in low voices. When Buck returned, he was frowning. "I have to get back to the Ranger camp. Can Stella stay with you for a few days?"

The nerve of the man. But Leta couldn't refuse. "Of course. But—how long?"

"I will come back as soon as I can." Blue eyes focused on her. "I promise." He nodded at his friend. "Jim will escort you home."

Leta straightened her back. "That's not necessary. I know the way out of town."

Buck looked at his friend, who nodded. She wouldn't be given a choice.

"I'm sorry, Leta." Buck tipped his hat and headed out.

CHAPTER FIFTEEN

SAN ANTONIO DAILY HERALD
May 20, 1875

We learn from Maj. Jas. Trainer that the Indians are very bad in his section of the country. They killed a woman on Mill Creek 12 miles from Mason.

Leta was trying to figure out how to keep Jim Austin from following her home when she spotted Dr. Tardiff.

The doctor had managed to withstand the pressure of the war raging in the county, treating any patient brought to him with equal care. Leta respected what little she knew of him.

"Mrs. Denning, I was just heading out your way. How is your son?"

Leta smiled at the memory. "He woke up this morning. I had to come to court today, but a—friend is staying with him to make sure he doesn't overdo." She supposed she could call Stella a friend.

"Good, good." The doctor smiled. "Are you done with court, then? I can come with you now." He helped Leta onto her horse. She turned around to face Buck's Ranger friend. "As you can see, I no longer need your assistance."

A hint of exasperation crossed the Ranger's face. Buck wouldn't be pleased, but she felt better back on her own. It was much better to do things that way.

By the time they arrived at the ranch, Leta had filled the doctor in on the court case and Rick's accident. "The important thing is that you have your cattle back. It sounds like you did everything that could be done for Ricky, but I'll check him over."

The yard looked impeccable; Andy had done a thorough job. Stella sat on a rocking chair on the porch, holding Leta's Bible in her lap. Ricky was curled up her feet.

When she saw the man with Leta, she stood. "I promise, this is the first time he's fallen asleep today. I figured an afternoon nap wouldn't hurt. I was going to wake him up in a few minutes."

Dr. Tardiff brushed her words aside and bent over Ricky, gently shaking his shoulder. Ricky sat up and rubbed his eyes. "Doc?"

"I hear you had a nasty fall yesterday." When the doctor announced Ricky was unlikely to suffer any lasting ill effects from the fall, Leta took her first deep breath in twenty-four hours.

⟵ ★ ⟶

Buck rode into Ranger camp and headed straight for Roberts's tent after he put Blaze with the other horses. Overhead the sun chased clouds across the sky, as pretty a fall day as he had seen in a while. Only the ground underfoot, still a little soft, reminded him that the storm had also struck this far north. He wondered what Captain Roberts wanted with him.

Roberts sat at the campfire with his senior officers. First one raised his voice, then another. Buck made sure Roberts could see him before he joined the circle.

"Morgan, you're back. It's about time." Roberts frowned.

"How's your family doing?" This came from Major Jones, whom Buck hadn't identified since his back was turned.

"It could be worse. They'll rebuild." Buck didn't intend to detail all the setbacks they had faced.

Jones shot him an amused look and grunted. He valued Buck's taciturn nature. "Come and join us. We're discussing how to use our resources."

Buck perched on an outcropping of granite. "Indian trouble?"

"Down Mill Creek way." Roberts tapped his knee with the butt of his rifle. "The Indians and Mexicans do a lot of the cattle rustling that gets blamed on townsfolk."

"We've promised to help them out here. Law-abiding folks in Texas want to know they can live in peace and quiet," Jones said. "They also want to be free of Indian threats."

Jones stood to his feet. "This is what we'll do. The main part of Company D will go on the Indian scout. Morgan here is already assigned to my company. Choose two men to stay with him—one of them your fastest rider. He can go after the troops if things heat up here again."

Roberts nodded. "I assume you'd like Austin and Sampson?"

Buck agreed. Once the meeting broke up, Jones pulled him aside. "I suppose you haven't made any progress in your investigation since you were away."

Buck gave a fleeting thought to the information he hadn't shared with Jones earlier—the names on Leta's list—but he did have something else to share. "Mrs. Denning has recovered her cattle, sir. The thieves—the Jordans—brought them into town, and she discovered them in a holding pen. That's where I was today, at their trial."

Jones arched his eyebrows, and Buck shook his head. "They didn't even bother to show up. I'm glad you're asking me to stay. That kind of behavior could trigger more violence."

"Same suspects as before, then." Jones considered. "Your first job while the company is gone is to keep the peace, but if you have a chance to round up any of the suspects, do it."

"Yes, sir."

"I hope you don't mind sharing my bed." Leta fluffed the pillows at the head of the bed. Derrick had insisted on soft goose down, so she could get a good night's sleep. The memory brought a smile to her face.

"Of course not." Stella pulled a brush through her long, light-brown hair.

Ricky was already sound asleep. When Leta tucked him into bed, all he could do was mumble, "Where's Ranger Buck?" before he flopped against the pillow.

Stella shared Buck's coloring and the faraway look Leta saw in his eyes sometimes. For the baby of the family, she handled the responsibilities of running a household well. "I just appreciate you taking me in. Men." Stella shook her head. "Buck must think everyone is like our ma, willing to take in any strays that wander by."

"I'm happy to oblige, but I don't have much space. We were planning on adding another room last year, before . . ." For the baby. After she miscarried, she no longer cared.

"Buck told me a little about it. You must be very brave, staying here with things so rough in town. Sometimes I feel like all the adventures have passed me by. Things are so quiet in Victoria these days."

Leta's eyes opened wide. "After a hurricane?"

"Oh, it's so settled. You know what I mean."

Yes, Leta did. What Leta would give for a nice ranch near a settled town, instead of this . . . wild frontier town. Yet this young girl, so mature in some ways, so youthful in others, craved excitement. "You'll get your fill of excitement while you're here." She hoped the awakening wouldn't hit Stella too hard. Just a hint of a scare would do—enough to shock Stella into appreciating a quiet life. That would be ideal.

"I hope you don't mind . . . I read my Bible before I fall asleep."

"Of course not. 'Morning and evening I will call to thee.'" Stella yawned. "As long as you don't mind if I fall asleep." She turned her back to Leta's side of the bed and curled up like a child.

A slim volume—that had only the New Testament and Psalms and Proverbs—lay on the nightstand. She turned to the fifth chapter of Matthew, Jesus' Sermon on the Mount. It helped when Jesus said, "Blessed are ye, when men shall revile you, and persecute you, and shall say all manner of evil against you falsely, for my sake. Rejoice, and be exceeding glad: for great is your reward in heaven." That's what happened to Derrick; he went straight from earth to his heavenly reward. She looked forward to joining him some day, but she prayed it wouldn't happen any time soon.

She continued reading Jesus' instructions on how men

should handle conflict. Things in the here and now fell short of God's design. Then she reached verses she had read before, ones she knew, but had conveniently shoved into a corner of her mind. "But I say unto you, Love your enemies, bless them that curse you, do good to them that hate you, and pray for them which despitefully use you." Fierce anger against the men who had killed her husband and stolen her cattle swept over her. She could identify with the psalms where David called down God's wrath. Jesus' instructions to "turn the other cheek" and show love for her enemies went against everything in her. She stopped reading, but the words echoed in her brain.

She pulled out her prayer list, a slim sheet of paper tucked into the front of the Bible. She had listed people she prayed for regularly. Ricky and Andy headed the list, of course. President Grant, Governor Coke, her pastor, a favorite teacher she remembered from school. Another person making a regular appearance in her prayers recently was Buck—his safety. Thanking God for all he was doing to help her. Asking God to protect her heart against the feelings springing up after the drought that followed Derrick's death.

But here God was telling her to add other names to the list. Sheriff Clark and his no-account deputies. Hinke, the Jordans, Fletcher—all the men she was certain had acted against her. Stealing life and livelihood.

God, no! Her stomach knocked against her heart.

"Hereby we do know that we know him, if we keep his commandments."

No, no, no. Everything in Leta rebelled against what God expected of her. *Make me willing. I can't do it on my own.*

She closed the Bible and turned off the lantern. Stella slept peacefully by her side. Leta's heart listed all the wrongs done against her, while her mind quoted God's words to her. Restless, she pulled back the curtain and looked at Ricky. *Please*

God, give me courage to do the right thing.

Outside something clattered against the fence, and she tensed. Just the wind, she told herself. Again, she heard the unmistakable neighing of a horse. Keeping in the shadows, she got up and crept down the wall and knelt below the window. A quick glance showed a strange horse in the yard.

Oh, God, what do I do? She grabbed the rifle from over the fireplace and slipped extra ammunition into the pockets of her robe. She waited by the door, holding as still as possible. She wouldn't confront them. She wouldn't put everyone in the house at risk. But she would shoot if attacked directly.

She waited for what seemed like an eternity. Through the window, she watched the moon rise high in the black sky. Only a quiet scuffling suggested any movement. At last she risked a glance through the kitchen window. The horse had disappeared. She would wait until morning light to investigate further.

Keeping the rifle in her hands, she retreated to the chair by Ricky's bed. Prayer came easily now, single words thrown up to heaven. *Protect us. Save us.*

Blackness turned to dark gray, and the rooster crowed in the yard. Leta shook the stiffness from her limbs. She went into the main room and splashed water from the bucket on her face. Now was the time to check for mischief, while the remainder of household still slept. After checking her rifle, she opened her door a crack. When no one moved, she pushed it open all the way.

A hangman's noose dangled from the nail where visitors tethered their horses.

CHAPTER SIXTEEN

The rangers not on guard spent their time as they wished when not on duty, but no man could leave the camp without the captain's permission. The boys played such games as appealed to them, horseshoe pitching and cards being their favorite diversions.

James B. Gillett, *Six Years with the Texas Rangers: 1875 to 1881*

I'm glad to help you, Buck, but I've got an itch to see some action. I'm tired of sitting around. You won't even play a friendly game of poker."

Buck smiled at Jim. "Just want to be sure you don't gamble away all your money."

Steve was cleaning his rifle. "Don't we have murderers to hunt down?"

Buck didn't answer right away. After he delivered Stella to his uncle's house, he wanted to have a talk with his cousin. He'd rather not have company for that conversation.

"Captain Roberts told us to stick together. I'll be keeping an eagle eye on you, so don't think about running out on us." Jim shook the pack of well-worn cards at Buck before spreading them out in a game of solitaire.

"He's just in love." Steve held his rifle to his shoulder, checking the sight.

Buck's head snapped up. Words of denial died on his tongue. Anything he said could be twisted; he'd best say nothing at all.

"Maybe so." Jim turned over a card. "He was right concerned about Mrs. Denning yesterday."

"Her husband was one of the first victims of the mob and now they've stolen her cattle. She's part of the job, that's all."

"Uh huh. That doesn't explain why you hightail it over there every time you get a chance." Steve shook his head. "You have it bad, you just don't know it yet."

"So you do have some names," Jim said.

Buck tensed. Jim knew, or had guessed, something.

"They must have read out the names of the cattle rustlers at court."

Of course. He relaxed. "Just one. Barnabas Benton."

"Does your uncle know where to find him?" Both men focused their attention on Buck, their gazes sharp enough to slice his secrets with an invisible sword.

"If he does, he's not going to tell a Ranger, even if I am his nephew. He's not sitting at his ranch waiting for us to show up and arrest him, if that's what you're asking."

Jim lit a cheroot and leaned back. "It should be easier for you to get that information than the rest of us yahoos." Buck stared at him, daring him to spell out what he meant. Jim shrugged. "Stands to reason. Your family's German. They're bound to hear things. I'm not saying they're involved."

"All the more reason why I have to go alone. If they know

anything, they won't talk with Anglos around."

Steve frowned. "We can't let you do that." He hooked his thumbs over his belt.

"Buck has a point." Jim gave up on the game and gathered the cards into a deck. "You go in alone, but we'll be close by, in case you run into trouble."

They made plans to leave after breakfast. "I, uh, have to go by Mrs. Denning's ranch first." Heat raced to Buck's cheeks. "I brought my sister back with me, to stay with our aunt and uncle. We stopped by the Denning ranch first, and since I rushed back to camp after court, she's still there."

"You brought her here?"

"She insisted on coming." Buck shrugged. "You don't know my sister."

"Takes after her big brother, does she?" Steve grinned.

Nothing more was said as they packed to leave. Depending on how things went at the two ranches, they might not make it back to camp before nightfall. "You might as well come with me and meet Mrs. Denning."

Jim sent him a sideways glance, and Steve grinned.

Buck expected Andy to be away from Leta's cabin, but he walked out of the barn as Buck rode in. "Buck. I didn't know when you'd be back." The boy looked almost glad to see him. "Something's got Leta upset this morning, but she won't say what's wrong."

"Court yesterday was a disappointment."

"It's not that. She was angry when she got home, but this morning was different." He shrugged. "I don't know. She might talk to you. She thinks I'm a kid."

Buck suppressed a smile. Had he seemed so impossibly young to his parents when he was that age? Probably.

Stella heard the commotion outdoors and ran outside. "Buck, you're back so soon!" She hugged him and took a step back. "And here I thought you'd let me keep up my adventure for a few more days." She whirled in a circle and looked at the other two men on horseback. "And who are these handsome fellows?"

One of them, with sun-streaked hair and looking good in a blue chambray shirt, tipped his hat. "Ranger Steve Sampson. I understand you're this monkey's sister."

"You just called her a monkey," said the other one, tall and dark. "Jim Austin, ma'am. I've known Buck these past five years. He's a fine man." He bent over and shook her hand. "But he never told me he had such a lovely sister."

Stella smiled. "Maybe because I was still in pigtails when he left home. Give me a minute to get Leta. She's been resting this morning." She hesitated. "She had a rough night, and I promised to look after things while she slept. I tell you, Buck, I truly wish I could just stay here a few more days. She needs the company of another woman."

A bleary-eyed Leta came out of the door, a shawl stretched across her shoulders, brown hair tumbling down her back, hand shielding her eyes from the sun. "Buck! You're back." She flew down the porch steps and across the yard, but stopped about a yard short.

Stella looked from one to the other. Leta was biting her lip to keep from blurting something in front of strangers. "Give me a minute to get dressed." She disappeared inside.

Buck nosed Blaze toward the barn and tied him to the railing of the corral. He entered the barn and came out a moment later with a handsome black colt.

Drawn by the irresistible lure of a horse, Stella joined him at the corral. "Is this the fella that threw Ricky?"

"Yup, this is Shadow." The colt nuzzled Buck's pocket,

whinnying softly. "Did you miss me? I don't have anything for you." Buck whispered to him, easing the blanket onto his back. Shadow didn't even twitch, and Buck added the saddle. The colt quivered but Buck stayed with him, continuing to whisper in his ear.

Stella watched her brother work with Shadow with pleasure. After Pa, he was the best horseman in the Morgan family, but he had chosen to use his talents in other ways.

Leta stalked across the yard. "What do you think you're doing?"

"Ranger Buck, you're back! Can I ride Shadow today?" Ricky raced across the yard and climbed on the fence next to Stella.

At the shout, the colt backed up a step.

"Not yet. I'll give him a test ride. Then if it's all right with your mother . . ." Buck looked over Stella's shoulder.

Stella glanced back and watched Leta crossing the yard. She joined Stella at the rail, gripping so hard that splinters must be digging into her hands. "Once. He can ride around the corral one time. The doctor said he should avoid strenuous activity for a few days."

A smile crept from Buck's eyes to his cheeks and mouth. Stella's friends said his smile made them swoon, but Leta looked too scared to faint.

"This I gotta see." Steve leaned against the rail on Stella's other side. Andy propped himself against the other side of the corral.

Buck swung up on Shadow's back. The colt took one step and stopped. Motionless in the saddle, Buck said something only the animal could hear. A long minute passed—two—neither horse nor rider moved. Buck took the reins in his right hand and made a clicking noise. Shadow moved forward one step, then two.

For the next half hour, Buck put on a show. After a circuit of the corral, he changed direction and walked the colt counter-clockwise. With each circuit Buck tightened the loop, increasing the pressure on the colt to follow his lead. Satisfied at last, he rode to the spot where Ricky perched on the rails.

"Let's do it, then. Stay quiet, though. Shouting scares the colt." Buck dismounted and lifted Ricky onto the saddle. The boy looked so small on Shadow's back. Beside Stella, Leta sucked in her breath.

"Looking good." Steve nodded his head. "You ride like you were born in the saddle."

Andy gave a quiet cheer.

"Tell him to move. Dig your heels in his side." Buck walked by Shadow's side.

Ricky did as instructed and the colt plodded forward. His grin stretched as wide as Texas, and Leta relaxed. With Buck sticking close, the boy completed the circuit of the corral. With every step, every bounce in the saddle, Leta fidgeted.

They completed the circuit within minutes. "Now get down," Leta said.

"Aw, Ma."

The expression on Ricky's face brought a laugh to Stella's throat, but she held it back. It took courage for Leta to allow her son to risk life and limb so soon after knocking himself out. She had seen the same expression on her own mother's face each time she did something foolish. Like the time she raced after a rabbit in the middle of a prairie dog town. She shook her head. Only God's grace kept her from twisting an ankle that day.

Buck lifted the boy down and grabbed the colt's reins before he unlatched the gate and gently pushed Ricky through. "You did good." He looked at Leta. "You won't have any more problems with the colt." Then he bent over the fence and stuck his finger in Ricky's face. "But you, young man, if I hear any more about you riding the horse without your mother's permission, I'll come and take this horse for myself. The Rangers can always use another good horse." Buck's facial muscles twitched, as if they wanted to smile, but he kept his face straight.

"Yes, sir. I mean, no, sir. I won't ride the horse when Ma tells me not too."

"Good." Now he released those muscles in a Rio Grande–sized grin. "You did good. I bet you worked up an appetite."

"How about some bread and honey?" Leta said.

Beside Stella, Steve stirred. Buck said, "We need to be on our way. Stella, we've imposed on Mrs. Denning's hospitality long enough. Are you ready to go?"

Stella's face lost her smile. She knew she should look forward to visiting Onkel Georg's family, but none of the girls were close to her in age She had enjoyed her time with Leta. Here she had adventure; at her uncle's ranch, she'd be a pampered guest, probably not allowed to help with the simplest chores.

Stella looked to Leta for support, but she was frowning. "I need to talk to you, Mr. Morgan. Alone."

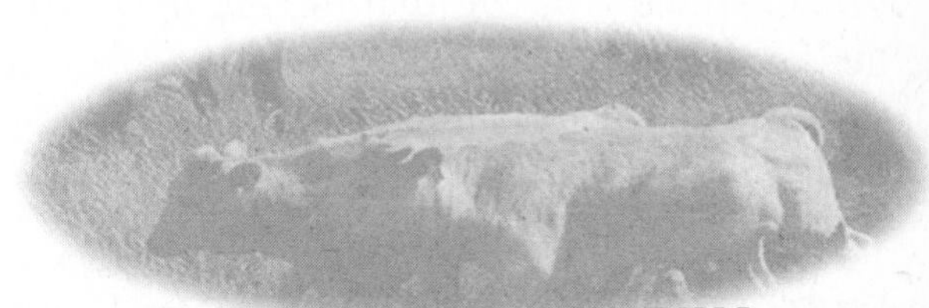

CHAPTER SEVENTEEN

Clark contacted the governor to request a reward on Cooley for Wohrle's murder. Coke obliged, offering a $300 reward on September 6, 1875.

Executive Record Book:
Richard M. Coke, Governor's Papers

Leta released her breath when Buck nodded.

"I'll get Ricky his bread and honey," Stella said. That girl knew what needed to be done before anyone asked.

Andy started to follow them, and Leta spun around. "This is a private conversation, Andy."

Her brother glared at her. "I need to talk to him too."

Leta trembled. She wondered if Andy knew what had happened last night. No, she decided. He would've told her. "Another time." She took Shadow's reins and entered the barn.

Buck joined her at the colt's stall and lifted off the saddle. "What's on your mind?"

"Last night." Leta's mouth went dry. "Someone came to the house. I didn't see who it was."

His face took on a hooded, concentrated expression, a world away from the way he looked when he smiled. "What happened?"

"I found this on the door this morning." The noose burned her fingers where she held it.

In a few savage motions Buck took care of Shadow's tack. "Tell me everything."

He made her relive every minute, every second, of the long night. She could practically smell the fear she had felt. She heard the *clip clop* of a single horse's hooves. The absence of any sounds from the farm animals. "They didn't harm anything. Maybe they didn't mean mischief."

"Aside from scaring you to death?"

A breathy chuckle escaped Leta. He didn't downplay her fear. "It's a warning, but about what? Don't try to get justice?" She thought of the missing defendants from yesterday's court case, and shivered.

Buck stroked his chin. "I saw the cattle in the pen on the way in. That's a good idea."

"Until they eat up all the grass." She drew in her breath. She'd worry about feeding them later. "It's close to time to send them to market. I won't breathe easy until I send them off." And until she saw how much money they fetched. On which side of the razor's edge between survival and loss, prosperity and poverty, would the sale fall? She shook herself. If she didn't close her mouth, she'd blab every one of her problems to this man, something she had vowed she would never do.

"Have you told anyone else about the men you identified? From the hanging last year?"

A shiver as cold as sleet in wintertime ran down Leta's back. "No." That was the source of her biggest fear. What if they knew she knew? What would they do? What would happen to Ricky if something happened to her? To Andy, for that matter? "I'm scared." Tears trickled from her eyes, in spite of all her resolutions not to cry.

"Aw, don't cry." Buck reached across the space that separated them and put work-roughened hands on her shoulders. Strong, steady hands. Slowly he pulled her head against his chest. She let herself lean into him, releasing the control she had clung to since Derrick had left her alone. The rough wool of his shirt absorbed her tears.

He preserved her dignity by releasing her when her tears stopped. She drew back, dabbed at her eyes with her apron. "God promises He's my protector. I keep reminding myself."

"With everything that's happened this past year, any reasonable person might question that statement." Buck's mouth twisted. "Not that I don't believe God. But sometimes what I believe and what I see don't match up. I figure God will clear it up sooner or later. But as far as being scared—there are three of us at the Ranger camp for now. One of us will be here at night. If we're called away, we'll let you know. No one should face this alone."

"You can't protect everyone in Mason County." Her protest sounded weak to her own ears.

"No, but you received a specific threat. It's what I want to do, it's what Captain Roberts would tell me to do, and most importantly, it's what God wants from me. So no arguing."

"I'm not going to argue with a Texas Ranger." She smiled weakly. "We'd better get inside before they wonder what's happened. You do know that I would love to have Stella stay, but I don't want to put her in danger. I've enjoyed having her here, these past couple of days."

"Maybe she can come back another time before she goes back home. After things have settled down."

"Maybe." Although she knew that was about as likely as snow falling tonight.

"It might take less time than as you think. Governor Coke has offered a reward of $300 for anyone who brings in Scott Cooley. Once he's out of the picture, things might settle down."

Leta felt the first ray of hope in a long time.

Andy was waiting by the corral when they walked out of the barn. "What's that?" He pointed at Buck.

Buck hadn't had an opportunity to put the noose away yet. "Nothing to concern you."

Andy frowned, hardening the face of a youth into an angry man. "I'm not stupid. Leta's been more crackly than leaves in fall all morning. And I thought I heard something last night." His hand lashed out, and he grabbed the noose. "Where was this?"

Leta came between them before Buck could raise voice or fist. "I don't want you involved."

"Somebody's threatening you, and I'm not involved?" Andy's voice rose.

"Quiet down before you scare the folks inside." Buck told him about the decision he had made for the Rangers to keep watch over the ranch. "We're going after the men who killed your brother-in-law. We won't stop watching out for you until they're where they can't do any more harm."

"Let me come with you." Andy stuck out his chin, every inch of his backbone stiff with determination.

Buck didn't have to look at Leta to know her reaction. He fought for words that wouldn't offend the young man's pride. During the War Between the States, he made the same arguments to his parents. He understood better than most the need of a boy to prove himself a man, but for the first time he caught a glimpse of his parents' agony over his constant pleas. Andy had a lifetime to prove his courage. Not at the killing ground that was Mason County.

The silence lengthened, and Buck realized he had waited too long to answer.

"If you don't want my help, I'll go find someone who does." Andy turned on his heels and climbed on his horse.

"Andy, wait." Leta darted forward. But he spurred the horse to a gallop, and the horse's hooves hit the ground like bricks.

"What have I done?" Worry colored Leta's brown eyes.

"Give him time. He'll come home soon." Buck spoke with a confidence he didn't feel. "Now let's go see if Stella is ready to go." He stopped by Blaze and dropped the noose into his saddlebag. The thing deserved a hot fire, but he didn't dare get rid of the evidence.

Leta opened the door to the cabin, and laughter drifted out, a world away from their worry about the noose. Buck paused, shaking off the sour mood from Leta's revelations.

Steve was talking, his arms sweeping in wide gestures. "—and that's how we caught the bank robbers."

Ricky clapped, and Stella smiled.

"Don't believe a word he says." Buck crossed the cabin. "It's nothing more than a tall tale for a campfire on a cold night."

Of Stella's trunk, Buck saw no sign. He'd bet she hadn't done a thing to get ready. "Stella."

She looked at him, the same defiance in her face as he had seen only minutes ago on Andy. "I told you, I want to stay—unless Leta says no."

Buck touched Leta's shoulder to lend her support. "I'm sorry, Stella," Leta said. "You need to be with your family. You'll be safer there."

She said the words, but the pallor in her face showed what it cost her to do the right thing. How lonely she looked. How determined. No one should be so alone. Buck vowed to spend his days in pursuit of her enemies and his nights guarding her welfare, for as long as it took. He wished he knew how he was going to make that happen.

Stella looked from him to Leta and back again, disappointment camping on her face. "Can I at least come to see you again?"

"I'm counting on it." Leta gave Stella farewell hug. "Enjoy your visit with your family." Her voice caught, reminding Buck of how small her own family circle was.

Stella nodded. "I'll get my bag."

Buck took Steve outside and explained in a few terse sentences the situation at the ranch. "I want one of us here at all times. At night for sure, and during the day if we can."

Steve nodded. "I'll stay here now, since you're going to your uncle's house." He grinned. "Although I wouldn't mind tagging along with your sister. You never said she was a beauty."

"Stella?"

"Do you have another sister around here somewhere?" Steve opened his arms to point to the yard. "Don't worry, I'm just kidding you. She won't be interested in a grizzled old ranger like me." He poked Buck in the arm. "But be prepared. She's going to have every young lad in the county coming to call."

Stella came to a standstill on her way out the door, waiting in the shadows where the men couldn't see her. Had Steve just called her pretty? Someone whom young men would come a courting? She blushed. She wouldn't mind if the Ranger showed some interest. He wasn't too old, not at all, but strong and handsome and brave. Like Buck, only a little younger. She sighed. Not much chance he would show interest in her as long as he was around her brother. She pushed the door open so that it bumped against the cabin wall and the two men looked up.

"Are you all ready to go?"

She pointed to the trunk at her feet. "All packed." Smiling, Steve helped her into the wagon. "Enjoy your visit with your family." He tipped his hat and took a step back.

Buck flicked the reins and the wagon moved. As so often in the past, he had withdrawn into himself, not speaking. After a bit, Stella spoke.

"Now tell me why I can't stay with Leta."

He shrugged. "I promised our parents to take you to the family. It's the only reason they agreed to the trip."

She scoffed. "You were fine with me staying with Leta the first night. Something happened. What?"

He frowned but didn't answer.

She kept an eye on the road, memorizing the landmarks. "If you don't tell me, I might ride back here on my own. I'll know the way." She lifted her chin.

He glanced at her sideways and laughed. "I believe you would." He pulled on the reins and the wagon came to a stop. She forced herself to sit still, not flinching as he stared at her. "You might be in a position to help."

"How?" She leaned forward.

"This—war—in Mason County is divided down racial lines. A mob of Germans started it, and now Cooley is working to even the odds."

She frowned. "But we're all Americans." She swallowed the protest. Germans against Anglos. "Is Onkel Georg involved?"

"Not Onkel Georg. Not as far as I know. But—Henry may be." Buck stared across the rolling hills. "There's more. Leta's concerned somehow."

An awful thought occurred to Stella. "Was Henry involved in the death of her husband?"

Buck's answered slowly. "Leta identified him. And someone is threatening her. It's not safe for you there. It's not safe for her, but I can't make her leave." He took a deep breath. "I haven't told Leta that Henry is my cousin."

Stella looked at the bleak expression on her brother's face. He cared a great deal. "How can I help?"

He glanced at his hand. "They know I'm a Ranger. They're careful what they say around me. But they might be less cautious around you. Don't do anything stupid. Just listen."

She considered, and then grinned. "This trip is turning into quite an adventure after all."

CHAPTER EIGHTEEN

Dan Hoerster said, "Tom, you tell Scott Cooley that the next time we meet one of us is going to die."

Thomas W. Gamel
The Life of Thomas W. Gamel

Cresting the rise to Onkel Georg's farm created a sense of coming home in Buck. The stone walls, well-tended fields, and half-timbered buildings reminded him of Oma and Opa's farm back in Victoria. In this household, German was spoken more often than English, although his cousins spoke accent-free English. He was worried now about getting Stella involved. She was still so young.

"We must be close." She turned this way and that. "I didn't expect them to be so settled. Ma makes it sound so—primitive." She gave a small hiccup. "I guess I was expecting something between home and Leta's cabin."

"German settlers are an industrious bunch. One of our

strengths." He grinned. "Give us a year on the land, and it will look more like five." He glanced behind him. "It's been hard for Mrs. Denning since her husband's death. She's not sure who she can trust."

He brought the wagon to a halt, taking in the valley carpeted with every shade of green and dotted with wildflowers. It was a beautiful spot, one of the prettiest in all of Texas. The land was well suited to raise cattle and crops. No wonder his uncle loved it here.

Hooves pounded behind them, kicking up dust. Stella coughed. A horse burst past them, headed straight for the ranch house. Henry.

"Where's the fire?" Stella frowned at the horse. "Is everyone around here that rude?"

Buck lifted a finger to his lips. His ears strained to hear the inaudible sounds, to separate birdcalls, the rustle of prairie grass, and wind in the trees from other, more dangerous noises. The excited barking of dogs. Answering neighs of horses. Voices speaking in bursts of German. All of it coming from ahead of them. He flicked the reins and urged the horses into a trot.

To give her credit, Stella didn't ask any questions, but only held on to her hat as the wagon rattled down the road.

When they pulled into the yard, Onkel Georg was arguing with Henry while Fred stood by silently. His younger cousin's eyes darted back and forth between father and brother. Much the same age as Leta's brother Andy, Fred probably felt the same need to prove himself and protect his family.

Tante Ertha bustled down the steps and interrupted the argument. "We have company. Can you not set this affair aside long enough to welcome your cousins?"

Henry tied his horse to the porch rail and walked to the wagon. "I passed you on the road."

Buck nodded. "Trouble?"

Henry frowned, but Tante Ertha interrupted before he could say anything. "Let it be. Your poor cousin has been on the road a long time. She must be tired."

As soon as Buck helped Stella from the wagon, Tante Ertha wrapped her in a hug. "It has been too long since we have seen your dear mother and father. How are they?"

Stella answered in German, the language their aunt had used. Tante Ertha and her mother had become friends shortly after their arrival in Victoria, and then she had married Onkel Georg. "Your mother also sends her greetings. As soon as I am settled, I have some things to give you from her." Stella pressed her aunt's hand. "I think both Omas miss their kinder."

Tante Ertha dabbed her eyes with the corners of her apron. "You must tell me all that is happening back in Victoria." She led Stella into the cool interior of the house.

Instead of following, Buck stayed behind with his cousin. "You looked like a man on the run back there."

After Henry studied Buck's face for a moment, he jerked his head in the direction of the barn. "I'll tell you about it while we take care of the animals."

Buck moved the wagon to a spot in the shade then unhitched the horses. Henry followed them to the water trough. "Who was chasing you?" Buck didn't lift his head when he asked his question.

Henry fingered the brim of his hat, glad it hid his expression. "Members of the Cooley gang."

"Cooley." The word came out on Buck's expelled breath. "You were fortunate to get away."

Henry narrowed his eyes, wondering why Buck avoided the obvious question: Why were they after you? Not that he would have given a complete answer.

"They have their eyes set on a bigger prize—the men involved in Tim Williamson's death. They might be going after Dan Hoerster next."

The horses had slacked their thirst, and Buck led them toward the barn. "Where is Cooley?"

From any other Ranger, the question would be academic. Buck meant it. But it didn't matter.

Henry shook his head. "I ran into them up close to Horseshoe Canyon." He took a brush and ran it over the flanks of his horse. "I'm lucky they didn't catch me and string me up. Even if my only crime is my German heritage."

"Maybe we can go up there later, see if we can pick up a trail." Buck filled the hay net for his horses. "Cooley's been as unpredictable as the first flower of spring."

"Bring a posse with you. Don't forget the man is single-handedly responsible for the deaths of good men around here."

"Better if we catch him in the act. If we can find him before he gets to Hoerster." Fierce determination blazed from Buck's eyes, the same strength it had taken their parents to cross an ocean and conquer a new world. In his cousin, it was transformed into something different, something very American, very—Texan.

Buck reached into his saddlebag and pulled out a tiny notebook. "Draw me a map—the location of Hoerster's ranch. Any hangouts you might know about, places they might plan an ambush. Mark the location where you ran into them."

Henry grabbed the notebook from his hands and sketched a readable map of the terrain. "No harm can come to Hoerster. Don't use him to snare Cooley."

Buck didn't answer right away. Henry must know the Rangers had a bad record in this particular conflict. "I'll do the best I can. But in return you must promise something."

Henry lifted his eyebrows.

"No harm must come to Leta Denning, her family, or her lands."

Henry wondered how much his cousin knew, or guessed. He held his gaze for several moments before nodding.

How lonely the ranch seemed. Leta didn't realize how much she missed female companionship until she had it and lost it. Stella had filled the cabin with joy and laughter. Don't fuss over it, she told herself. Look at all the ways God has blessed you.

Ricky played in the yard. Leta insisted he stay close to the house for a few days, until the doctor had a chance to look at him again. When she promised he could ride Shadow after dinner, he grabbed his marbles and set up a game in the yard.

All too soon he would start school, the first step in the process of growing up and away. With Buck and Steve's dependable help around the ranch, she felt she could relax for short periods. She had decided to stop questioning their presence and instead accept it as a gift from God. After they left, she'd have to hire help to take their place.

As for Andy—maybe it was time for her to let go. He was young, but like her, he'd had to grow up fast. Sometime soon she'd sit down with him and have a serious conversation. See if she could tease out his dreams. Free him to go someplace far away from the factions splitting Mason County in two.

"Ma, come play with me." Ricky waved at her. He had drawn a lopsided circle in the dirt and placed precisely six marbles in the center.

They played marbles for maybe five minutes before the familiar figure of Buck on Blaze's back galloped into the yard.

"I didn't expect you back so soon." She stood, brushing the dust from her skirts.

"Something has come up—I need for Steve to come with me." He stopped. "I'm so sorry. Maybe Andy can stay closer to the house until Steve can come back."

God was her fortress. "He'll be back tonight. I'll do as you say."

Buck stared at her for a few seconds, and looked like he was debating with himself.

"We're going after the thieves. Maybe even some of the German mob."

Terror seized her throat, and she couldn't say any more. "Get that other Ranger—Jim, was that his name? Before you go after them. Where are they hiding?"

He glanced at the ground. When he looked back up, determination lined his face. "We think they might have holed up in a remote part of Loyal Valley. Near Columbine Canyon. Stay at home until you hear back from me."

"Stay safe. I'll be praying."

The weight of worry grew heavier as his figure grew smaller in the distance.

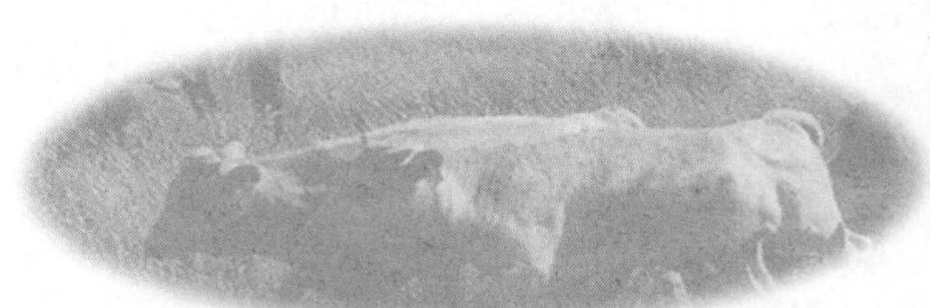

CHAPTER NINETEEN

GALVESTON DAILY NEWS
October 12, 1875

It appears that the contest is gradually becoming one of nationalities, the Germans being pitted against the Americans. Which is in the right is "one of those things no fellah can find out." Even the parties themselves are not a unit on that subject.

Buck was grateful that Steve left him alone. He had just told Leta the wrong location of the thieves' supposed hideout. What had possessed him to tell such a lie to Leta?

Because of Andy, that was why. He couldn't escape the suspicion after a cold examination of the facts. While Buck was riding to the D-Bar-D, Leta's ranch, his mind drew a map from point A to point B to point C. A—Henry's name hadn't come up in any of the accounts of the German mob, and Cooley's men had no reason to suspect him. B—Leta had listed Henry as one of the men involved in her husband's death. C—less than a week later, Henry had been chased by members of the Cooley gang.

Buck hoped he was wrong, but he feared his conclusions were built on a firm foundation.

Drizzle fell, sprinkling his jacket like a shirt before ironing. He shook off the droplets.

"Want to talk about it?" Steve broke his silence.

Buck turned his mind from the questions about Leta. "Which do you think we should do first? Cooley or Hoerster?"

"Hoerster. If your information is correct, find Hoerster and we might find Cooley. I only hope we get there in time to prevent more bloodshed. If we had a list of the people involved with Williamson's murder, maybe we could round them all up and keep them safe."

"If we could identify the people involved with Williamson's murder, we'd have to arrest them." The corner of Buck's mouth lifted. "Some people think Cooley is saving the county the cost of a trial."

"If I believed that—"

"—you'd be on the Indian scout with Roberts."

"Thanks for your confidence in me."

Even with the long summer daylight hours, dusk was approaching before they reached the campsite on the Llano. They explained the situation to Jim as they headed out. "From the map I have, I figure we can reach Hoerster's ranch by dawn."

"Am I coming with you or do you want me to bring word to the captain?" Jim said.

"Come with us. From what my cousin said, Hoerster is in imminent danger." Buck drained a cup of the campfire coffee and chomped down a bowl of cold beans. He wouldn't mind forty winks, but that would have to wait. Long days and even longer nights—that was a Ranger's life.

Night was full dark when they reached the entrance to the Valley. His uncle's ranch lay to the west. How soon would the information he had planted with Leta come to fruition? Maybe never. That was the best outcome.

Their route took them within a mile of his uncle's ranch house. The buildings lay in darkness, vague shapes in the darkness of the moonlit night. Where was Henry on this night? At home, safe in his bed, Buck prayed.

A light mist fell, and clouds covered the moon. The lack of light slowed their progress until dawn spread pink fingers to the east. They rode to the southwest corner of the county.

Jim stopped and pulled out his flask. He broke a piece of jerky in pieces and handed them to Steve and Buck. "It seems like we would have seen some sign of trouble by now."

"I agree. I wonder if we made the wrong call." Steve looked at Buck.

"We'll find out, soon enough." Buck shook his head. "If we can prevent more killings, that's more important than catching up with Cooley." He closed his eyes and scanned the map he had memorized. "We're close now. No more than a half hour's ride. We keep going." Buck tapped the pocket where he had tucked the notebook. "Cooley's hideout is bound to be on the opposite side of the county. Away from the German settlements. If we don't find him here, we'll take a brief rest and start over."

Left unsaid was the fact they were no closer to locating Cooley.

They covered the remaining distance to the Hoerster ranch

in under twenty minutes. An eerie quiet greeted them, none of the hustle and bustle of early mornings around a ranch.

They circled the farm buildings—nothing, no one in sight. They paused, checked their guns. "Let's do it." Buck spurred Blaze out of cover.

Right hand on butt of rifle, Buck stood in the center of the yard, expecting someone to come out and greet them. At a gesture from Buck, Steve headed for the barn. Jim went up to the house and knocked on the door. When no one answered, Jim went in. "Looks like no one's been here for a while. Maybe he's hiding out from Cooley."

Steve came out of the barn, shaking his head.

They regrouped in the yard. "So we head back to camp and start over?" Steve said.

Buck's thoughts swiveled to the information he had planted with Leta, and he shook his head. "No. I know where Cooley might head next." He didn't explain why. "But we need clear heads before we approach him. We'll rest for two hours, then head out again. A shorter ride this time."

They grabbed oats from the barn to supplement the grass. Buck fried some bacon for them all. Then he leaned against a tree, keeping his hat on to cushion his head against the rough bark of the trunk.

Steve settled down beside him. "Tell us about Cooley. No more secrets. I'll die by your side if it comes to that, but I gotta know the truth."

Jim joined them at the tree. "I don't want to ride another half day and not find anything at the end of the road. You like to play things close to the vest, but it's time to tell us what's up. Where are you taking us, and what do you expect to find?"

Leta breathed a sigh of relief when Andy showed up at dinnertime. With the renewed threats, she wanted those important to her close by. God willing, the danger would end soon. The Rangers would capture the leaders of the gangs, and without heads, the followers would drift away.

And justice would prevail and everyone brought to a rightful end? She swallowed a laugh. Her faith in justice had about disappeared a year ago. At least Andy sat at her kitchen table cracking jokes and teasing Ricky instead of chasing after Cooley. "Let's you and me take a ride after we eat."

Ricky turned pleading brown eyes in her direction. "Ma, can I?"

Leta wanted to scream no. Instead she said, "Where?"

"I found a vixen with kits. Thought you might like to see them." Andy looked over his plate at Leta. "It's only a couple of miles. Near the river."

Baby kits. How cute. "I'm coming with you."

"Ma, I'll be safe."

She put the plates in water to soak. "I want to see the babies too."

Ricky's eyes opened wide. "You like foxes?"

"Baby ones." She grabbed her journal. She didn't often draw, but this might be one of those times. She found a sketch she had done of Ricky, running her fingers over his features. She wished she had done more sketches of Derrick.

Now when she tried to bring Derrick's face to mind, instead of his open features and steady brown eyes, far-seeing blue eyes took their place, a hat obscuring his forehead.

She tucked three cookies in a handkerchief and filled her canteen from the pump before climbing onto her horse.

"You took forever." Ricky squirmed and Shadow snorted.

Before she could open her mouth, he straightened his back and Shadow settled down. Leta smiled. "Let's go."

Andy led them to a quiet spot where they could watch. "You have to be quiet. If the mother fox hears you, she'll chase them inside quicker than a lightning strike."

Ricky nodded and settled between his mother and uncle. "I don't see anything." His whisper could have filled a church.

Andy lifted his fingers to his lips.

Leta's pencil caught Andy's expression, his open eyes, his boyishness. With each passing day, she saw less of the boy he had once been. Yellow tinged the leaves hanging overhead. The breeze caught one and twisted it on the stem, and it fluttered to the ground. Before long they would cover the ground.

Ricky sucked in his breath, and Leta knew the kits had made their appearance. Turning a page of her journal, she looked toward the burrow. A pointed, whiskered nose poked out. A thin red leg batted at the nose. The baby tumbled out head over head. All babies were cute, but she loved watching the way littermates played together.

If only her baby had lived. Ricky needed a sibling. Tears sparkled in her eyes. She dashed at them and sketched the kit tumbling in front of the burrow. If only all evenings were this quiet and pleasant. "Maybe it will all end soon."

"What's that?" Andy scooted onto his knees.

"This whole business with the cattle thieving. Buck said they have a lead."

"When did he say that?" Wariness came into Andy's expression.

"After you left."

"Ranger Buck said I can ride Shadow whenever Ma says it's okay. He said I'm a good rider." Ricky puffed his chest out. "He said the thieves were in Loyal Valley, near the caves. He told Ma."

"Loyal Valley." Andy frowned. "Where the Dutch ranches are."

"Are they close, Ma?" Ricky raised his voice. "Will they come back and hurt us?"

The vixen raised her head. She pushed the kits back in the burrow.

Ricky twisted back. "Where did the baby foxes go?"

"You scared 'em, little guy. We might as well go home." Andy stood and helped Leta to her feet. "It's getting late anyway. It'll be full dark soon."

She glanced at the sky. Clouds obscured the light, darkening the sky earlier than usual. "You're right. Let's get home."

She stayed up later than usual, finishing the evening chores. In bed, she turned to the Song of Solomon, where she thought there were verses about foxes. Yes, there they were, in the second chapter: "Take us the foxes, the little foxes, that spoil the vines: for our vines have tender grapes." Poor little guys. She'd have to catch the kits if they raided her chicken coop or ate their plants.

God made them all, hunter and prey. Germans and Anglos. She sent up a prayer for the Rangers on the hunt. Maybe this yearlong nightmare was coming to an end.

She went out to the main room for a drink of water and stuck her head around the corner of the blanket. She couldn't resist the urge to check on Ricky. To reassure herself that he was still breathing.

He was curled up on his side of the bed.

The other side of the bed was empty.

Where had Andy gone?

Jim shook Buck's shoulder. "Your watch."

The three rangers had arrived at the watch point—a small ledge with a good view of the valley below—shortly before dawn. After Buck explained the situation—his suspicions that

Andy Warren was in contact with Scott Cooley—Jim and Steve agreed that reconnaissance was a good idea.

"Quiet as a giraffe." Jim yawned. "Maybe things will get busy now that it's daylight."

"Or not until tonight." Buck scratched his chin. "A cup of coffee sounds good." His mind flashed to the last meal he had enjoyed, in Leta's kitchen. If his suspicions about Andy were true, she wouldn't welcome him so warmly next time. He wasn't sure how he wanted this stakeout to end. In the capture of a gang responsible for multiple thefts and murders? Or in a dead end, alleviating his suspicions about Leta's brother?

In justice for the many, or mercy for the few?

He was glad such decisions were up to God, not him. He prayed God would direct the action on this day.

"Splash some cold water on your face. That always helps me." Jim stretched out next to Steve and pulled his saddle blanket over his shoulder, his rifle where he could grab and shoot.

Rainwater had collected in an indentation in the rock face. Buck scrubbed it into his face. It did help. He found a comfortable spot where he could scan the valley below. He settled down, reciting his way through the Psalms—his favorite activity while waiting. Light crept across the valley, revealing trees and hollows and rock outcroppings. Of the three ways to the caves, he dismissed the route that crossed his uncle's ranch. Cooley wouldn't worry about someone not involved with the Williamson murder—unless Leta told Andy about her suspicions about Henry.

He'd better keep his eyes on all three routes, just in case. Buck sent up a prayer for his cousin's safety, until his guilt or innocence could be proved in a court of law. Once through several Psalms, he rotated his position so he could view from a different direction.

When he reached Psalm 23—the bit about green pastures and still waters—ironic in this setting—tree branches dipped and Buck spotted gray and brown shapes coming through the trees.

"They're here."

CHAPTER TWENTY

I open this letter to say that James Cheyney was shot this morning at his home about 1½ miles from town. Verdict of Coroner's jury: "Shot by parties unknown."

Correspondence between
Henry Jones and Governor Coke
September 24, 1875

Three guns lined up at the edge of the ledge. "There's over a dozen people down there," Buck said.

"How do you want to handle it?" Jim eased back.

"We want to avoid a shootout." From this viewpoint, Buck couldn't make out any features. "Could be some of my uncle's men."

"We didn't wait all night to second-guess ourselves now."

Buck nodded. The first rider emerged from the copse of trees. "It's Cooley, all right. They won't see us as long as we stay on foot."

"No riding to the rescue."

Steve grunted. "No one to rescue today." He led the file. "I see the Warren kid."

Buck's gut clenched. "So he came along." How many of the murders had he witnessed? Murder begot murder. He thought of King David's admonition to his men. "Deal gently for my sake with the young man, even with Absalom"—after his son had plotted to take over the throne. He never could understand that, until now. He prayed that the men would give up without a fight.

He knew they would not. Not men led by a former Ranger. Not someone who knew how the Rangers would react almost better than they did themselves.

"I see movement, coming from the north," Jim called from behind Buck.

The three of them watched the approach of the second group. There were three men on horseback, working their way through bushes.

Not bushes. Cattle. "They're not with Cooley. Not unless he's become a cowboy in the past week." His uncle and his two cousins were headed straight into a trap. He jumped onto Blaze's back. "We got to get down there. Now."

Buck's mind sped through the possibilities as Blaze made his way sure-footed down the mountain. He had to reach his cousins before they were ambushed. When Cooley saw Germans moving cattle, he would assume they were the cattle thieves as promised and open fire. They had demonstrated their philosophy often enough: kill first, ask questions later.

Onkel Georg was much too close to Cooley.

A single gunshot rang out. Buck wished Blaze could fly down the mountain. If he urged the horse to go any faster, he would slip and fall. Cooley's group was racing forward, guns drawn.

By the time they reached level ground below the ledge, the

two groups had reached the open pasture. His uncle motioned to his sons to move back; the men with Cooley increased speed.

Now within firing range, bullets started flying. Frightened by the gunfire, the cattle ran in several directions, cutting off Fred.

Cooley raised his gun and aimed.

"No!" Buck spurred Blaze who spurted forward.

The piercing sound of a gunshot filled the air. Buck felt as if he was living a nightmare as he watched the confusion before him.

Fred slumped from his horse and hit the ground. Jim and Steve surged toward the gunmen. "Texas Rangers! Halt!"

They were still too far away from the scene for their words to have an effect on the gang. But Andy glanced at the man who had been so kind to him in the past, and fear spread across his face.

"You go see what you can do for your cousin. We'll take care of Cooley." Steve turned his horse west and galloped away in pursuit.

Buck watched as the riders quickly disappeared into the distance. Signaling his horse for action, Buck gently spurred his side and together they raced to aid Fred.

Stella wished she could have stayed with Leta. At least there she felt like she was contributing something to the household.

Buck wanted her to sniff out any suspicious activity by his cousin. But Henry didn't talk with her. How likely was that to happen? No man was going to tell his young cousin, "Oh, by the way, I was part of a lynch mob."

Tante Ertha couldn't tell her anything. She knew no more about the violence than a fly trying to make its way out the window. But Lisel, her cousin Henry's wife . . . maybe. Maybe she would talk.

But so far, Lisel was about as likely to spill her husband's secrets as she would share the details of childbirth to an unmarried girl. Stella would have to be her most charming, empty-headed self. Too bad she couldn't have saddled up and gone out with her uncle and her cousins. That way, she might pick up clues.

"What are you thinking so seriously about?" Tante Ertha looked up from the biscuits she was rolling out.

"Thinking how fun it would be to go out with the men." Stella put her hand to her mouth and quickly turned her attention back to the eggs she was separating. The hens had laid a bumper crop, and Tante Ertha decided to make a sponge roll and a meringue pie.

Tante Ertha laughed, a light, tinkling sound that revealed her soprano voice. "I used to do the same thing. Say whatever thoughts came to my mind. It almost cost me your mother's friendship." She dusted the bottom of a glass and starting cutting biscuits. "But she was so kind as always. Your poor mother worries for you. Wande says you are still a tomboy at heart." Even with the gray sprinkled in her red hair, Tante Ertha remained young at heart. Stella enjoyed her company.

Lisel took the bowl of egg whites. Her face revealed nothing more than serious concentration as she whipped the egg whites. A good German hausfrau.

"I confess, I'd rather be outside most days." Stella looked out the window. "I like growing plants more than cooking them."

"Wande loves a garden. Does she still sell vegetables at market?"

"Yes. Everyone in Victoria comes to her for her *Gewuerzgurken* and fresh vegetables." A pang of homesickness swept over Stella. If she found adventure and love here so far away from home, she would never spend her Saturdays visiting with their neighbors in Victoria again.

Horses raced into the yard. Buck among the riders. A slender body slumped in front of Onkel Georg: Fred.

Tante Ertha moaned and ran for the door. Lisel looked up from the egg whites, which had formed soft peaks.

"Fred's been hurt." Stella dunked the last egg yolk in the bowl and headed for the door.

Before she made it outside, Onkel Georg filled the frame, Fred's still body in his arms. Buck followed close behind. Stella jumped out of the way, and her uncle brushed past her, carrying his son into the parlor where he laid him on the couch. "Henry, go for the doctor."

"Dr. Tardiff won't be at his office." Stella cleared her throat. "Yesterday he said he couldn't come by the Denning Ranch this morning because he had promised to check out a couple of cases of measles."

Tante Ertha was on her knees leaning over her son. "Friedrich? Can you hear me?" She pressed her ear to Fred's chest. The room came to absolute stillness as she listened. When she lifted her head, they released a collective breath. "He's still alive."

Lisel brought in a bowl of steaming water, soap, and a mean-looking knife. Buck came to life. "I've done this before."

Stella stumbled. Her knees buckled at the sight of the knife taking its first cut.

"Come, cousin." Henry put his arm around her shoulders.

"No. Let me stay." He led her to a chair and helped her sit. Closing her eyes, her lips moving in prayer. He returned his attention to his brother.

Fred looked so impossibly young, younger than his years laid out still as he was, as innocent as Henry's two little girls. As Buck worked, Fred's breath came out in ragged gasps, a bit like a fish trying to breath in air. Henry's own breath labored as his brother struggled.

When at last Buck finished, Ma took his place by Fred's side, his head in her lap, holding his hand, head bowed in prayer.

Cooley had a lot to answer for. Henry wanted to go get Schmidt and Hinke and chase him down. Make him pay.

His father noticed Fred's slight movement and shook his head.

Fred wouldn't last long.

Henry wanted to plant a bullet straight between Cooley's eyes.

Stella wasn't a stranger to blood. She had bandaged her nephew's scrapes and even set a broken leg one time.

But she'd never dug a bullet out of someone. She wasn't living up to the standard set by her heroine Clara Barton, a ministering angel to the men she nursed during the War Between the States.

After Buck finished, he washed his hands in the bowl of water and dried his hands, then came toward her.

"Tell Tante Ertha and Onkel Georg I'll be back as soon as I can."

"Ranger business?"

"There's nothing more I can do here. Steve and Jim went after Cooley. If they catch up with him, they'll need help." He stepped closer to her. "There's something else you should know. Andy Warren was with Cooley."

She gasped. "Leta's brother?"

He nodded. "I hoped I was wrong but . . . I'm afraid Andy and maybe Leta too are meting out justice without benefit of law. I don't want you back there until we've sorted it out."

"Buck?"

He paused on his way out the door.

"Can't you wait a little while? Until . . ." She nodded in the direction of the parlor. She hated the tremor in her voice. "They need you. I need you." She began crying.

Buck cradled her quivering body in his arms. He knew he could not leave yet.

Jim Cheyney had been shot, not Dan Hoerster. All of Mason was in an uproar.

Leta pushed down the fear. She needed to finish her weekly shopping. Miss Moneypenny, the teacher, had agreed to meet with Leta and Ricky on Saturday. Perhaps she was overanxious, but she wanted to learn how Ricky was doing. She was determined that Ricky could read the Bible and do basic sums. More, if he wanted it. She'd love for him to become a doctor or a lawyer or a pastor. Big dreams for a poor rancher's son.

She'd feel better if they lived closer to the school. Maybe she should seek a job in town that would support them. Give up the ranch, especially if Andy . . . moved on. She didn't know what she would say if he came home tonight.

Her head hurt. Texas had always been her home, but for the first time, she wished she lived in a more settled part of the country. Maybe if she sold the ranch.

No, if she sold the ranch, she'd be lucky if she was left with enough money to buy train tickets. Maybe Ricky could ride for free. Still, she didn't know where she'd go or how she would support a family.

Andy and Ricky would wither in the confines of a city,

away from the space to ride and the rhythms of ranch life. So would she.

No. Mason County was home, and like marriage, it was for better or for worse.

CHAPTER TWENTY-ONE

MASON COUNTY NEWS
January 6, 1893

Mankind ever stands appalled before the impenetrable mystery of death. No voice has ever broken the somber silence of the grave, but God in the wisdom of His Revelation has responded to the yearnings of the soul and faith gives us a vision of the "city not made with hands, eternal in the heavens."

A sharp cry rent the air, shocking Buck out of his light doze. Tante Ertha flung herself across Fred's still form, sobs racking her body. "Why? God in heaven, why? He was just a boy who did no harm to anyone."

Dr. Tardiff had come at last in the early evening, but offered no hope. "Keep him as comfortable as possible . . . and pray." The family kept watch all night, while Fred's breathing slowed. From what Buck observed, his death was quiet and peaceful. No fever, no delirium—only his life seeping senselessly away.

Fred's needless death weighed on Buck. He would stay with his family long enough to bury his cousin—and then he would add very personal reasons to chasing down Cooley.

Not only Cooley, but also the people with him—including Andy Warren. He was close to Fred in age, and yet far removed in experience. Why, God, indeed? Why Fred, who had never harmed anyone, and not Henry? Not that Buck wanted Henry to die, but it would have made a kind of poetic justice.

Some people would call the death of poor Fred God's will. Buck didn't believe that way. God allowed it to happen, but it was no more His will than Satan's rebellion in heaven. The Rangers had ignored Cooley's part in this hoodoo, bad luck, long enough.

Buck closed Fred's eyes and placed his arms under his chest and knees before picking him up. "Where do you want him laid out?"

Tante Ertha pointed down the hall to the bedroom she shared with Onkel Georg. Buck used his bulk to shield the family from the sight of Fred's limp body in his arms. After spreading a clean sheet across the quilt, he laid down his cousin. He had seen plenty of dead bodies before, but rarely one so young, and never one from a gunshot wound. He closed his eyes. "Lord, I trust Fred is with You now. So I won't pray for him. But his family here is hurting."

Buck's conscience reminded him that other families in Mason had suffered loss. Most of them had done something to bring anger on themselves. The mob activity had started over cattle theft and been raised to the level of murder.

Guilt overwhelmed Buck as he gazed at his cousin. As a

Ranger, he had made life-and-death decisions before. Command and responsibility carried risk, and he had killed men in battle.

But this . . . the closest Buck had felt to this guilt was when he saw a Comanche mother and child killed during one of their scouts. The brave's family was no threat to white settlers. After the event, Buck debated resigning his commission. He held off until he could speak with Major Jones. By the time he saw the major again, he had changed his mind.

The door opened, and Tante Ertha and Lisel entered. "We'll take over from here. Thank you for everything."

Buck turned his head, so they wouldn't see the tears that blurred his vision. His aunt wouldn't thank him if she knew the truth. That he was responsible for Fred's death. Anger and guilt propelled him toward the door.

"We'll hold the funeral tomorrow. Henry is going to town, to ask if Reverend Stricker can come say a few words. We can't wait any longer than that." Tante Ertha's voice broke. "It will be the first family member buried in our cemetery. We've only had one ranch hand die. We've considered ourselves so blessed, and then this happens . . ."

"We have to accept God's will," Lisel said.

A gasp from the door alerted Buck to Stella's presence. She opened her mouth, but Buck shook his head and guided her back to the main room. Under her breath, she sputtered, "God's will doesn't include murder."

Thou shalt not kill. Buck didn't like to think of all the men who had died at his hands. "No, but God promises to work everything for good. That gives people comfort." He pulled her close, cradling her head against his chest the way he had when she was little. "Even when illness took two of Ma's siblings and the Comanche captured Aunt Billie, our parents never gave up their faith in God." His hold on her tightened. "I have to believe in God's goodness. Or else nothing makes any sense."

She clung to him, crying. His sister had gained a new and terrible knowledge, akin to that Eve gained from the tree of the knowledge of good and evil. She pulled away and patted his chest. "Go capture the guys who did this." Her voice turned cold. "No other family should go through this. Not if you can do something to stop it."

"I'm on my way. As soon as I get a letter off." He borrowed pen and paper from Onkel Georg. In a quiet corner of his room, he wrote the letter he should have written long ago. He would detail everything he knew and suspected. He would beg Major Jones to commit the Rangers to stay in Mason County until things settled, one way or the other.

Major Jones:

The Texas Rangers must go to Mason County to preserve the peace and to remain until further notice. The situation is critical. Company D should abandon the Indian scout and return to Mason with all speed.

I realize you may choose to bring action against me for not passing on the names Mrs. Denning gave to me earlier. I have no excuse, except a desire to confirm her suspicions and to catch Cooley in an act of violence. Anything you do cannot be worse than the death of my cousin because of my cautious approach.

I also recognize that you must pursue Heinrich Fleischer's (Henry Fletcher's) involvement in the German mob.

I cannot endure watching the remainder of my uncle's family destroyed. I am tendering my resignation immediately.

Sgt. William Meino Morgan

He addressed an envelope. He would send it the next time he reached a post office. First he would find Jim and Steve. He wouldn't abandon them until Company D returned. He grabbed a stamp from the parlor desk and stuck it on the envelope, blowing on the ink of the address to let it dry.

"I am so glad to meet you, Mrs. Denning." Fresh out of school in Arkansas, Miss Moneypenny had started teaching Mason's school the previous week. Arkansas was far enough way that she might not have heard about the war in Mason County. She hadn't mentioned the most recent death, Jim Cheyney, and Leta wouldn't mention it if she didn't.

"I wish all our parents were as interested in their children's schooling as you are. Of course, it's early in the year."

They'd be more interested if they weren't worried about survival. "Education is an advantage I want my son to have. He likes stories. I'm hoping he'll like to read."

"He already knows the alphabet." Miss Moneypenny glanced at the chalkboard, where all twenty-six letters of the alphabet were written in block letters as well as cursive. "What letter does your name start with?" Miss Moneypenny smiled at him, confident of his answer.

"D. Like dog."

Miss Moneypenny cast a confused look at Leta. "Ricky starts with R, not with D."

Ricky giggled. "My real name is Derrick. D-e-r-r-i-c-k. I know how to spell it." He ran to the chalkboard and wrote it down.

"He's named for his father. We called him Ricky, to tell them apart."

"His father died when the awfulness started last summer?"

So the young woman had heard about the town's troubled history. "If you know our recent history, Miss Moneypenny, I'm surprised you came to Mason."

"It's Julia. Let's talk. But first—" She walked to her desk and pulled out a spelling book. "Ricky, I need your help next week. Here are our spelling words. Can you read them?"

He looked at her scornfully. "Of course. C-a-t, cat. R-a-t, rat. B-a-t, bat." He read through the list with ease, and Leta allowed herself a moment of pride.

"I'd like you to memorize them in order and make up sentences. And for a treat, why don't you go outside while you work on it."

Once Ricky had closed the door, Julia took a seat beside Leta. "My reason for coming to Mason may sound foolish. I felt called. Of all the people damaged by war, children always suffer the most. Several of them are in my class. I was hoping to bring healing to children from both factions, but . . . none of the German families have sent their children to my school." She looked out the window. "I fear they will learn to hate from their parents unless something changes. Mason will need its own Reconstruction, and I pray we do a better job than the folks in Washington did."

Leta sat back. Was she passing on her own hatred and distrust to her brother and son? "Don't you believe in justice?"

"Justice, yes. Revenge, no. 'Vengeance is mine; I will repay, saith the Lord.' Romans 12:19." Julia turned into a schoolmarm for a moment. "I know this all started when people thought a trial ended in the wrong verdict."

Oh, Derrick.

"But if people start keeping score—it will be like things were after the War Between the States. From what I have heard of President Lincoln, things would have gone much better if he had lived to see things through, instead of President Johnson."

"Here in Mason, we started out with a sheriff who took one side over the other."

"So I've heard. We'll have to pray God sends someone new. But my job—besides prayer, of course—is to help the poor young ones left behind. Including Ricky. He chatters a lot—that's his biggest problem."

"Use whatever discipline you feel is needed." Nothing Leta tried made much difference, but this teacher seemed so competent.

"I will, if it's necessary." Julia smiled. "He gets bored easily. My biggest job will be to keep him too busy to get bored." The laughter in her eyes said how much she enjoyed the challenge.

"I'm so glad we had this chance to talk. I'll be praying about your calling. God brought you here for a special purpose, I'm sure of it. And now I won't keep you any longer." Leta stood. Julia and Stella, both young women with drive and determination, must be about the same age. Leta didn't think she ever felt so certain of herself, so open to new experiences. Ricky was blessed to have Miss Julia Moneypenny for a teacher.

Ricky dashed inside the school. "I know the words, Miss Moneypenny." He listed ten rhyming words. Eyes twinkling, he said, "I made up a poem with the words."

"Wonderful!" Julia clapped her hands. "Ask your mother to help you write it out, and bring it on Monday."

"I'll do that."

Maybe the future in Mason held promise after all.

CHAPTER TWENTY-TWO

SAN ANTONIO DAILY EXPRESS
November 23, 1875

Then again on Saturday night a party supposed to be the Cooley party came to town heavily armed, but were pursued by the Rangers and three of their number captured, and as rumor has it, Cooley himself was wounded. The Rangers are still in pursuit . . .

Buck stared at the loose pebbles under his feet. He had caught up with Jim and Steve about an hour before. Looking across the valley, he realized the spot he had chosen was a poor place for an ambush. After the shooting started, Cooley lit out over the rocks. Jim and Steve followed, looking for a place where the two of them could take down more than a dozen men. But they lost the trail heading around the mountain.

"If it was just a matter of bringing them in dead or alive, we could have done it. But we figured killing them would just start the whole cycle all over again."

"They need to be tried and punished in a court of law." Buck shook his head. "It's my fault. I should have set the meet in a different place." He thought of Andy and the approach from the Denning ranch. The route cut across the Llano and ran through trees and pastureland, easy enough for a tracker. "I should have come with you."

"Don't say that. You had to see to your cousin." Jim tilted his head in his direction. "How's your family taking his death? Breathing fire and vengeance like everybody else?"

Henry probably was. Buck's stomach clenched. "Might be. And I don't altogether blame them." When the other two exchanged glances, he held up a hand. "I'll stop them, if they try."

Jim pulled his horse up. "We're a ways from our camp. I'm worn out. I say we stop here for the night and rest up. I got the makings for coffee and bacon in my saddlebag."

They all agreed and soon they had settled for the night. Buck dug in his saddlebag and pulled out a pouch. "I've got rice to add."

"Remember the time that new recruit cooked all that rice?" Steve grinned.

"It's grown into such a tall tale that there was enough rice to soak up all the water in the Gulf of Mexico." Jim chuckled. "I remember."

"Growing up, I ate too much *aroz con frijoles* to not know how to cook rice." Buck dumped a measured amount into the water Jim had boiling on the campfire.

"I'll add the frijoles." Steve settled a crock of beans in the pot with the rice. "We'll have ourselves a feast. Hot food, strong coffee, and a full night's rest. What more could a Ranger want?"

Buck thought about the letter of resignation waiting in his pocket. He looked at the sky, clear tonight, with the Big Dipper pointing to Ft. Worth and Indian Country and other stops north all the way to the North Pole. From childhood he'd dreamed of joining the Rangers, rejoicing when Governor Coke reinstituted the service. He had lived his dream for the past twelve months.

And now he was ready to leave. All because of a widow woman, her outlaw brother, and her accusations against his own flesh and blood.

Buck couldn't tell Steve and Jim about his decision to leave the Rangers without spewing anger across the still night. His natural reticence won out, and he said nothing.

Stella had stayed busy in the kitchen, fixing supper last night and breakfast this morning. Between meals, she cooked enough food to feed all the Fleischer clan, ranch hands, and any neighbors who happened by for the funeral. Ma would be impressed with her efforts.

Bypassing American dishes like peach pie, oatmeal cookies, and cole slaw, Stella concentrated on Oma's Texas-style strudel and a chocolate torte.

Someone knocked at the front door. She headed that way, but Lisel arrived first. "*Guten morgen*, Herr Hoerster, Frau Hoerster."

Frau Hoerster headed straight for the kitchen, bearing a pot of *Rubensuppe*, beet soup. Soon the sideboard was groaning with food—good, solid, German dishes. Bringing food to comfort the grieving was a tradition probably as old as Abraham and just as universal. If only the sight of food didn't make her feel sick.

Mason's German community filled the parlor. Several women came alone, unescorted, their husbands dead at the hands of the Anglo gang. Stella didn't wonder that they were angry. She dashed in and out of the kitchen, cleaning plates and refilling dishes as they ran out. The men gathered in groups of two or three, but Henry stayed glued to Lisel's side.

The door opened and Buck came in. He caught Stella's gaze and nodded. Tears prickled behind her eyelids. She hadn't realized how alone, how sad, she felt, so far away from her parents and everything familiar, until that moment. As far as Fred's death, she wavered between grief and shock. She wanted to feel more grief, but she just hadn't known him all that well.

Reverend Stricker arrived, and Tante Ertha gestured for her to bring him a drink.

"He has a sweet tooth." Lisel handed her a plate of their best china with strudel, and Stella poured a glass of lemonade. Nothing but the best.

Homesickness for her beloved Onkel Peter, for Ma's mouth-watering apple pie, her father's deep smile, swept over Stella. She handed Reverend Stricker the plate and pushed through the crowd into the yard.

Buck joined her a few moments later. He sat down with her on the swing Onkel Georg had built on the porch. She wanted one of her own some day, when she had her own house. Would she live in a nice house like Onkel Georg's or a simple cabin like Leta's?

As long as she shared her home with a husband she loved, she wouldn't care. A porch swing or two didn't matter in the long run. It could wait. She leaned against Buck's side. She wouldn't mind finding someone like him—strong, dependable, kind.

A sob caught in her throat. Daydreaming beat the grieving

in the parlor. She closed her eyes and breathed in the scent of newly dewed grass.

Buck nudged her. "It's time."

The family's guests exited the house. Their cousins with their families came at the end. Lisel leaned on Henry's arm, their young son and daughter dressed in somber colors and exhibiting a formal demeanor. Last of all, Reverend Stricker accompanied her aunt and uncle.

Buck helped Stella to her feet and they fell in with the mourners. They walked to the newly dug grave. A pine box, placed there earlier that morning by a couple of ranch hands, waited by the hole. A plain cross, with "Friedrich Fleischer, 1859–1875," carved in the wood. Sixteen short years. "I'm glad we can be here, for Ma's sake."

Buck nodded. Reverend Stricker stood at the head of the grave. "I remember the first time I met Friedrich. He was preparing for his confirmation. He loved the Lord, no lad better, but he couldn't remember the order of the minor prophets. He was so worried I would refuse his confirmation over such a little thing." The pastor continued with simple anecdotes, introducing her cousin to her in a way she hadn't known. Pastor Stricker was a shepherd to this flock, much as Onkel Peter was back in Victoria.

When he quoted the Twenty-third Psalm—familiar to Stella in both German and English—she joined in the recitation. "Der HERR ist mein Hirte; mir wird nichts mangeln." With his prayer, she felt comforted.

After the amen, Buck touched her arm. "I must leave again. I'm not certain when I'll be back."

The reality of the dangers her brother faced was reflected by the pine box being lowered into the ground. She didn't voice a pointless warning. "I'll be redoubling my prayers that this will reach a peaceful conclusion."

He waved as he headed for the barn. "Amen." His voice trailed behind him.

⟵ ★ ⟶

Buck patted the pocket where his letter to Major Jones waited. He couldn't mail it until tomorrow. He could rejoin Jim and Steve, but he didn't have the heart. Neither was he ready to stay at his uncle's house and listen for any plans his cousin might be hatching. His soul felt raked over coals, and there was only one place he wanted to go. Leta's simple cabin.

All the way across Loyal Valley, crossing the Llano, riding the final miles to the ranch, Buck reminded himself of all the reasons why this wasn't a good idea. Her brother was a suspect in the Cooley murders; Cooley's gang was all but convicted in a court of law. He had seen Andy with his own eyes. For all Buck knew, Andy could have fired the shot that killed Fred, although he had observed only Cooley with rifle raised.

Guilt warred with anger over Fred's death. He blamed himself. He had no reason to expect his uncle and cousins to show up in that pasture. But on the other hand, if Leta hadn't passed the information on to Andy, who in turn told Cooley, his cousin would have gone about his business, tending to his family's cattle, with no harm. Matching his master's mood, Blaze galloped at full speed until they arrived in Leta's yard. The sun lowered in the sky, a cool breeze blowing pleasantly through the trees, redolent with the odors of a well-ordered farm. Leta leaned against the corral fence, where Ricky rode Shadow at a brisk trot.

The boy saw Buck first. "Ranger Buck! You came back!"

Buck slowed Blaze, ignoring the enthusiastic greeting. He scanned the yard, confirming what he already knew—no sign of Andy or his horse. He didn't bother dismounting. "Where is your brother?"

Leta looked at him as if she didn't recognize him. "Ricky, go get ready for bed."

"Ma-a!"

"You have school in the morning. It won't hurt to get to bed early, while you're still recovering from that fall." Her smile didn't reach her eyes. "Miss Moneypenny is depending on you to help her with the spelling lesson tomorrow. The black bat chased the black cat—"

"—who wears an orange hat while he eats a big fat rat."

"Take care of the horse first," Buck told the boy. The look Leta threw at Buck when she twisted around made him wish he had kept his mouth shut.

As soon as Ricky disappeared into the barn, she spoke in a furious whisper. "I don't want my son any more worried than he already is."

"So you don't know where Andy is. When did you see him last?"

"Why do you want to know? Do you intend to boss him around too?"

CHAPTER TWENTY-THREE

Taking away thirty men weakened my force so much that I abandoned my proposed scout, and . . . thinking it probable that I might be able to gain more towards restoring peace and quiet to this distracted community than could be done by a Lieutenant I started next morning on a forced march for Mason with twenty men of my escort, Co. A.

Letter from Major John B. Jones
to Adjutant General William Steele,
September 28, 1875

"Do you think that's what I'm trying to do with Ricky? Boss him around?" Buck sounded genuinely surprised that she would say such a thing.

"You're not his father. You don't have that right." She bit off the words.

"I don't want to see anybody else hurt." He felt his face flush, and he turned away from her, his shoulders rigid in the grip of some strong emotion. Leta had never seen Buck like this.

Ordinarily he was kind, considerate—controlled. He had almost convinced her that he cared about her and her family. She didn't know why she'd ever thought this man was attractive.

He took deep, ragged breaths. She waited him out. She would wait to see if he had an explanation. He had earned that right—just about. The color in his neck returned to a healthy pink.

Ricky came out of the barn. She forced herself to smile. "Go ahead to bed. I'll come in before long." They didn't speak again until the door closed behind him.

"My cousin was killed yesterday. The latest victim of this ridiculous war."

Whatever explanation Leta expected, she never imagined this news. Her anger drained away. She put her hand on his arm, but he shrugged it off.

"You don't understand. Your brother was there when he died. For all I know, he fired the killing shot."

Leta's mouth shut. She took a step back. "That's impossible. Andy's not a killer."

"You don't even know where he's been. You said so." His eyes were as cold as polar ice. "I saw him there, Leta. I'm not making it up."

"You must have mistaken someone else for Andy."

His eyes darkened. "He was wearing that bright yellow jacket I've seen hanging from the peg by your door. The one the color of a harvest moon. Is it there today?"

"I told you. He's not here. Of course he has his coat. But he's not the only one with a yellow jacket." Even though she had stitched that one herself, from a golden-colored flour sack.

"He was riding a sorrel, like Comet."

"There are other sorrels."

"Not that many. You forget, my family raises horses. That's an unusual color combination. Every other horse was dark."

He leaned forward, danger sizzling like static between them. "I saw his face, Leta. It was him."

She stood her ground. "I don't believe my brother has committed murder. He's mixed up. He lost his father and my husband. I thought you could help him." She bit her lip, feeling the sharp pain of Buck's accusation. "I didn't expect you to accuse him of murder."

"My cousin was even younger than your brother. I will find the men who killed him. Of all people you must understand how I feel."

Leta returned glare for glare. "Good luck with that. My husband's killers still walk free." She turned on her heels and walked to the cabin, willing him to walk away.

The cabin had darkened in the deepening dusk, and Leta lit a lantern when she entered. "Ma?"

Leta carried the light behind the curtain and stood by Ricky's bed. "What is it, sweetheart?"

"Why are you mad with Ranger Buck?" Ricky was curled up on his side of the bed. "Did something happen to Uncle Andy?"

Leta resisted the urge to reassure him, to promise that Andy would be home any day. "I'm not sure where Andy is." She made herself smile. "But he's always come home safe and sound before, hasn't he?"

Ricky straightened, sitting up in the bed. His head hit the top of the headboard. She reached out and brushed the hair from his forehead. He looked more and more like his father every day.

"Ma." His voice sounded thin, uncertain. "I think I know where Andy went."

Leta set the lantern on the nightstand and sat on the chair still by the bed. "Where?" *Lord, please let him have gone hunting or even to a saloon or run away.* Anything would be better than . . .

"He said he knows who killed Pa. And he said he'd joined the gang that's hunting them down."

No. Leta fought to keep a neutral expression on her face. "When did he tell you this?"

Ricky squirmed toward the middle of the bed, a little farther away from her. "After Ranger Buck left the last time. He told me not to tell." Ricky hung his chin on his chest. "But I don't like it when you argue with Ranger Buck."

Buck was telling the truth. She stood abruptly. "I'll be right back." She reached the door in three strides and yanked it open. "Buck? Are you still here?"

Buck couldn't explain his reason for staying behind, mucking out stalls and feeding the animals. The work wasn't neglected, only behind, as if someone alternated daily tasks in order to keep up.

The Bible said to take care of widows and orphans. No matter how mad Leta and her brother made Buck, he couldn't let it go. So he cleaned the stalls, laid down fresh straw, using the time to consider his next move. He should go into town, spend a night at the local boardinghouse, mail his letter. Then he would be free to head for parts unknown, to wherever God led him next. The open road didn't hold the same appeal as it had ten years ago.

Talk to her. God's inner voice urged him.

I tried, God. She didn't listen.

Remember when Paul warned to speak the truth—in love? You weren't loving.

She doesn't want to talk with me. I lost my chance.

"Buck? Are you still here?" Leta's voice called through the darkness. There was only silence to answer her. "I know you are. Blaze is still in the corral."

Buck glanced through a crack in the barn roof at the heavens. *I'll try.* He emerged from the barn. "Here I am."

"There's something you need to hear." She jerked her chin at the cabin and disappeared into the inky darkness.

What was going on? God had opened the door, and he must follow. "Lord, let me speak Your truth. With Your love. I'm too angry to do it on my own." No wonder he kept his mouth shut as much as he did. No good came from blurting out whatever came into his mind.

He scraped the muck from the barn on the ground outside the door and knocked.

"Come in." Leta's voice was muffled, coming from behind the blanket.

Buck pulled back the blanket and went in. His face a pale oval in the dim light, Ricky sat with his back against the headboard. "Are you mad with my Ma?"

A choking sound came from Leta's throat. Maybe she was as uncomfortable with their earlier confrontation as Buck was.

This boy deserved the truth after all he had been through. "Maybe I was, earlier. I'm sorry about that. God set me straight about that." Shrugging, he smiled. "God's whipping shed is a lot worse than my pa's belt."

That brought a weak smile to Leta's face, and Buck relaxed a little.

"Ma doesn't wear a belt." Ricky giggled.

Buck glanced at her and smiled. "Your mother's got a good heart." He sat down at the end of the bed and looked into Leta's dark eyes. "She doesn't like to punish people unless she's sure they've done something wrong." He stared at her, hoping to communicate his willingness to open the discussion again.

She blinked. In a low voice, she said, "And if I think it will change bad behavior. Everyone deserves a second chance." She turned her eyes from him and took Ricky's hand. "Tell Ranger Buck about Andy."

"Do I have to?" Ricky's lower lip trembled.

"It's important."

Buck sat back, trying to keep an open mind.

Ricky looked from his mother to Buck and back again. "Andy said he knew who killed my pa, and he was going to join the men who were hunting them down."

Leta slumped over, her arms crossed over her chest. Oh, Leta. Buck wished he had been wrong about Andy. And if Buck hadn't tested Andy's loyalty, Fred might still alive. He gritted his teeth until it hurt.

"When did he tell you this?"

"After you were here the last time. He made me promise not to tell." A tear trickled out of his right eye. "Is Uncle Andy okay?"

Buck weighed his answer. "He was, the last time I saw him." He paused. "Did he say who he was meeting?"

Ricky looked at Leta, who nodded, his face solemn. "The man who used to be a Ranger like Ranger Buck. The one who came back. Colley?"

"Scott Cooley," Buck said with a glance at Leta.

Leta tucked the quilt around Ricky and disappeared behind the curtain to get him a drink.

Buck slipped out behind Leta. He cocked his head at the door but she shook her head, so he took a seat by the fireplace and stared into the ashes in the fireplace. He had interrogated plenty of men before, but hearing the truth from Ricky's innocent lips broke something in Buck.

Leta brought the glass to Ricky. She stayed with him quite some time, while the sky turned dark black. Rather than lighting a lantern, Buck remained in the dim interior, a small stream of moonlight leaking through the window. The soft murmur of voices ceased and Leta reappeared.

"You're still here." A soft chuckle sounded in the darkness. "Why are you sitting in the dark?" She lit the lantern. Buck blinked against the bright light.

She sank into the rocker and began moving back and forth, tapping her foot in time to the motion. He waited. The silence he kept wrapped around him like a shield seemed the wisest course.

"You were right." The speed of the rocker increased. "Andy is part of Scott Cooley's gang. It's my fault. I never should have written down the names of the men I suspected killed Derrick."

The fact he had set Andy up tasted bitter on his tongue. "What a mess. Your brother running with Cooley. My cousin, dead." To think he used to complain to his cousin Riley because he missed fighting in the War Between the States. Four years of neighbor killing neighbor instead of the one year Mason County had suffered so far.

"I met with Ricky's teacher yesterday." The creaking of the rocker stopped, and Leta stood to get coffee for them both. "Julia—Miss Moneypenny—said she wanted to see if she could help us avoid what Reconstruction has done to the South. She's good, Buck. She's going to help Ricky and the others get through this." She ground coffee and put it into the pot, filled it with water, and put it on to boil. "But I'm afraid it may be too late for Andy. He's been angry for a long time."

CHAPTER TWENTY-FOUR

AUSTIN DAILY STATESMAN
October 17, 1875

The Germans, who as a class are farmers, and have small gentle stocks of cattle, accused the stockmen of stealing their cattle, and complained that the courts afforded them no protection.

Silence fell between Buck and Leta, both wrapped as they were in their own thoughts. The coffee finished brewing. Leta poured two cups and cut a few slices of bread, bringing out butter and honey and a slab of ham she was saving for Ricky's lunch bucket. She'd boil an egg for him. Buck looked hungry. Leta wondered if with the death of his cousin, Buck would turn into another Scott Cooley—quitting the Rangers and chasing after the men who had killed his cousin. In her deepest heart, she couldn't believe she was feeding the enemy at her table, but a small doubt remained. He finished the ham and drank a second cup of coffee. He wiped his mouth with a handkerchief he pulled from his pocket. "Thank you for the food."

"You're welcome. But please . . . leave now. I need time to consider what you have said."

His face twisted, showing his conflicting emotions clearer than any words he might say. "Do you mind if I come back from time to time?"

"So you can check if Andy comes back?" She shook her head. "I'm sorry. I shouldn't have said that. But I do want you to leave for now."

He stood and headed for the door. "I'll be seeing you." He smiled, the smile that warmed her straight down to the coldest reaches of her heart. "I wish things were different."

"So do I." He twirled his hat on his finger. "I would like to speak with Andy. I don't want to hurt him. Maybe I can convince him to change his ways." His smile changed to that twisted, halfhearted version. "I have to at least try."

She shook her head. "I can't betray my brother."

"I understand. May the Lord lift up His countenance upon you and give you peace. That's an old benediction." With a final nod of his head, he disappeared into the night.

God's peace, in this time and place? How foolish could the man be? A part of Leta wanted to call him back, to tell him he could return anytime he wanted. He was the best thing that had happened to her in a long time.

The rest of her—the part that had followed her father from town to town and watched her husband die—knew different. He was a man, no more, no less. A Ranger bent on avenging his cousin, any means used justified by a commission from the governor. She shivered.

She lit the stove under her kettle and changed into her night shift. Once the water warmed, she unwrapped the bar of rose-scented soap she saved for special times. Dragging the pins out of her hair, she let it cascade over her shoulders. Derrick had loved to run his hands through her hair when it was down. He said it was no wonder God called hair a woman's crowning glory. She picked up a loose strand—tangled, unwashed. She never would have let it get this way when Derrick was still alive.

She lifted the soap to her nose and breathed deeply. She and Derrick had spent their wedding night at a hotel in Austin. The claw-footed tub had amazed her, and she had luxuriated in rose-scented water and lavender soap. Every year on their anniversary, Derrick brought her a bar of rose soap and one of lavender. This rose bar was the last she had from her husband.

Derrick was dead, Andy had disappeared, but she was still here. In spite of the late hour, she longed to feel clean, to be cleansed of all the horrible things that had happened over the past twelve months. A sponge bath would help her relax. She worked the soap into a lather and washed up. After pouring the water out the door, she refilled the basin again and washed her hair. Back in the rocker, she rubbed her hair until it was nearly dry, then brushed through the tangles. She brought a strand to her nose, breathing in the rose scent. She wove it into a braid for the morning.

Leta's Bible beckoned to her from her nightstand, but she didn't want any more reminders about leaving vengeance to God, loving her enemy, and doing good to those who used her wrongly. *Lord, You have to change my heart. I'm no saint.* She tossed and turned, sleeping in short snatches, until the rooster crowed.

Her eyes flew open. From behind the curtain, she heard Ricky's deep breathing. At least he had no trouble sleeping.

He'd had a late night. She'd give him a few more minutes while she fixed his lunch bucket for school.

The hens had produced extra eggs this morning. A small sliver of ham remained. She'd fry that up and scramble it with the rest of the eggs. She whipped up cornbread and added buttered bread to the lunch bucket. With the addition of two peaches she had picked last week, he had plenty to eat. Today she would bake fresh bread.

She chopped the ham and stirred it with the eggs, then went to wake Ricky. As he woke up, she melted butter in her frying pan and poured the egg and ham mixture in. Fragrant aromas teased a grumble from her stomach.

Over breakfast, she quizzed Ricky on the spelling words—he knew them all. She left the bread dough to rise when he left for school. "Take things slow coming home. Don't make Shadow run fast. Promise me?" She kissed his cheek.

"Aw, Ma." He raised his hand to his cheek and rubbed at the spot where she had kissed him.

"I'll have sugar cookies ready for you when you get home." She watched him ride away at a slow pace, which she suspected he would increase as soon as he left her line of sight. If only his speed on a horse was the greatest danger facing him.

The day sped by, baking bread and cookies interspersed with doing daily chores and Monday laundry. The barn was surprisingly clean; Buck must have done this last night. His help around the ranch had made a big difference. *And I told him not to come back.* Without Buck's help, or Andy's, she would have to hire help. But whom? Maybe she could advertise in a county removed from the suspicions swirling among Mason County's population.

After dinner, she pocketed several wrapped cookies and took her horse down the road to meet Ricky for a picnic as he came home from school. On the way, she checked to make sure nothing else had happened to her cattle. When she reached the bend in the road that led toward town, Ricky still hadn't appeared. At the side of the road she spotted a cluster of wildflowers. They'd make a pretty centerpiece on her table. She hadn't had any new flowers since Ricky brought her dandelions last spring.

After tying her horse to the tree, Leta stood among the wildflowers, blackfoot daisies and goldenrods and black daleas, breathing in their fresh scents, not caring when she sneezed. They had sprung to new life after that horrible storm late last month, extending the summer growing season. Mist blew on the breeze, hinting at an afternoon rain.

"Hi," a boy's voice said. "Are you Ricky's ma?"

Leta turned in the direction of the voice. A slender boy, a little older than Ricky, stood on the road.

"I am." She joined him on the road. "What's your name?"

"Peter Madison. My friends call me Pete."

Leta smiled. "Hi, Pete. Have you seen Ricky since school let out?"

He looked at the ground, shifting from foot to foot. "Not exactly."

The good mood Leta had fostered since last night disappeared. "When did you see him?"

"He asked me to give you this." Pete thrust a piece of paper at her. "I hope it's all right, Mrs. Denning." He twisted his body and took off at a run.

The mist turned to raindrops that landed on Leta's head like pebbles. She unfolded the piece of paper. Ricky's pencil scrawl shouted at her.

I go to Andee here.

He had drawn a picture of a cave surrounded by cottonwoods, next to a river.

A scream pushed up from Leta's heart through her throat and out her mouth. She jumped on the horse's back, bunching up her skirts to ride astride, not caring about propriety. Her horse sprang to action, racing for town, pushed by the storm winds at her back.

⟵ ★ ⟶

"Ricky! Ricky!"

Buck stopped in his tracks, two steps away from dropping his letter to Major Jones at the post office. He turned and saw Leta on horseback, riding up the main street of Mason and calling for her son wildly. He rode up to her on Blaze.

"What has happened to Ricky?"

Leta couldn't speak. She thrust her hand toward him. He brought Blaze a few inches closer and leaned forward to take the note. He read the brief message.

"He's gone after Andy?" Buck blew out his breath.

She nodded, looking around her. "He left for school this morning as usual. I was riding into town, to take Ricky on a picnic, and ran into one of his friends. A boy a little bit bigger than Ricky."

Buck thought back to the street scene. "I saw some boys on the edge of town. A couple of them maybe that age. Let's see, brown hair, long arms, brown shirt?"

She shook her head again and started toward town, at a pace they could talk. Her head turned from side to side, looking at open fields and distant farmhouses. "His hair was kind of blond. Wearing a blue shirt, squinting, like maybe he needed glasses?" She turned it into a question, looking at him for confirmation.

"Sorry, no." They reached the edge of town, where the schoolhouse was located. She slowed down. That made sense. "Do you mind if I come with you? I want to help . . ."

His voice trailed off at her helpless expression. "You could try to make sense out of Ricky's map." Pinching her lips together, she said, "Or you could come with me."

"I'll come with you, then. Another body can help."

"I didn't expect to see you in town. I thought you'd be off somewhere else, far away, taking care of Ranger business."

Buck thought about the letter of resignation still tucked into his pocket. He had spent a night and day debating about whether or not to mail the thing. Once again, circumstances had intervened. He was still officially a Ranger. "Following up some loose ends, that's all."

Another time he might tell her today was spent reading through the transcripts of the trial last year that had precipitated the violence. The law was confusing, the evidence inconclusive, and even so, the men brought to trial were convicted and fined. Only Derrick Denning was found not guilty.

Buck thought the jury did a fair job. But a number of German citizens felt that—despite the convictions of cattle rustling and punishment in the form of fines—that wasn't enough. The guilty parties should pay with their lives, the mob decided, and began their reign of terror.

Fred was only the latest victim of that trial. Ricky's, and even Andy's, behavior, grew out of the circumstances. Murder demanded justice. When justice was denied, it brought about vengeance.

They arrived at the schoolhouse, and Buck helped her down from her horse. "Let me see if Julia is here." She straightened her skirts and opened the school door. "Julia? Miss Moneypenny?

"Mrs. Denning."

Leta nodded and Buck followed them into them into the classroom. The odors of chalk dust and pencil lead assailed him, sending him back to his own days in the classroom. A map of the United States included the states of West Virginia, Nevada, and Nebraska, which had joined the Union after the War Between the States broke out. During his childhood, the maps kept changing: the United States, the Confederacy. Several flags had flown over Texas since the first European French had built a fort in the seventeenth century. The atmosphere in the schoolhouse felt familiar, welcoming—safe.

"This is Buck Morgan, a Texas Ranger. Tell us, did Ricky show up to school today?" Panic laced Leta's eyes as she relayed the encounter described by Peter.

"No, Ricky didn't come to school today." The curly haired teacher looked confused. "I assumed he had fallen ill."

CHAPTER TWENTY-FIVE

I find the houses closed [with] a deathlike stillness in the place and an evident suspense if not dread in the minds of the inhabitants. Every man is armed but so far as I have been able to ascertain there is no body of armed men in or near the place, at present.

Correspondence between Major John B. Jones
and Adjutant General William Steele
September 28, 1875

Buck wanted to rip the teacher apart, to demand why she hadn't questioned Ricky's absence. But he knew his anger was foolish. The poor woman had done nothing wrong.

Miss Moneypenny was young, perhaps even as young as Stella. She sank onto the chair behind her desk in obvious distress. "I thought about checking with you if Ricky didn't come again tomorrow. He was so excited when we visited on Saturday, I thought he would walk to school even if he had to walk barefoot over hot coals. No wonder Peter was fidgeting so today."

Buck told himself to calm down. He had no claim on Ricky. He was a family friend—no more, perhaps less. One missing child wasn't the concern of a Texas Ranger, committed to protect his state, his community—not just a single family.

He turned his attention back to the conversation.

"—this looks like Loyal Valley." Leta looked at Buck. "Like the place you were telling me about." Her eyes dared him to disagree.

He picked up the sketch. "Trees, water, cave. There must be a dozen places like this scattered across Mason County."

Leta's lips thinned. "There aren't any I know of outside of Loyal Valley, the heart of Deutschland. And my son went there."

Buck clamped his teeth together, biting off the words he wanted to spew. The so-called German mob wouldn't hurt a child. Violence caught innocents as well as enemies in the crossfire. Arguments didn't matter. Actions did. "How can I help?"

Leta turned serious brown eyes on Buck. "I want you to take me to the place where the shootout took place. He's near there, I'm sure of it."

"That's not a good idea."

She continued as if he hadn't spoken. "We need help. I would suggest you bring Steve and Jim, but they don't know the land. You already tried tracking them down, and couldn't find them. So—would your family be willing to lend their ranch hands? I know they are in mourning." A small smile softened her lips. "Besides, I need to borrow a split skirt from Stella."

Leta let her horse follow Buck, trusting him to lead her straight. She was following her heart, trusting the man who had labored over training Shadow for Ricky. She hoped she wasn't traipsing after the man who wanted to capture her brother at whatever cost.

She shook her head to clear her mind of doubts. Buck would do his very best for Ricky, she was certain. So many hours in the saddle left her sore; she hoped a split skirt would make riding more comfortable. But she would ride until she fell off the horse, if it meant finding Ricky.

Buck didn't break the silence, but maybe conversation would take her mind off her sore muscles. "Tell me more about your family. I haven't heard of any Morgans in the area, but there's a lot of people I don't know. What's their ranch?"

Buck's back stiffened, causing an awkward bump in the saddle. "They live at the Lazy F Ranch."

Lazy F . . . That meant their name probably began with *F.* She sorted through the possibilities. "Is it John Faris?"

He shook his head.

"It must be Frank Eastwood, then." She couldn't think of any other potential families.

"No."

"I give up. Who is it?" The horses were climbing as they left the banks of the Llano and heading into Loyal Valley.

His face stayed firmly ahead. "George Fletcher is my mother's brother."

"Fletcher." The name echoed in her mind. It couldn't be. It must be. "Henry Fletcher is your cousin? You're German?" She reined her horse to a stop.

Pulling up Blaze, he looked at her.

"Yes, and yes. Half German. My uncle was born Georg Fleischer and came to Texas in 1845. But he's as American as you and I are, Leta. He changed his name to an English form to make himself fit in."

Leta stared down the road, not seeing anything. "Henry has

different ideas." She wanted to turn around, to run home. "How could you not tell me? Your cousin helped kill my husband."

"I knew it would upset you. My cousin and your brother both got caught up in events. I doubt either one of them intended murder."

"Your cousin was there when they put a noose around Derrick's neck and hung him from a tree."

"Andy was there when they pulled guns on Fred."

She shook her head. "It doesn't matter. I can't go there. Henry must know who I am."

Buck's heart wilted at the panic in Leta's voice. "This is not about Derrick or Andy or Henry. They're just ordinary people, Leta. My family will help you look for Ricky."

"We're calling a ceasefire in the middle of a war?" Leta looked at the hill in front of them. If only she could do this by herself and didn't need anyone's help.

"I will talk with them first, if you feel safe waiting here."

She looked to her right and then to her left. "I am in German country hunting for an outlaw mob that might have my son." Some of the anger seeped out of her, and she shrank back on the saddle. "I'm scared to stay alone."

"Leta, I won't let anything harm you."

She looked at him a long moment. "I know." She straightened in the saddle. "Let's go."

"Buck's back." Stella bounced up from the chair where she sat gazing out the window. Two days of sitting in the house, dressed in a borrowed black skirt with her plainest blouse, had left her restless.

"William is here?" Tante Ertha struggled to her feet and joined Stella at the window. Her tear-blurred eyes blinked. "And he brought company with him. His Ranger friends? We must get him some good coffee."

Steve? Stella's heart tripped at the thought of seeing that good-looking Ranger again. She narrowed her eyes, looking at the second horse and rider.

"It can't be a Ranger. It's a woman." Lisel looked over her shoulder.

"It's Leta Denning." Stella looked again, checking for Ricky on his prize colt. She saw no sign of the child. That was odd.

"I don't know any Dennings." Tante Ertha sounded confused. "Does she like coffee?"

"Yes." There was enough food left from the funeral to feed a hundred guests, and Tante Ertha hadn't allowed the coffee pot to empty. "She'll be fine."

"She's one of the Anglos," Lisel said. "I know of her. Why does Buck bring her here?"

The riders grew close enough for Stella to see their features. Leta's pinched face startled her. This was no social call, nor a call on a family in mourning.

Tante Ertha went to the kitchen to prepare refreshments for their guests. Stella walked to the porch and opened her arms wide to greet her friend. Leta hung back for a second, then accepted her embrace. "Oh, Stella, it's good to see you." She glanced at Buck. "Please tell them I'm here."

"Come inside. You look ready to fall down where you're standing." Stella decided Leta looked like a woman who had suffered a tremendous loss—like Tante Ertha. "Where's Ricky?"

Leta hesitated in midstep. "I don't know. I'm hoping your family can help us find him."

Buck's hand stayed gently on Leta's arm, and he cradled her against his side as he led her through the door.

Stella followed, joining them at the kitchen table.

As Stella had expected, Tante Ertha had cut large pieces of chocolate torte and fixed a coffee tray, two china cups and saucers with a pitcher of cream and a sugar bowl. "I don't know how you like your coffee, Mrs. Denning. William, I know you drink yours black."

"William?" Leta looked up at him. "Is that your real name?"

"I was born William Meino Morgan, named for both my grandfathers."

Tension threaded the simple words. Stella rushed to smooth it over. "But when Aunt Billie came home from the Comanche, Buck didn't like having a 'girl's' name. So he insisted everybody call him Buck."

"I didn't get you coffee, Stella. Let me get you a cup." Tante Ertha jumped up from the table.

"That's not necessary." But Tante Ertha was already pouring from the coffee pot. Stella leaned closer and whispered. "I've drunk so much coffee I think I'll be awake until I go back to Victoria."

"It is delicious coffee." Leta cut a tiny corner of the torte but laid down her fork without touching it. "Will they help me look for Ricky? Or let their ranch hands help?" Tears sparkled in her eyes and slid down her cheeks. She turned to Stella. "We think he might have come here." She took a piece of paper from her pocket and straightened it out on the table. "We think this is on your uncle's ranch."

Tante Ertha brought a full cup of coffee to the table. She glanced at the paper. "That looks like a drawing Fred made of the smugglers' cave when he was a boy. He used to go camping there." She slumped down in grief, and Buck helped her into a chair.

"I heard what happened to your son. I'm sorry for your loss. I can't imagine losing a child." Leta's voice quavered. "That's why I'm here. My son ran away today, and we believe he was headed for that cave. I need your help."

Lisel stood in the door, framed by the light coming from the parlor. "How dare you come to a house of mourning. You're not even one of us. For all I know, your son was involved in Fred's death."

CHAPTER TWENTY-SIX

Some fifteen men, very suspicious-looking fellows, passed through Loyal Valley en route for the Upper Llano where it is thought they will make a camp and probably take up winter quarters. Several horse thieves of notoriety have lately gone from San Saba, Lampasas and other places in that direction also. I wish you as soon as practicable to make a scout in that section of country.

Letter from Major John B. Jones to
Neal Coldwell, Commander of Company F
October 25, 1875

Buck beat Stella in jumping to his feet. "He's just a boy. A small, scared little boy."

Crossing her arms, Lisel glared at them across the table. "If he's only a child, how did he get here? And why did he come to our ranch?"

"It's all right, Buck. They deserve to know. My son came searching for my brother." Eyes fixed on her plate, Leta spoke with a soft voice. When she looked up, pain ravaged her face. "Andy was with Scott Cooley when your son was shot." The words scraped out of her throat.

Stella's head snapped back. Andy had joined up with Cooley?

"But my son." Leta stopped, silent sobs shaking her shoulders. "My son is only six years old. He worships Andy and Buck. He misses his father." A single sob burst from her lips. "Help me, please. Before anyone else is hurt."

Stella didn't need to hear any more. "I will help."

"You're staying here," Buck said. "It could be dangerous."

Stella glowered at her brother. "I'm an extra pair of eyes. I'm sure the ranch hands will help with the search. You can at least ask."

Leta's face showed her gratitude, and heat rushed into Stella's cheeks. "Let's get ready. How can I help?" She took Leta's arm and guided her away from the Lisel's scowl and Tante Ertha's helpless hovering.

"Can I borrow a split skirt?" Leta followed Stella to the guest room.

Buck barred the door as Lisel attempted to follow Stella and Leta.

She sputtered. "Her brother was one of the men who killed Fred."

"But Ricky is an innocent child. He's only trying to find his uncle and convince him to come home. He doesn't know he's headed into a den of murderers."

"You're sweet on her. That Denning woman." Lisel clamped her lips together. "Does Henry know about her brother?"

The Dennings had already suffered the mob's wrath. Henry knew that, but Lisel might not. This wasn't the time nor place for that revelation. "How I feel about Mrs. Denning is irrelevant. Finding her son is what matters. I'm done talking." Behind him, Leta and Stella appeared, dressed in split skirts, hats in their hands to keep the rain off their heads. They were ready, and he hadn't yet talked with the ranch hands.

"I'll get some food together." Stella looked hard at Lisel. "We have plenty."

The hands—Jeff and Slim—readily agreed. Back in the house, Buck checked his uncle's study for the guns he stored there. The men had firearms, but neither Stella nor Leta were armed. Remembering his first encounter with Leta, he knew she could handle a rifle. For Stella, he chose a Colt.

When he came out with the weapons, Leta stared. "We can't get into a gunfight. Ricky could be shot in the crossfire."

"We have to be prepared." Stella accepted the Colt and tucked it into her waistband.

Reluctantly, Leta accepted the rifle. She showed the map to Jeff and Slim. "Mrs. Fletcher said this was the smugglers' cave. Do you know where that is?"

"Sure do." Slim nodded. "It's a two-hour ride from here. Far enough for a young boy to feel he was spending the night in the wild, close enough for his mother to allow it." He scrunched his face. "It's close to where we were ambushed the other day."

Leta blanched.

"They're long gone." Buck's words did little to reassure her.

Leta glanced at the sky. "In two hours, it'll be dark. The rain doesn't look like it's letting up any time soon. I don't know which is worse. If Ricky caught up with Cooley, or if he's alone, lost, far from home."

Determination chased fear out of her face. Her face was so expressive; he wondered if she knew how much she revealed just in the simple blink of an eye. Or maybe he had grown sensitive to her moods because he had grown to care more for her than made any kind of sense. "Let's move out. Keep your guns ready and stop at the first sign of movement."

Slim led the way. Buck hoped the presence of two women in their party would alert any lookouts that this wasn't a posse. That Andy would recognize Leta. Buck trained his eyes on the passing landscape, looking for any signs of passage. The rain obscured most signs, but Buck was surprised not to find evidence of the passage of a number of horses and cattle. "Is this the route you took the other day?"

Jeff shook his head. "Nope. Slim's leading us by the most direct route. The cattle couldn't travel this way."

Blaze wended his way through oak and willow trees. The vegetation provided cover from watchers, but it also made it hard to spot any sentries. Buck listened to the sounds of the woods, but heard nothing beyond the rushing wind. Unease heightened his every sense.

Rain plastered her braid to Leta's back, below the edge of her hat. Stella sat straight in the saddle, hat tipped over her forehead, but her head went back and forth, scanning side to side. She'd make a decent scout. He had shown her the basics, and she had continued learning on her own. She was more comfortable hunting a buck than cooking it, although she could do both.

"Over there." Leta pointed to a clump of creek plum shrubs. She turned her horse and increased speed, hooves splattering mud against the horses' shanks as far as her skirt. Glancing in the direction she was headed, Buck saw a metallic glint that suggested human passage over the rocks. It could be anything. Guns.

Buck spurred Blaze into a gallop, pulling out his Winchester as the horse ate up the distance. He reached Leta in seconds and pulled on the reins of her horse. "It—could—be—a—gun." The words came out in gasps.

She slowed a fraction. "I spotted a patch of blue. It's the same color as the shirt Ricky was wearing. That metal? I think it's his lunch bucket."

Shielding his eyes against the rain, Buck peered through the glistening skies. He saw a patch of light blue, the right size for a small boy's chest. He spurred Blaze, who jumped into action and together they barreled forward.

Several horses galloped behind him, and he assumed the others had veered off the path to join them. Blaze outpaced them all.

A familiar, high-pitched whinny greeted them. Shadow. The black colt poked his nose out of the brush and trotted forward to greet Blaze.

A horse whinnied. Leta's mount responded in kind, and she recognized the sound a second before Shadow raced out of the bushes.

Buck jumped down and dropped Blaze's reins to ground tie him. He crashed ahead.

"He's okay!" Buck yelled.

"Ranger Buck! How did you find me?"

Tears ran into Leta's eyes at the sound of Ricky's voice, and she raced ahead. Ricky sat on the ground, his blue shirt pulled over his head to protect him from the rain, but he was still shivering. In his right hand, he held flint. The twigs in front of him looked anything but dry.

She knelt beside him and took him in her arms. "Don't ever do anything like this again."

"I wanted to find Andy, Ma. I know you're worried." His mouth quivered. "But I didn't see him."

Others were coming, but Leta focused on her son. Buck took over fire-making duties while she rocked him.

"I took extra peaches and some cheese and the rest of the bread. I'm sorry, Ma."

"No, that was smart." What was she saying? She should tell him how stupid his behavior was, how dangerous. She wasn't sure if the moisture on her cheeks came from tears or the rain. "But it was dangerous riding across country. You didn't know where you were going."

"But Andy told me all about it. He said he was going to help find the men who killed Pa. I wanted to go with him." His lower lip stuck out. "That's more important than school any old day. But then it started to rain, and I couldn't see where I was going. So I decided to wait the rain stopped. I was lighting a fire so I wouldn't get too cold."

"And now we have fire." Buck blew on the small flame and fed it a few twigs. "You did a good job finding wood."

"How cozy you look." Stella joined the circle.

"Miss Morgan!" Ricky leaped from Leta's arms and hugged Stella. He was clearly relieved to see his "rescuers."

"You had your mother awful worried, buddy." Stella took his face in her hands. "Say hello to Jeff and Slim. They helped us find you."

"Hi, Jeff. Hi, Slim." He giggled at the name.

Slim bent his tall frame over. "Hi there, Ricky." They shook hands before he turned to Buck. "Do you want to spend the night out here, or go back to the ranch?"

Go back to the Lazy F and the Fletchers? Shivering at the thought, Leta hoped the others would put it down to the drenching rain. "Is there any kind of cover nearby?"

Buck grinned. "I have a tarp in my saddlebags. It will be enough for the ladies and Ricky. Slim, Jeff, you probably should get back."

"Nope." Jeff's hand tightened on the butt of his rifle, and Leta understood. "We'll stay with you until daylight."

She glanced at the dark gray sky. "Thank you. For everything."

Buck's saddlebags proved as amazing as a magician's hat. He handed over the tarp to Slim and Jeff, who fashioned a canopy that directed the rain away from them and the fire. While they set up camp, Buck cut strips of bacon and tossed them in a fry pan. After they sizzled to a healthy brown, he stirred beans into the pan. Stella opened her saddlebag and added sauerkraut. Ricky reached for his lunch bucket. He still had the heel of the loaf of bread. The aromas alone cheered Leta.

"We're having a grand adventure, aren't we, Ma?" Ricky stirred the beans with the spoon Buck had given him.

She didn't have the heart to scold him. "Yes, we are." Muscles sore, clothing still damp, wind tearing at the tarp but not dislodging it, she curled up with Ricky in her arms and thanked God for protecting her once again.

CHAPTER TWENTY-SEVEN

Came out of the gallery and heard a lot of shooting uptown —poor Dan Hoerster killed.

Lucia Holmes's diary
September 18, 1875

Sun teased Buck awake in the morning, bright, warm, sunshine, already baking his waist overalls dry. A glance to his right revealed Slim and Jeff had already headed back to the ranch. They had kept watch all night, a gesture Buck appreciated.

In other company, Buck would strip to his long johns and hang his clothes to dry. He glanced at the tarp. Small puddles had formed where it sagged, but it had done its job. Ricky was tucked under his mother's chin, her braid hanging over both their shoulders.

As if she sensed Buck watching her, Leta opened her brown eyes, smiling at him. She sat up. "Do you have any more magic in that bag of yours?"

He gestured with the coffee pot. "Coffee to keep us warm." He dug into Stella's bag and found the other half of the cake she had grabbed yesterday. "Is this enough, or do you want some bacon? Rice?"

Her eyes lit up at the sight of the cake. "More cake? Oh, I'm getting spoiled. And I haven't had to cook for two days." She detached herself from Ricky and climbed out from the tarp. Biting into the cake he handed her, she closed her eyes, savoring the delicious taste.

Once she swallowed, she opened her eyes, some of the simple delight gone. "Having Ricky run away like that helps me focus on what's important. Life. Family. But nothing has changed, has it? Andy is still on the run."

He nodded. "And Henry . . ." He stared in the direction of the ranch. "I have to accept his involvement in your husband's death."

"I didn't know Henry was involved with the mob from the beginning." Stella joined them at the campfire. She broke off a piece of cake and began munching. "I didn't know about your husband, Leta." Her eyes teared up. "I'm so sorry."

The cake in Buck's mouth had turned to stone. "What have you learned?"

Stella glanced at Ricky's still sleeping form, and her face softened for a moment. She chewed a second bite of cake. "I've heard some chatter. The men didn't seem to notice me hanging around." She shrugged. "I spent a lot of time in the kitchen. Or maybe they forgot I understand German." She looked at the sky. "Or maybe I pretended I understand less than I do."

Leta's eyes flickered back and forth between the two. "You asked Stella to spy on your cousin?"

The corner of Buck's mouth lifted. "If he's guilty, I can't ignore it." He stopped. "I hope you'll forgive me for wanting further proof."

"You listened to me."

He shrugged. "Of course." He nodded at Stella. "I also want to know if Onkel Georg is involved, or if Henry is acting without further family involvement." He sounded like he never resigned from the Rangers. "So what have you learned?"

Stella brushed the crumbs from her hands and off her skirt. "They didn't talk about the past in detail. No who, what, when, or where. Plenty of whys, of course—I've had an earful of everything about those so-and-so Anglos. Do you mind?" Without waiting for an answer, she snatched his cup of coffee, since they only had the one cup to share among them, and continued.

"They've had enough. Now Cooley has killed someone who wasn't involved with the Williamson killing in any way. A kid. And they want to fight back." She drained the cup, poured in fresh coffee and handed it to Leta. "A couple of men argued that would only lead to more revenge killings by the Anglos. But Henry won the day." She reached out and touched Buck's hands. "I'm sorry. He's one of the leaders."

Buck took the cup Leta handed to him and drained it without speaking.

"What are you going to do?" Stella spoke, but Leta's eyes asked the question.

Buck only shook his head. The sadness he felt at that moment was something he couldn't put into words.

Leta cast one last look at their impromptu campsite. She had lived all nine of a cat's lives in the past twenty-four hours, but finding Ricky unharmed and having a good night's sleep had restored a few of them. As expected, the worst consequence of yesterday's events was her sore muscles. She stared at the saddle, wishing she could reach the seat without climbing.

Buck came beside her. "Let me help." He lifted her as if she was as light as a cotton ball and set her on the saddle. "You were incredible yesterday."

Heat flooded her cheeks, and she turned away. Calm down. "How do you balance the demands? Justice pulls on you from both sides. Don't you feel split down the middle?" She turned her face in time to catch a look of such pain crossing his features that she felt like she had seen his soul. She averted her face, knowing she wasn't meant to see that.

"I'm both. I'm neither. And I have to decide what to do about it. Justice may be blind, but vengeance comes in a thousand forms. But how do I know which is which?"

She was glad she was on the horse. Otherwise she might throw her arms around him, and that would be a bad thing. "You'll figure it out. God promises to give wisdom to anyone who asks." Now she was quoting platitudes. "I mean, it won't be easy. God won't write His will in the stars. But whatever decision you reach, God will help you get there."

"So you found the boy." Henry repeated his question to Jeff.

"He's a plucky kid. Wet and freezing, he managed to find shelter and was trying to start a fire." Slim tilted his hat back. "Reminded me of you when you were that age."

Henry's mouth twisted. Derrick Denning had been a mistake, but he couldn't go back and change it. And once he had witnessed that rough justice, he couldn't back out. Hadn't wanted to, until Cooley arrived and then Fred died.

"Did you see any sign of Cooley?"

Slim and Jeff exchanged a look. "We couldn't see much in the rain. Do you want us to go out and check?"

Henry considered it for a minute before he shook his head. "No." He had a better idea: get Schmidt and Hinke involved.

Together they could concoct a plan that would address the problem of Scott Cooley and Andy Warren.

He wanted a plan in place before he addressed his cousin again.

CHAPTER TWENTY-EIGHT

The undersigned citizens of Loyal Valley are under the impression that you are in command of the State Troops sent to this county to suppress disturbances and to aid in keeping up peace and good order.

Petition, Citizens of Loyal Valley
to Major John B. Jones
October 4, 1875

After escorting Stella, Leta, and Ricky to their respective ranches, Buck headed south for a meeting with Major Jones at the Kirschberg Ridge. A face-to-face meeting would relieve Buck of the necessity of posting his letter of resignation. He hoped resigning would relieve him of his feeling of responsibility for how things turned out in Mason County. For his family. For Henry and Andy, two good men caught up in evil actions. For Leta. For all the other good people of Mason County afraid of their neighbors.

He wasn't the only Ranger. Others could be more objective, not torn in half by the two factions.

After riding far into the night and getting up before dawn the next morning, Buck was nearing Major Jones's camp. Buck slowed Blaze's pace as he rode down Kirschberg Ridge, doubting he would find the major. Pausing, he stared through the gathering dawn when he reached the crevasse where they had met the last time. Only a few weeks had passed, although it felt like years.

"Morgan, as I live and breathe, I began to think you had died in the hurricane." Jones's words were friendly, but his eyes held no warmth. "I've sent Company D back to Mason for the duration."

"I'm glad to hear it." Buck dismounted. "That's one of my recommendations." He tapped the pocket that held his letter.

"I was sorry to hear about your cousin."

The major's matter-of-fact voice pierced Buck's defenses more than effusive words of sympathy would have. A lump the size of a quarter formed in his throat. "There is more to the story."

Jones gestured for Buck to follow him deeper into the mesquite trees, where a cheerful fire awaited. "Fill me in."

"This explains most of it." Buck held out the envelope, but Jones waved it aside.

"You could have posted the letter. Report."

The major's clipped words left Buck with no choice. He tucked the envelope back in his pocket. Stalling for time, he sat by the campfire and poured a cup of coffee, although he was ready to report. He had spent the hours on horseback sorting through facts for the information he knew Jones would demand.

"I was there when Fred—my cousin—was killed."

Jones raised his eyebrows but didn't comment.

"I set a trap for Cooley and his men."

"But Cooley is still at large." Jones frowned. "Back up. Tell me about this trap."

Buck drew in his breath. From the time he had first seen the list in Leta's handwriting, he knew this moment would be inevitable. "Mrs. Denning has identified five men involved in her husband's murder." He named them: the two Jordans, Hinke, Schmidt. He hesitated.

"That's four of them. What is the last name?"

Buck buried his nose in the coffee cup and took a deep draft. "Henry Fletcher."

Jones's breath hissed, and he learned forward. "Your cousin?"

"Yes. I used some unorthodox methods to confirm his involvement." Buck explained Stella's presence at the Lazy F. "She has overheard conversations between Henry and other members of the German mob—Johann Schmidt, Adolph Hinke, Peter Jordan. Her impression is that he is a leader within the group."

Jones grunted. "I know you better than to think you set up a trap for Cooley for the mob's benefit. You still haven't explained that."

If Buck felt guilty for betraying his cousin, betraying Leta pierced his heart like a thorn. "I suspected Mrs. Denning's brother. He's seventeen and hot-headed, bent on revenge—and he disappears for days at a time."

"You thought he had joined up with Cooley."

"It was a possibility. I mentioned that members of the German mob were hiding in Loyal Valley. I sent them to a remote spot on my uncle's ranch."

"Young Warren passed on the information to Cooley. What was your cousin doing there?"

"Unknown to me, my uncle chose that day to check on his

herd." Buck forced himself to stay still under the major's penetrating gaze. "Fred's death falls at my feet."

Jones grunted. "It sounds like an unfortunate accident."

"If you say so, sir." Buck sipped his coffee again.

Jones allowed a moment of silence to fall between them before he spoke. "You went with your uncle when he was wounded. What happened to Cooley?"

"Austin and Sampson trailed them, but lost them on the rocks."

"Cooley perfected his talents in avoiding detection during his time with the Rangers." Jones pointed to Buck's pocket. "I can guess what's in that letter."

"I can't be impartial in this investigation. One of the suspects is my cousin. One of the victims is my cousin." And he wasn't sure how he felt about Andy.

"And you fear your feelings for Mrs. Denning are clouding your judgment."

Buck's head snapped up.

"You have faced down Indian scalping without blinking, but this hideous little war has twisted you like a pretzel. You've fallen hard." The major made a sound halfway between a laugh and a snort. "Don't worry. We all do, sooner or later."

"Whatever happens, someone I care about will be hurt, more than they already have been. Both sides want vengeance. I want justice, but I'm not sure what that is anymore."

"Which is why we leave the decision to judge and jury."

Now Buck snorted, and Jones looked at him. "I know a court case started this vendetta last year. The system isn't perfect, but it's the best we've got." Jones coughed. "People in Mason don't have much reason to trust the courts or the sheriff. That doesn't mean they can take the law into their own hands."

"I agree, sir. I just don't know how much good I can do.

Or—"The words dragged from a place deep in his soul. "Maybe I don't know if I want to anymore." He reached into his pocket for the envelope.

"Wait a moment." Jones put up a hand and stroked his beard. "Keep that letter. I'm not ready to let the Rangers lose one of our best men. I agree, you need time away from Mason. I'm reassigning you to Company E. Take a week. Take longer, if you need to." Jones clamped his hand on Buck's shoulder. "Have a good, long talk with your God on the way. I've found a long trail, an open sky, and a conversation with God above can settle most of life's knots."

Buck didn't speak, thinking of the hours he had already spent storming heaven over this question. "I've been asking." He removed his hat and scratched his head. "But if God's been speaking, it must have been in a whisper."

"One thing I know about God." Jones grinned. "He can get louder if He needs to."

Buck checked his hat and rolled the brim. "I'll do as you ask. On one condition. If I still want to quit when I come back, you won't try to stop me."

"Fair enough."

Thunder rolled. Another afternoon storm threatened. Jones tilted his head to one side, smiling. "See? God's started increasing His volume already."

Although Ricky ran a slight fever, his cough cleared up on Tuesday night, Leta decided to send him back to school on Wednesday.

"Ma! I'm ready for school." Ricky appeared in the kitchen, the buttons on his shirt off by one space. He checked his lunch bucket. "Egg salad." He wrinkled his nose.

Leta relaxed, glad for an ordinary day. "Boys who run away don't get special treats."

Ricky had slept better than Leta did, since she kept waking every half hour to check on him. She knew she was hovering over him, but he had a boy's penchant for getting into trouble.

Leta sighed at another day of work lost, but a discussion with Julia was essential. She also wanted to place an ad for ranch hands before another week passed. Maybe she could place an ad that read, "Andy. All is forgiven. Please come home. Leta." Even outlaws must read the paper. They'd want to know what was being reported, true or false.

As they rode into town on Wednesday morning, she glanced around. Feeling like a schoolgirl, she hoped Buck would appear. The very thought of seeing him again cheered her spirits. She had to focus on something else. "Say the poem to me again."

"The black bat chased the black cat who wears an orange hat while he eats a big fat rat."

"And how do you spell cat?"

"Cat. K-a-t." He stuck out his tongue.

Leta stifled a laugh. "Be serious."

"Cat. C-a-t. Give me words I haven't studied."

Pleased that he had asked for a challenge, Leta pondered what to ask. They had studied the short *a* sound. Would they study long *a* next or a short *o*? O, she decided. The long *a* sound could be spelled too many different ways: bait, date. "How about dot?"

Ricky's eyes lit up. "D . . ." His face screwed up in concentration, and he leaned over Shadow's neck as if he had the answer. He straightened. "Dot. D-o-t."

"Very good."

Coming up with simple spelling words was harder than she would have guessed. At least it kept her from thinking about Buck all the way into town.

Eventually they arrived at the schoolyard, where Julia welcomed them with a warm smile. Ricky raced to say hello while Leta approached at a moderate pace. "Go on inside, Ricky. I need to speak with Miss Moneypenny. Alone."

Julia's eyes grew wider and wider while Leta described Monday's adventure. "You must have been terrified. I'll keep a close eye on him. And if he misses another day of school, I'll find out why."

"You can't come all the way out to the ranch."

Julia's cheeks warmed. "I'll find a way to get word to you. And I'll keep Ricky after school for the rest of this week, as you asked." Julia glanced around the schoolyard. "But it's time to start school. Until next time." With a smile, she rang the bell and watched the children go inside.

Oh, to be able to join Ricky in school, to once again lose herself in the innocence and simplicity of childhood. Leta squared her shoulders. God had given her a responsibility, and He would see her through. He must.

She walked down the street and past St. Paul's. Maybe she could stop in and speak with the pastor. Hopefully a man of God could see beyond her identity, even though he ministered to a largely German congregation. She opened the door, hoping to find the pastor in. "Hello?"

A man of uncertain age with thinning blond hair appeared from behind the altar. "Mrs. Denning, is it not?" He smiled. "I am Johann Stricker. How may I help you?"

Leta nodded. "I need some counsel. If you are willing to speak with me."

"Why would I not? 'All that the Father giveth me shall come to me; and him that cometh to me I will in no wise cast out.'"

Embarrassed that she had questioned his sincerity, Leta sat on the front pew and stared at her hands. Where to start?

"Will it help if I tell you I know of your loss at the start of the hostilities? Does that have any bearing on why you wish to speak with me?"

"Yes." Relief that she had made the right decision flooded Leta. "My parents died shortly before I married my husband, so my brother lived with us. Derrick was more of a father to Andy than our own father had ever been. On the night they came for Derrick, he witnessed what happened."

"And he has been misbehaving." The pastor made it a statement, not a question.

"It's worse than that. I didn't place much trust in justice here. We talked about getting vengeance for Derrick's death. I didn't think it was anything more than talk. But he hasn't been home for days, and I have reason to think he's joined up with Cooley." She put her hand to her cheek, turning away from Reverend Stricker. "I have failed the responsibility God gave me. And my son is so confused." She started crying.

"Ach. You must feel a little like God felt when Eve and Adam ate the fruit from the tree. You gave him everything, and he has broken the law."

CHAPTER TWENTY-NINE

SAN ANTONIO DAILY EXPRESS
October 6, 1875

On Wednesday morning September 29, Daniel Hoerster, one of the best and most favorably known citizens of the county, was shot and killed at Mason; and at the same time Peter Jordan was shot at, escaping however with but a slight wound.

A sharp report, followed by a second, and a third, penetrated the church walls.

"No. Not again." Reverend Stricker looked out the window.

"Those were gunshots." Near, too near. Fear seared through Leta.

The look in the pastor's eyes said he recognized the sound

as well. "I am sorry, but I must take my leave of you. Perhaps I can offer some comfort or assistance." His face set in resolute lines, he dug a finger under his collar and stood.

"I will come with you."

"Mrs. Denning, it's not safe."

What if Andy had been shot . . . or had done the shooting?

The pastor's face softened. "You must keep yourself safe. Perhaps Miss Moneypenny needs help with the children. They will have heard the shots as well. As soon as it is safe, I will bring you the news." He opened the door for her. "I know you are worried about your brother."

"Thank you." Her brain dredged her memory for the right word. *"Danke."*

"You are most welcome, Mrs. Denning. God promises He is with us always. And that includes even this day." He laid a hand on her shoulder.

God is with me. Leta imagined Jesus walking by her side while she crossed the yard to the schoolhouse. She glanced at the sky. "Why do You let such evil happen?"

A sense of God's abiding peace came over her. God had stepped into evil. The One who was perfect and holy had come to earth and lived among fallen people. The God who came to earth as a helpless newborn would walk with her through this troubled time. Was it selfish to pray Andy wasn't hurt?

Arriving at the school, she opened the door as quietly as possible. Ricky stood at the front of the class, his voice reciting his poem in singsongy fashion. " . . . big fat rat." His eyes widened when he saw her. "I got it perfect, Ma!"

"Yes, you did." She smiled.

Julie clapped for attention. "Now I want you to write sentences of your own, whatever your spelling words are." She passed down the rows, speaking to one child, then another, before reaching Leta. "What brings you back?"

"Did you hear . . ." Leta's eyes turned toward the window.

"I didn't hear anything. We were singing."

"Gunshots," Leta whispered.

Julia placed a hand on her throat.

Only an hour earlier, Leta had longed for the simplicity of the schoolroom. She should have known better. The children of Mason County didn't enjoy that luxury. A couple of times Ricky glanced at her, but she shook her head. Grinning, he picked up a piece of chalk and scribbled on his slate. He was struggling over some basic arithmetic problems. Once sums went over ten and he couldn't count on his fingers, she didn't know how he would manage. Reading came much easier to him.

That train of thought kept her occupied for all of three minutes. Then the possibility of Andy shot or dead intruded again and she glanced out the window, willing Reverend Stricker to reappear.

Ricky was still bent over his slate when she spotted the pastor. Nodding at Julia, she went outside. "They didn't notice the shots," she said.

"God protected them." The pastor smiled. "I cannot say the same for all on this day."

"Andy." Leta breathed his name.

He shook his head. "Peter Jordan was wounded and—Dan Hoerster died immediately." He took her hands in his. "I saw your brother. Cooley and his men are riding around town as if they will answer to no one."

At his words, Leta wilted, her ankle tilting to one side on the gravel. Reverend Stricker held her arm to steady her. "I should not have spoken so plainly. Please, let us return to the church, where we can speak in private."

"Thank you." Leta reached for the sense of God's presence that had touched her earlier.

I am here. Do not fear.

Strength seeped into her legs and back.

Stricker walked quickly, his smile encouraging her to follow. She moved to the cool interior, her eyes blinded in the shadows of the church. A blurry figure moved in her direction, then sharpened. She made out a familiar yellow jacket, hair dangling in front of dark eyes. Andy!

Leta rushed forward and threw her arms about her brother. "Thank God you are alive. I have been so very worried about you."

He moved back. His appearance hadn't altered, but he had changed in a myriad of ways. He had become a man in the brief span of time of their absence from one another. He pushed her away, with gentle arms. "I can't stay."

"You must." She stepped back, fighting her desire to command him to her will. She had to respect his right to make his own decisions. And pray for God to change his way before he hardened into an outlaw.

"Leta. I've seen things, done things . . ." Andy took her hand and led her away from the pastor. "Derrick's murderers are still alive. I can't rest as long as they still walk the land as free men."

"I heard that Peter Jordan was wounded today," Leta probed.

"Bad luck." Andy's half smile expressed the paradox of that statement.

"But Dan Hoerster has never been anything but good to us. Extended us credit at his store when we needed it."

Andy's face hardened. "He was involved with Williamson's death."

Cooley's vendetta was still exacting its toll.

The church door opened again, and Ricky burst in. "Uncle Andy!" He shouted like he was in the schoolyard.

How had he escaped Julia's supervision? Leta stepped to the window and saw children streaming from the schoolhouse. "She said I could come over here and eat with you." Ricky opened his lunch bucket and frowned at the contents. "You take half the sandwich, Andy. I'll share the rest with Ma."

"That's all right, kid. I'll get something to eat later." Andy disengaged himself from Ricky.

"You are coming home with us, aren't you, Uncle Andy?"

Leta looked at her brother, daring him to disappoint his nephew. "I can't force you to live with us. But will you at least join us for the evening? Or even stay a few days until I can hire ranch hands?"

Andy glanced to the front of the church, where Reverend Stricker knelt at the altar. "I promised him I would listen. I'll do as you ask." He stretched to his full height, several inches taller than Leta. "I can't say more than that."

"That is all I ask."

The long trip to south Texas from Mason County gave Buck plenty of time for a lengthy conversation with God. He still didn't have clear direction, but he was more at peace. He arrived at Company E ready to get to work chasing the enemies of Texas and securing her borders.

Buck sought out Captain Neal Coldwell and explained his presence. "I have been seconded to your company by Major Jones for the length of your current scout."

"Morgan. I've heard good things about you. I'm glad to have you with us." Captain Coldwell introduced him to the members of the company. "Rest while you can. We leave before first light. We'll see action on the morrow."

The captain's promise of action the next day didn't come to fruition. About noon they ran across an Indian pony, sore used of back and foot. The sweat on the horse had dried, and their scout decided the Comancheros had passed that way about sunrise. "They're thirty-five or forty miles ahead of us and still moving. We'll be lucky to catch up with them today."

"Let's keep pressing forward," Coldwell said.

The men of Company E rode for the day without stopping to eat until they found a creek late in the day. Buck didn't know how long they could have continued without finding a water source—not much longer. The good news was, the Comancheros they chased faced the same conditions.

"We'll spend the night here," the captain said. "We'll leave before first light."

One kid—tall, bony, and so young he had little more than peach fuzz on his chin, stretched out next to Buck. Buck closed his eyes, knowing the value of rest on scouts like this. He recited Psalms to himself, drifting off.

Beside him, the boy stirred. "Sergeant Morgan?"

Buck came awake. "Yes?"

"You ever fought Comancheros before?"

"A few times." Buck resigned himself to the inevitable questions.

"What is it like?"

"In some ways it's easier than you expect. Once the fight starts, you just react, and it feels like it's over before it hardly even started."

The boy didn't say anything for a minute. "You must have seen men die."

"Yes."

"Were you afraid?" The last question came out as little more than a whisper.

"Every time." Buck repeated it under his breath. "Every time." Louder, he said, "But I did my job, and so will you. You have the makings of a fine Ranger."

After that, the boy let him sleep.

Shortly after noon the following day, the shout went down the ranks. "Comancheros ahead."

Captain Coldwell gave the orders: ride double file. No talking. Sneak up on the Comancheros if possible.

They closed the distance: One thousand yards . . . eight hundred . . . they might keep the element of surprise.

At five hundred yards, their cover broke.

Coldwell raced down the line, shouting orders. "Dismount! Shoot low! Kill as many horses as possible!"

Almost the same exact words Captain Roberts had used on Buck's first scout. It had worked then. It should work today.

The lust of battle rushed through Buck's veins, and he jumped from Blaze's back, rifle cocked.

A Comanchero rushed at him, rifle aimed.

Mason County disappeared from Buck's mind as he fired his weapon.

CHAPTER THIRTY

I find it impossible to get a consistent or reliable account of the troubles and am sorry to have to report that very few of the Americans whom I have met yet manifest any disposition to assist in the arrest of the perpetrators of yesterday's deed.

Letter from Major John B. Jones to
Adjutant General William Steele,
September 30, 1875

While Leta brought her ad to the telegraph operator, Andy stayed at the church.

Reverend Stricker walked out with Leta. "I'll make sure he stays put."

"Thank you. Again. Please pray that I find reliable hands. It's either that, or I have to give up." Unfortunately Mason didn't have a newspaper of its own. Fredericksburg had a paper, but she doubted the largely German population would care to work for an Anglo rancher. She wanted to advertise in the Austin Daily Statesmen, San Antonio Daily Herald, and the Burnet Bulletin. After Rab Turner, the telegraph operator, named the price, she checked her money and decided to skip the Austin paper.

"If you're looking for help around the ranch, you might go around to the stores. They could put you in touch with people who are looking for work," Rab said.

"I'll do that." Thinking of local stores brought Dan Hoerster to mind. What a horrible waste of another life. Would Mrs. Hoerster welcome her condolences, one untimely widow to another? Leta decided to try. After receiving confirmation of receipt of the telegrams, she headed for the Hoersters' store to offer her sympathy.

As she rounded the corner for the store, Leta hesitated. The townspeople must have seen Andy with Cooley, as surely as Reverend Stricker had. She reached for that peace, that reassurance of God's abiding presence, she felt earlier. All the more reason why she should reach out to her sister in Christ. After sending up a brief prayer for God's protection, she crossed the street to the store.

A CLOSED sign hung on the door, but a soft light lit the interior, and the quiet murmur of voices reached Leta. Countless people had passed in and out of her cabin following Derrick's death; names and faces had blurred, but their support had carried her through the darkest days. She would offer the same to Mrs. Hoerster. Gathering her heart with her skirts, she climbed the steps.

An older matron, a woman Leta didn't recognize, was keeping guard at the door. Her eyes widened when she saw Leta. "You. You are not welcome here."

Leta froze on the steps. "I don't wish to intrude. I only wish to offer Mrs. Hoerster my condolences. I know what it is to lose a husband in this horrible conflict." She felt like a

Yankee soldier must have felt approaching the house of a Southern widow, out of place and unwelcome. No wonder so few people paid attention to God's command to love their enemies.

"Who is it, Irma?"

"It's Leta Denning, Mrs. Hoerster." Leta took the silence that greeted her announcement as an invitation and made her way through the crowd. All eyes upon her, she didn't stop until she reached the new widow. "I came to town today on business, and so I was here when the shots were fired." She swallowed, finding the words hard to say. "Your husband was a good man. This is a terrible thing that has happened."

"Your brother was with them." Mrs. Hoerster's guardian frowned.

What do I say, Lord? "Regardless of whatever my brother has done." Leta closed her eyes and prayed for courage. "Or whatever anyone represented in this room may have done, we all agree that such a loss of life is wrong. I for one will no longer seek the men who killed my husband."

The words surprised her as soon as she spoke them. Murmurs floated around her. She laid a hand on Mrs. Hoerster's arm. "I will pray for you."

"And I for you."

Mrs. Hoerster's soft whisper followed Leta out the door.

Buck relaxed among the men of Company E. Spirits ran high after the successful completion of their scout.

"If we keep this up, pretty soon we'll have the Comanchero problem under control. We might even work ourselves out of a job." Abe Zeller lifted a flask to his lips.

Whiskey wasn't uncommon among the Rangers, but the fact didn't make Buck dislike it any less. A Ranger might be called to battle on a moment's notice. A liquor-addled brain diluted his focus. At least the men who gambled kept their heads clear.

Captain Coldwell sought out Buck. "Appreciate your help today. The way you and that horse of yours corralled the head honcho when he was trying to escape, that was a pretty piece of work." He grinned. "But hear tell, you come from a family of horsemen. The Rangers are proud to have a Morgan, horse and man, among their number."

Buck tipped his hat to accept the praise.

"I was pleased to have your assistance. Didn't expect to see anyone from Company D for a string of Sundays, with the trouble going on up in Mason. Is it as bad as the papers report? Murders in broad daylight with no one called to account?"

Fred's fallen body flashed into Buck's mind, and he grimaced. He nodded but didn't speak.

A rider entered the camp and headed straight for the commander. "News from Major Jones, sir."

Coldwell took the missive and opened it. He glanced at Buck. "News from Mason. Cooley has struck again, this time getting to a Dan Hester."

Hoerster. Buck mentally corrected the pronunciation. Not that he blamed Major Jones. Onkel Georg had Americanized his Christian name to George and his surname to Fletcher.

The captain finished reading the letter. "Apparently they pranced around town for several hours, celebrating, scaring everybody into staying inside, and no one stopped them." He whistled. "Roberts has his hands full."

Conflicting emotions roiled through Buck. Was Andy involved in the firefight? Would Henry seek vengeance? Buck wondered if Major Jones would require his immediate return.

No such request came, and Buck wasn't sure if he was relieved or disappointed. He could stay here forever, doing worthy, brave work. He could continue until he was too old to sit in a saddle, without shedding a tear.

Unfortunately, it no longer satisfied him.

The commander folded up the missive. "He's asking for three volunteers to take the place of the men who admitted to a prejudice in favor of Cooley." He peered at Buck keenly.

"Send me back." At last Buck had a clear sense of God's leading.

"We need to get hay for winter." Leta bent over her account book. Andy had more than fulfilled his promise to her, staying for the better part of a week since the Hoerster shooting.

Andy slapped his work gloves against his waist overalls, stirring up dust Leta would have to sweep out later, but she didn't complain. Reverend Stricker had advised her to leave conviction to God. Leta was trying, but it was hard.

"I was worried after that big rain last month." Andy took a swig from his glass of cool well water. "But most of it dried out. There are three pastures ready for the sickle."

Her little brother. The same brown eyes that melted like hot chocolate when he smiled, the same cleft in his chin like their father, the way his eyebrow wrinkled when he was thinking about something—like now. She wished she could turn the clock back ten years to the day Derrick Denning had ridden into their lives. If only they had gone somewhere, anywhere else, someplace that would have avoided the heartache of the past year.

If wishes were horses . . . Leta met Andy's gaze with a steady look of her own.

"I will get as much hay in as I can. I know you depend on it for the winter. But then I've got to leave."

Leta nodded. She'd been pleased he had stayed with them

as long as he had. "Will you ride with Cooley again?" She forced the words past the lump of coal in her throat.

"Our interests run parallel with Cooley. Some of the same men involved in lynching Derrick got to Williamson."

"But that's the job of the law. To hunt them down." Leta traced the names from her list with her finger. "I told Buck what I remembered about that night."

Andy scoffed. "A lot of good that did. He's left for parts unknown from what I've heard. The Rangers are on our side, at least some of them."

Leta considered mentioning the deaths of Fred Fletcher and Dan Hoerster. The American faction weren't the only ones who had suffered because of the war. But so far they hadn't talked about either incident, and Leta wasn't ready to bring it up right now. She satisfied herself with saying, "There are two sides to this."

Andy leaned back and gaped at her. "How can you say that? They killed Derrick."

Leta's own words came back to haunt her. "Maybe I've finally learned that two wrongs don't make a right. Adam didn't make things any better in the garden when he ate the fruit after Eve did."

"The same Bible you're quoting says an eye for an eye, a tooth for a tooth—a life for a life."

Leta sighed. "I will not argue with you about it. I appreciate the help you are giving me. I care too much for you to let you act without speaking my mind, but I will not stop you from going. You are old enough to decide for yourself what is right and wrong." A sad smile crept across her lips. "And to live with the consequences of your actions. For too long I've protected you as if you were still a child."

Andy's brown eyes were alight with the love that bound them together. "I believe you mean it."

"Of course I do." Standing, she pulled him close for one long embrace, then let him go. "Use your freedom well."

CHAPTER THIRTY-ONE

SAN ANTONIO DAILY EXPRESS
November 30, 1875

They were . . . well mounted and armed to the teeth (not figuratively speaking either); dressed roughly, with hair and head unkempt, they certainly presented an appearance more like guerillas [sic] than officers of the law . . . these men were a portion of Capt. McNelly's brave band, and were on the search for the authors of the Mason County troubles.

Three men arrived on Leta's doorstep on Tuesday morning in response to her newspaper ads. One of them she hired without hesitation—Bob Unger, the son of her nearest neighbor, hoping to earn some extra money before his Christmas wedding. "I can't promise to work past the wedding."

She smiled at the earnest young man—only a year or two older than Andy, the kind of man she would love to see Andy grow to be. "I appreciate all the help you can give me. I'll continue looking in the meantime. Andy will take you out to the hayfields for today."

The other two applicants posed more of a quandary. Mac Burnett had drifted south from Kansas, working with cattle before moving on when the mood struck him. She decided to try him for a week.

The third candidate had a handful of sterling references, from his commander in the Union army to his sergeant with the Cavalry. Recently he had mustered out and hoped to find work as a cowboy. But he was a former slave. Leta had seen slaves in the days before the War Between the States, but she had never spoken to one face-to-face.

Toby Lincoln had dark skin, but his speech was pure Texas. "You've no cause to be worried none about me. I don't need no room and board; and I'm handy at anything that needs doing around a ranch."

"What brought you this way?" He must have passed a hundred bigger ranches on his way to the D-Bar-D. Given the high turnover on ranches, other ranchers must have offered him a job.

"Why, I asked the Good Lord to show me the place He needed me. And His footsteps led to your front door." Toby chuckled.

Leta laughed, the first happy sound she had made in what felt like weeks. "If there is anything God has been teaching me lately, it's that a person's color or country of origin shouldn't matter. I'm not going to tell God He sent me the wrong person. Welcome aboard, Mr. Lincoln."

Late that afternoon, Ricky ran into the cabin. "Ma! There's

strange men working in the field with Andy."

Leta laughed. If this continued, it would become a habit. The thought made her laugh again, and Ricky started giggling with her. They laced hands together and danced around in a circle. "All around the mulberry bush." Ricky's face lightened like the little boy he was.

"I hired some men to work at the ranch." That meant Andy would leave soon, but she'd worry about that when it happened. "Let's have a party tonight. Today is a good day."

"I like parties." Ricky smiled. "Will we have presents?"

"No, but how about cake and fried chicken and corn on the cob instead?"

"In the middle of the week?" Ricky's eyes widened. "Hurrah!"

Leta quizzed him on this week's spelling words—some of the ones she had suggested to him last week, so she added a few new ones to challenge him. "You're so good, I think you need to sit down with a dictionary and copy words."

Ricky's nose wrinkled. "Ma."

Daylight had faded from the sky before the men came in from the fields.

"Praise the Lord, we finished the first pasture." Toby's smile was as bright as the moon rising in the sky.

"Mr. Lincoln, I know you said you didn't require room and board, but I'd be proud if you would join us for dinner tonight."

Andy whistled when he saw the spread.

The men spoke with a ready camaraderie. Any concerns Leta had about men with such different backgrounds disappeared. The cabin rang with laughter and deep male voices raised in song and tall tales. Ricky's gaze darted among them, as if committing every detail to memory. It was good for him to be around more men.

In spite of the male-laced conversation around the table, Leta found herself listening for one particular voice, one that had departed for distant places. Telling herself to forget about Buck didn't work. He had come into her life and made an impression. Then he had abandoned her, as she had known he would. She had been a fool to let herself come to depend on him.

But when she remembered his patience in training Shadow, his dedication in finding Ricky on the day he had run away, his rare smile . . . she knew she would do it all over again.

Buck traversed the state for the second time in three weeks. Blaze ate up the miles, riding with speed and purpose as they covered the distance back to Mason.

He traveled north from Nuevo Laredo to Cotulla, through towns where he heard as much Spanish as English. When he spotted the first half-timbered farmhouse, he knew he had reached the southern edge of the German settlements. Turn east, and he could reach his parents' ranch in Victoria in a couple of days. But he kept Blaze's nose faced forward and pressed on to Neu-Braunfels for nightfall. In this community, he could revel in his mother's heritage. He allowed himself a small smile. The original German settlement in Texas, named after German nobleman Prince Carl Von Braunfels, offered food even better than his mother's. He scheduled a stop whenever he could.

After leaving Blaze in the livery, Buck sought his favorite restaurant. The waitress brought a plate covered with enough food for two men, and he ate every bite. Satisfied, full, and tired, he could have slept on rocky ground. On the soft feather mattress, he slipped into sleep.

Desire to cover the miles to Mason, to once again see Leta's face, drove Buck out of bed at an early hour. With a fond thought for breakfast sausage and soft-boiled eggs, *kaffee kuchen*, and fragrant bread fresh from the oven, he packed to leave. Rolls snagged the previous evening would have to suffice.

Buck stopped by Austin, but learned that Major Jones had left for Mason County. Good. He wanted to make Jones aware of his decision as soon as possible. Swinging by their meeting place below Kirschberg Ridge, he was greeted by smoke swirling up through the mesquite trees.

Major Jones sat without moving as horse and rider approached. Buck slowed down as he came closer, debating the explanation for Jones's presence at their usual meeting place.

Jones's expression didn't change, but Buck grinned as he slid from the horse. "You knew I'd come back."

"Not only that you would come back, but how long it would take for you to come to your senses." Jones extended a hand. "Sit down and tell me about it."

Buck gave a detailed account of the raid on the Comancheros, down to the number of outlaws killed, wounded, and captured. "A couple of the men sustained minor wounds, but they succeeded in shutting down the thieves. This gang had been tormenting local farmers for some time." Buck poured himself a cup of coffee and settled back. "I had almost forgotten what it was like to make a difference." Staring at the major over his cup, he said, "What's been happening in Mason?"

Jones grimaced. "The good news is that that the court impounded Sheriff Clark for false imprisonment."

The look on Jones's face told Buck that it hadn't ended well. "But he slipped away."

"There's more?"

"Someone wrote to the governor and accused me of favoritism."

Buck shook his head. "I'll testify to the steps you've taken to ensure an impartial Ranger force."

Jones looked mildly amused. "I can see to my own defense. But your support means a great deal to me. Now about your plans . . ."

When Buck finished detailing his plans an hour later, a smile had returned to the major's face. "Sounds like the Lord had a lot to say to you. God go with you, son."

Buck's last doubts disappeared with the major's words.

"I've come to take you home."

Pa towered over Stella.

"But Pa." Stella scrambled to marshal her arguments against dragging her back to Victoria. Ever since Fred's murder, she'd expected something like this. Pa probably thought she should have packed her bags and gone with Buck when he headed south.

"I was helping. There's been a lot of company." She'd overheard ringleaders of the German mob discuss their response to the continuing atrocities, but her father didn't need to know that. "Buck was ordered down south, and no one here could take me home." Anger flashed through Stella, because Buck had broken his promise to delay writing to her parents.

"I'll have a few choice words for my son when I see him again, leaving you here, after he promised to protect you. It's a good thing Georg sent me a letter." Pa looked every bit as big and strong as Buck did—competent and dangerous. Barely under control. "Get packed. We're leaving in the morning."

Tante Ertha burst into action. "Ach, no, Jud. Now that you are here, you must stay for a day or two at least. You must meet the little ones, and see how Georg has built up the ranch . . ." Her voice trailed off as Pa shook his head. "Please, Jud, we have not seen your family for so long. Please say you'll stay until the day after tomorrow."

Stella watched as Tante Ertha's words cooled down Pa's anger like water, and she stifled a smile. She would have an extra day in Mason. Anything could happen in a day.

CHAPTER THIRTY-TWO

If any complaint has been made to the Governor against me I should like to know the nature of it and by whom it was made, and I think I have a right to know in order that I may be able to vindicate myself.

Letter from Major John B. Jones to
Adjutant General William Steele,
October 20, 1875

Pa's chuckle held a hint of the fiery anger he had arrived with, rueful and smoky. "Both of our families will never forgive me if I don't come home with all the details. But I am worried about safety. What steps have you taken to protect yourselves from any further attacks? Can I take a shift of watch during the night?"

Oh, Pa, you don't want to know what Henry has done. "But Pa, you don't know the lay of the land."

He stared at Stella as if he had forgotten she was there. "I've got eyes in my head, and my aim is sure and steady."

Tante Ertha clucked. "You must speak with Georg about these things."

Onkel Georg refused Pa's offer of help. "You must have left as soon as you received our letter, and ridden hard. Even with your marvelous Morgans, the ride must have been grueling. Rest tonight. Join us tomorrow night so you can report we are all safe. What happened to Fred was a most unfortunate accident. This . . . gang is seeking revenge for the death of Tim Williamson. Fred was not involved in any of that."

But you and Henry were. If only Buck would return. Stella wanted to give him a full report before she left for Victoria.

Maybe she could get word to Buck another way. "Pa, how would you like to meet the men Buck is working with? They're back in Mason." Maybe she could see Steve Sampson again. The thought sent a shiver of pleasure down her arms.

"You only want to delay going home as long as possible." But Pa smiled as he said it. "Is Major Jones in the area?"

"I'm afraid you're out of luck. He's on his way back to Austin."

Stella whirled around at the familiar voice.

Buck draped his right arm around Stella's shoulders and tugged her close. "Pa, what are you doing here?"

Leta's heart raced as she stared down the road where Buck had disappeared earlier that afternoon. His plan was breathtaking, risky, foolish—brilliant. She doubted it would solve all the problems in Mason County, but it might turns things around for the people who mattered most to the two of them.

Toby would say God had given her another unexpected answer. She'd talk the details over with him, hoping he could shed some wisdom on the current situation.

Four figures appeared on the horizon. She didn't know

how long Burnett would stay—probably not much longer. If Buck's plan worked, Andy might stay. Even if he left, Toby and Bob could handle the lighter winter workload. Toby worked with the ease of someone with long experience, and Bob had youth and strength on his side.

As the men came closer, Leta spotted Ricky between Andy and Toby. Since the first day, he had spent the hours after school with the men in the fields. Swinging his arms, he tried to match their swagger.

Leta could imagine the conversation. Like herself, Ricky found the experience of meeting a former slave fascinating. He had endless questions, and Toby didn't mind answering. "Why is your skin so dark? Are you a Yankee? Did you ever see Abraham Lincoln?"

God had made all people—white and black, Anglo and German. They were all related, all the way back to Noah and Adam before that. The thought appealed to her. The warring factions in Mason wouldn't appreciate the reminder that they were all members of the same human family.

Only, like Cain and Abel, brother still killed brother. Mason County's violence was almost as old as man's first sin. It went right along with God giving them the freedom to choose. Every one of them, including herself, had chosen to sin.

The fact there was sin didn't make it any easier to live through. It wouldn't bring back Derrick. But it also didn't mean anyone else should die here and now.

The men had arrived in the yard.

"See you tomorrow." Toby tipped his hat to Ricky and went to the corral to retrieve his horse.

Leta stepped into the scraggly grass of the yard. "Toby, please wait. I have some business to discuss with you gentlemen after supper. Nothing special, just beans and cornbread."

"Good food and even better company." He tipped his hat.

"I'd be happy to oblige, ma'am. Nothing pressing back at my campsite."

"Wonderful." Leta's stomach fluttered, and she prayed for God's wisdom to guide their conversation.

If she had the food to spare, she would have prepared another Sunday-dinner type feast; but beans, cornbread, sweet tea, and a fresh peach pie with cream would have to suffice. When they finished the last bites, Toby stacked their plates. "You got something on your mind. I'll clean up, and you start talking. I'll be listening."

"Thank you."

Five pairs of eyes fastened on her, including Ricky's. She wished Ricky could be somewhere else; but the plans they made tonight could endanger him. She risked danger in the hopes of achieving peace. If only life didn't have to be so complicated.

"Do you want me to take the boy outside, ma'am?" Toby waited before pouring hot water over the dishes.

"No." The word dragged out of her. "Not yet." She shifted to the bench where Ricky sat, both elbows plunked down on the table, and pulled him close. "Promise me you'll listen. I'll answer any questions you have later."

Andy nodded, anxious brown eyes bobbing up and down, and she patted his hand for reassurance. "I expect you have all heard about the war waging across Mason County this past year."

Andy blinked and leaned forward. The three hired hands looked at each other.

Leta swallowed. "My husband was one of the first victims, last summer. He was involved in the court case that got the community riled up."

"Them dirty Dutchmen, you mean." Andy scowled.

"Many of them were of German origin, yes. And so far, no

one's been arrested, let alone tried and brought to account for his death."

"Scott Cooley's done a pretty good job taking care of that." Andy's words hung in the air.

"Scott Cooley isn't a lawman, though. It wasn't his place. Although I understand his desire to see justice served. I felt—I feel—the same way." She drew in a deep breath. "I've learned about the death of a young man, almost the same age as you, Andy. Fred Fletcher. He hadn't done any wrong, any more than Derrick did. He got caught in the crossfire."

Andy's scowl deepened, turning his face an ugly red. "His brother did."

Henry Fletcher. Tears formed in Leta's eyes, but she blinked them away. She wished she had never identified the men who killed Derrick. Too many people had been hurt. Of the men she recognized, only Peter Jordan had been attacked—and escaped with little more than a scratch. "Do you think it was right to blame the lad for what his brother did?"

"It's like they say about Indians—they're only good when they're dead. Germans, leastwise here in Mason, will just keep multiplying trouble." Andy's jaw stuck out.

"I think Miss Leta has some ideas how we can stop that. Let's have a listen." Toby swiped the dish towel over the last pan and joined them at the table.

"Fred Fletcher was Buck Morgan's cousin." Leta waited, giving her words time to sink in. "The Fletchers had a hand in Derrick's death. I'm not denying that." She looked at each man, lingering when she stared at her brother. "But you were there when Fred Fletcher was killed."

Andy shot to his feet. "Who told you that?"

"Buck saw you, Andy."

He groaned. "He'll sic those Dutchmen on me for sure."

"No, he won't."

"Why? Because he's a Ranger?"

"Don't be ridiculous." She frowned. "We had a long talk. What both of us want, more than justice or vengeance or whatever you want to call it, is peace between our families. We want to see you—and Henry—quit this path you're on."

"It won't happen." Andy bared his teeth. "It's gone too far. They hate us as much as we hate them."

"We have to try. I've invited the Fletchers to join us for dinner tomorrow. We'll have a picnic here at the D-Bar-D. And if you care about me at all, Andy, you will attend, even if it's the last thing you do before you leave."

"You can't make me." Andy stomped out the door.

"Do you want me to go after him?" Bob asked.

Leta shook her head. "He'll either come back, or he won't. I've finally realized Andy's not my little brother anymore, but a man who will make his own choices." She knelt down and pulled Ricky into her arms. "Go ahead and get ready for bed. I'll be there in a few minutes, and we can pray for your uncle Andy."

His sad brown eyes looked at her. "Are we safe, Ma?"

"God is with us." She hugged him again and gently pushed him behind the curtain. "I'll come back in a few minutes."

Leta rejoined the men at the table. "The three of you also have a choice to make. I would welcome your presence at the picnic, but I'll understand if you choose to stay away. This isn't your fight. Especially you, Bob."

"I want peace as much as anybody. I don't want to start out married life wondering if somebody will ride across our land and decide they don't like our accents. Count me in."

"I'm always ready for a good fight." Burnett touched the gun he kept belted to his waist.

"This is supposed to be a peaceful gathering." Leta wished she could demand everyone leave their guns at home, but most men of her acquaintance would feel naked without them.

All of them looked at Toby. "You don't have to ask. If you like I'll stay close by. Just in case."

Leta prayed that the primary players in both families would come and be as ready as she was to see peace reign between them.

CHAPTER THIRTY-THREE

I think a very excellent man for sheriff will be elected Mr. James Baird, at present the only candidate . . . With his election I look for a more orderly and law-abiding spirit to spring up and hope, but dare not say however, that peace will be restored.

Letter from Henry Holmes to
Governor Richard Coke,
September 24, 1875

"You want what?" Henry glared at Buck. "Young Andy Warren was one of the ones who killed Fred. I recognized him."

Buck stood his ground. "It's possible that someone in our family was involved with the death of Mrs. Denning's husband last summer."

Henry squirmed under his cousin's gaze.

Pa whirled around, surprise evident in his face. "You? You were part of the group that took out Denning?"

"You had a part in the death of that poor man?" Tante Ertha's voice boomed across the room. "You *dummkopf*. You brought those evil men onto our land." She burst into German that needed no translation, even if Buck hadn't understood it.

She turned to face the Morgans. "And you. We are no longer in Victoria, and it is not 1846. We have worked hard to build a life here, and these—Anglos—want to take what we have worked so hard to build. They are angry with us for not agreeing about the War Between the States. They do not forget, and they have not forgiven us for voting against secession." She mumbled in German. "If more people had voted with us, things would not have gone so poorly here. Your Riley Morgan wouldn't have come back from the War a skeleton of a man."

Pa threw back his head and laughed, and some of the tension left the room. "Well said, Ertha. This is a new day. But I have to believe peace is still possible. I say we go tomorrow."

"Of course we will go." Tante Ertha planted her fists on her hips. "We must ask and give forgiveness, as God would want us to."

Henry's deliberate nod didn't give anything away. He would attend the picnic. How much more, Buck couldn't say, but he was praying God would work a miracle of healing.

Stella spent the morning in the kitchen preparing for the picnic.

"I should have prepared American dishes." Tante Ertha bustled around the kitchen, second-guessing the mounds of sauerkraut and links of bratwurst she had prepared to bring.

"If we can't enjoy each other's food, we have no hope of peace."

Tante Ertha looked even more uncertain than before.

"Leta is kind. One of the nicest women I have ever met.

She welcomed me, a total stranger, like I was her little sister," Stella said.

"How could she not love you? You are a darling." Tante Ertha packed the dishes into a basket. "I have been praying for this meal all night. I do not know if I slept more than thirty minutes, and Georg also did not get any rest."

Stella pulled her aunt into an impromptu embrace. The present situation would test her own mother. This kind woman didn't deserve the awful things that had happened, one son's death and the other's complicity in murder.

No one deserved this lunacy, Stella reminded herself. That was why today's meeting mattered so much. Maybe with the womenfolk involved, the men would listen and not simply react. She prayed so.

The question of transportation posed a thorny problem. Ordinarily they would travel by wagon, allowing Tante Ertha to pack as much food as desired. But Onkel Georg was adamant: a wagon was too vulnerable to attack, too slow to move in case a quick escape was needed.

"Nothing's going to happen," Buck said. "I wouldn't suggest this if I thought there was any danger to the ladies."

"Maybe I should hoist a white flag so they'll know not to fire on us." Pa attempted a joke but no one laughed.

"These men, they would use a flag to track our approach and open fire before we could react." Henry scoffed.

"We will tie the picnic basket to a pack horse. Women and children will ride in the center while the men guard the perimeter." Onkel Georg frowned at everyone, daring them to disagree.

Buck agreed it was a sensible plan, and as soon as the morning chores were finished, they started out. The trip passed without incident, and they arrived at the D-Bar-D shortly before noon.

Leta stood on the stoop to the cabin, wearing a yellow calico Stella recognized as her best dress, waving a greeting. Ricky waited by her side. Several men were ranged in a semicircle in front of the cabin. She was surprised to see Buck's fellow Rangers, Steve and Jim. Three strangers who must be the ranch hands Buck had mentioned rounded out the group. Like Henry and Onkel Georg, they were armed, looking as uneasy about this meeting as Henry was.

But where was Andy? His absence compromised the purpose of the meeting. Something moved near the barn door, and Andy walked into the sunlight, his rifle propped from elbow to shoulder. Beside Stella, Onkel Georg sucked in his breath.

Ricky chose that moment to run to Andy's side. "Uncle Andy, are these the dirty Dutchmen you told me about?"

"I told you." Henry's breath hissed loud enough for Stella to hear. "This woman you claim is so willing to listen has poisoned her son's mind."

Buck had pulled Blaze a couple of steps back, and Stella had to strain to hear his low response. His gaze was fixed on Leta. "Look at her, Henry. She's heartsick."

"Because the boy gave her away." Henry put his fingers to his teeth and whistled, the sound piercing the air.

Stella shifted in the saddle. She heard the low rumble of hooves striking the earth. Buck stared at Henry. "You didn't."

Flat hazel eyes looked at Buck. "I couldn't allow my family to come in here unprotected."

Stella had heard enough. She left the huddle of riders from the Lazy F and dismounted, leading her horse by the reins as she approached Leta. She was counting on the fact that no man of either party would shoot an unarmed woman. "We're going to have unexpected company."

Andy's face quickly deepened from tan to a dusty pink to a deep red. He let loose with a call of his own, something akin to a barn owl. The barn doors burst open, and men Stella didn't recognize stormed through the opening.

The stunned look on Leta's face told Stella everything she needed to know.

Their attempt at a parlay for peace had turned into a showdown between the factions.

Leta pounced on Andy. "You promised."

"I promised to be here. I didn't say I'd come alone."

She heard a stir behind her. Riders burst through the elms and formed a line behind a man about Buck's age. Henry Fletcher had betrayed her peace gesture. Anger and fear tightened her stomach.

Andy swallowed, and for a second, she saw the frightened little boy behind his gruff façade. "They're coming to string me up."

Buck remained on horseback between the two factions. Leta and Stella flanked him, Leta facing Cooley and Stella the Germans. The Rangers Steve and Jim moved next to the girls.

"You said this would be a peaceful gathering." An older man who looked so much like Buck that he must be his father joined them in the center. He nodded at Leta. "Ma'am."

Leta looked at Buck pleadingly. "That was our intent, Mr.— Morgan?"

The man nodded.

A man separated himself from the pack behind Andy. He tapped her brother on the shoulder and together they walked forward. He held his arms up, gun at his waist but not in his hand.

Henry Fletcher rode forward at the same time, together with another man Leta didn't know by name.

"Cooley." Buck greeted the man with Andy.

So this was the infamous Scott Cooley. He didn't look like a hardened killer.

"Morgan." Cooley's voice was as flat as a sheet of paper. "Have you come to take me in?"

Henry Fletcher scoffed.

Buck's nose widened as he drew in a breath. "I'm not here today as a Ranger, but as a man of peace."

"Then what are they doing here?" Henry Fletcher gestured at Steve and Jim. "Looks like you were trying to round us up. Catch us all with the same net."

Men from both factions inched forward, guns in hands.

Leta untied the apron from her waist and held it over her hand. Putting iron into her voice, she said, "There will be no fighting here today. Anyone who has not come in peace must leave." Her legs quivered, but she willed them to hold still. "I swear to you by the graves on that hill, I am not seeking vengeance. Again I say, if you haven't come here in peace, you must leave."

Buck dismounted in a single movement and stood shoulder to shoulder with her, his finger on the trigger of his Winchester. "You heard the lady. Remain, with a promise of peace, or leave—if anyone moves his gun so much as an inch he will answer to me."

Steve and Jim joined Buck. Toby, looking like the battle-hardened soldier he had once been, crossed the yard, followed more slowly by Bob and Burnett.

Cooley took Andy aside and whispered a few words in his ear. Leta held herself still, aching to come between them. This was the man who had lured her brother to murder. Shoulders slumped, Andy walked away in the direction of the cabin.

Cooley stopped in front of Leta. "I'm sorry for your loss, Mrs. Denning. Your brother's a good boy, and he'll become a good man some day. But it'll be without my interference." He saluted her and turned his back on the German mob, signaling his men to head out.

Henry Fletcher slipped his gun back into its holster and nodded to the man beside him. The tall blond glared at Cooley's back, but jumped on horseback. With a whistle, he melted into the forest with the other members of the German mob.

Leta let out a breath. The men who had killed Derrick had come to her ranch, and she let them walk away. The taste of bitter ashes filled her mouth.

But they had walked away, without a single shot fired. She and her family had survived the encounter. She went weak at the knees. Buck appeared, throwing his arm around her waist and pulling her against him before she could fall.

"We did it." Her voice squeaked out the words.

"It's a start." Buck tilted her chin until her mouth met his.

Vengeance and hate, peace and justice, all melted in the warmth of Buck's love.

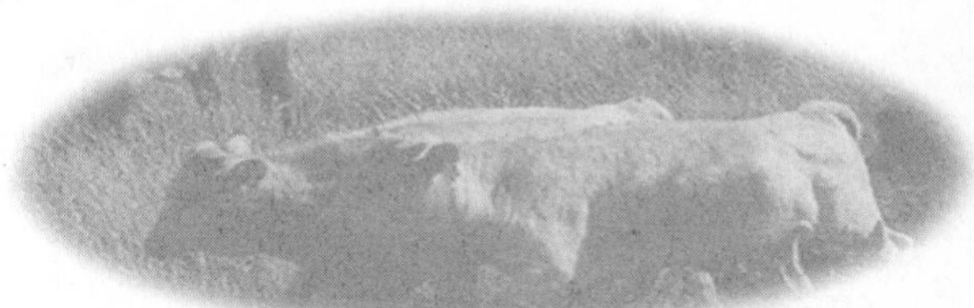

CHAPTER THIRTY-FOUR

Lawlessness at Mason is being superseded by order and morality. A Methodist revival is progressing up there, and the late evil-doers are doffing the six-shooter and getting themselves checked for a blessed immortality.

Telegraph from Sheriff M. B. Wilson
to Major John B. Jones,
May 11, 1877

Buck reluctantly separated himself from Leta's arms. People around them looked alternately amused and confused. Ricky looked mostly bewildered, confusion mixed with a darker emotion flickering in his eyes. Toby bent down and spoke in his ear. Ricky shook him off.

Leta reached for him, but he evaded her, and Buck's heart shivered with pain at the rejection. Ricky had experienced far too much for any small child to accept. Buck and Leta's embrace had punched another hole in the boy's fragile spirit.

Buck took a step toward the cabin. Leta stepped in front of him, shaking her head. "No."

Did she already regret their brief kiss? He searched her face.

She reached out, the work-roughened fingers of her right hand caressing his cheek. "Not now. Help Toby with the meal." She pointed to the basket of food Tante Ertha held on her arm. "I'm looking forward to meeting the rest of your family. I'll go talk with Ricky." A last caress that landed as softly as a kiss on his cheek, and then she lifted her skirt off the ground and strode to the house.

Buck gestured to Stella, while he kept his eyes on Leta's straight back and confident bearing. Behind him he heard movement, the neighing of horses and soft laughter.

"Let me carry that." Andy appeared at the periphery of Buck's vision, smiling as he carried a basket for Tante Ertha. They were getting ready for the picnic without his involvement, leaving him free to enjoy this moment of peace with Leta at the center of his thoughts.

She had almost reached the cabin when the door burst open. Ricky had decided to join the party. Good.

But Ricky was holding a gun.

"Ricky!" Panic strung Leta's voice. "Put the gun down."

"That Dutchman killed my Pa. Uncle Andy said so."

The gun boomed. Buck lunged at Ricky, knocking the gun from his hands, and pulled him to his chest.

The boy broke into tears, hiding his face against Buck's chest.

The kid shot the gun.

Henry stared at his leg. Blood spattered his legs but he felt no pain.

At his feet, Andy Warren clutched his left calf. Blood

streamed through his fingers. He stared up at Henry, as if expecting him to finish what his nephew had started. Tante Ertha looked from the stranger to her son and back. "He jumped in front of you." She looked around, in a daze. "Where is the pump?"

"Over here, Tante Ertha."

"Let me see." Henry bent down to examine the wound.

The dark cowboy Toby crouched on the other side. "This is okay. Take care of it, and you'll be up before you know it." He looked over the young man at Henry. "I did some doctorin' while I was in the Army."

If Henry needed any further proof, the flush on Andy's face spoke volumes about his lack of experience with gunfire. This was no hardened killer. He was just a kid, as raw and innocent as Fred had been. "You jumped in front of me?"

Pain twisted Andy's face into a grimace. "I couldn't let Ricky shoot you. He didn't know what he was doing." He closed his eyes. When he opened them, guilt sat on his features. "He was just repeating what I told him."

Henry's heart went still for a brief moment. He had deserved the bullet the child had intended for him, and more. "You were right. I was here when Derrick Denning died."

"I know that, Mr. Fletcher." Leta Denning knelt beside her brother and offered him a drink of water. "I saw you."

She locked gazes with him, and he couldn't look away. "Why didn't you tell Buck? He's a Ranger."

A sad smile shadowed her face. "I did. He set up the trap at the ranch, when your brother was killed." She held her brother's head against her chest. "My desire for revenge only poisoned my brother and then my son with hate." Tears sparkled in her eyes. "I forgive you, but it came too late." She started rocking.

"I'll take care of Andy, Mrs. Denning." Toby took Andy in his arms and carried him into the cabin.

Leta stayed on the ground, staring at her hands, Andy's blood staining on her fingers. "It's my fault."

"I don't deserve your forgiveness." Henry stumbled to his feet, mouth as dry as if he was the one losing blood.

"None of us do." Leta's voice was tear-streaked. "But God means it when He says 'Vengeance is mine.' He exacted every last ounce of punishment when Jesus died on the cross." She made an all-encompassing gesture. "It's not up to me."

"What about the law?" Henry asked with a choked voice.

Leta nodded. "They're supposed to administer justice. Ordained by God, as Paul says. But governments are human. So they make mistakes." She swallowed and blinked. Fixing Henry with her stare, she said, "I don't know if the law will catch up with you or any of the men involved in Derrick's death. For now, all I care is that the violence stops."

Henry drew in a ragged breath. "For my part—I will promise the same. Any action the German mob chooses to take won't include me." He offered her his arm, and helped her to the cabin.

Leta sat by Andy's side while Toby cut the material from the wounded leg. He didn't speak as he worked, snipping, cleaning away the blood and dirt, probing the hole where the bullet lodged. Andy twisted.

"Sorry, son, this is going to hurt."

"I already know that." Andy bared his teeth.

"It's okay to scream. Or cry."

"Or squeeze her hand until you break all the bones." Buck brought Ricky into the partitioned area and took a seat beside Leta. "That was a brave thing you did back there."

"Uncle Andy?" Ricky's voice quavered.

"He shouldn't see this . . ." Leta couldn't believe Buck

brought Ricky in while Toby was still at work.

"I think he should see what happened to the person he shot. Don't you?"

Buck's cool blue eyes bored into hers, sending shivers down her arms. Ricky had to face what he had done.

Trembling, Ricky fixed his eyes on Andy's bare leg. "I didn't mean to shoot you, Uncle Andy."

Toby took his pocketknife from the boiling water where he had cleaned it. "You ready?"

Ashen-faced, Andy nodded, and Toby set to work.

A low moan escaped Andy's lips, and he crushed Leta's fingers. Opposite her, Ricky patted his arm in sympathy. About the time she began to lose feeling in her fingers, Toby straightened, a smile playing around his lips. His knife speared a blood-smeared bullet. "We got it." He bent over Andy and squeezed his shoulder. "That was bravely done. It's going to hurt a little more while I clean out the wound, but then we'll bandage it up."

"Should we send for the doctor?"

Toby and Buck exchanged looks, one veteran to another. "He should be fine. All the more the doctor could do is give him something to ease the pain."

"No doctor." Andy shook his head. "There's supposed to be a party today. Go have fun."

Leta wanted to go. Meeting the Fletchers was the whole purpose of the event, after all. Looking into their faces after her son shot at one of them, it was doubly important. But Andy was family.

"I'll stay with him. You go on now," Toby told her.

Ricky was still staring at the bullet Toby had laid on the nightstand. He reached out a finger and touched it, horror clouding his eyes. She'd have to think more about it, but she was certain any further punishment she meted out would pale in comparison to watching Toby operate on Andy. Picking up the bullet, she held it palm up. "This bullet could have killed a man today." She unfurled his fingers from her left hand and placed the bullet in his palm. "I want you to keep this and remember what almost happened today."

When he didn't respond, she said, "Go ahead. Put it in your pocket."

Nodding, he slipped it in his pocket and wiped his palm on his pants.

Leta went out to greet her guests and neighbors, the nucleus of a new beginning for Mason County.

CHAPTER THIRTY-FIVE

HOUSTON DAILY TELEGRAPH
June 14, 1876

The notorious Scott Cooley died this morning about one o'clock, at the house of Esquire D. Maddox, nine miles north of Blanco, of brain fever.

"We won't bother you again." Henry Fletcher held Leta's hand firm in his grasp. "We're well out of it. I can't promise that the fighting will end, but no one will bother the D-Bar-D again." A sad smile played around his mouth. "I'll make sure of it."

Henry bit into a chicken wing Leta had fried, what felt like days ago instead of only that morning. "Delicious." He suited the action to his words, licking along the length of his finger.

"Heinrich, I taught you better than that."

Leta laughed. She chewed the bratwurst that the Fletchers had brought for the picnic. She enjoyed the hearty meat that made a welcome change from the beans and chicken that constituted the staple of her diet.

"Trust me, you have to try the strudel." Buck dipped a fork into the pastry and bit into it. "Not quite as good as Ma's, but delicious nonetheless." He gestured to the older gentleman Leta had observed earlier, whom she hadn't yet met.

"Leta, this is my father, Jud Morgan. Pa, this is Leta Denning."

The man was an older version of Buck, his hazel eyes a shade darker, his hair more silver than blond, but the same sun-colored skin and easy manner. Leta liked him immediately. "We have already met. I'm pleased you could join us, Mr. Morgan."

"Jud, please." He tipped his hat in her direction, then set it back on his head. "You have done a brave thing here today. We can only pray that other people hereabouts learn from your example."

"Time will tell." Her face warmed. "Words aren't enough to make up for everything my family has done to yours."

"It goes both ways, if we were keeping count. But I learned to set that aside the hard way a long time ago. With God's help, it's possible."

"Yes." This man made her feel like change, real change, was possible.

"I'll pray that this ranch becomes your own Salem."

"Salem?" Leta scrambled for the word.

"It means peace. Leastwise, I think that's right."

"It does." Leta had recovered the memory. "I heard a sermon about it once. About Melchizedek, king of Salem. I like that. I may have to change the name of the ranch. New start, new name: the Salem Ranch."

"Peace Ranch. I like that." Mr. Morgan winked and slung

an arm around Buck's shoulder. "I like her, son."

Buck's tanned cheeks turned a brick red, but warmth flooded his eyes when he looked at Leta. "You may be right." When Buck looked at her that way, she forgot about everyone else in the yard. She forgot about the past ten years, as giddy as a girl who'd never been kissed. "I'm going to steal her away from you for a few minutes, Pa."

"Give me a minute." Mr. Morgan grinned, then turned serious. "I have a proposition for you, Mrs. Denning. I know what it's like to have a young man around the house who can't wait to leave home."

He glanced at Buck, who remained impassive, except for a twitching of his lips.

"We were blessed that Buck was too young to fight in the War Between the States. Your brother hasn't been so fortunate. Feeling his manhood and ready to fight for his family and doing it the best way he knew how."

That was one way to look at it. "And I didn't make it easy for him. I still treated him like a boy."

Buck snickered. "My Aunt Marion, back in Victoria, would say Pa still treats her like a little girl. Stella probably would say the same thing about me. It comes with being the oldest."

"Maybe. But . . ."

"The point is, your brother made some bad choices, but that doesn't make him a bad man. If you're agreeable, I'd like to offer him a job at my ranch in Victoria."

Andy could accept a job at the premiere horse ranch in south Texas. "That's an incredible opportunity. He doesn't know a great deal about horses . . ." The words were stumbling out of her mouth. "I don't want you to be disappointed."

Mr. Morgan chuckled. "Don't worry about it. I've trained plenty of ranch hands in my time. I taught Georg most of what he knows about horses."

Pa's confidence was teasing a smile out of Leta, and she looked more relaxed than she had all day. Buck had told his father a little about Andy's situation, but he hadn't known he would offer him a job on his ranch.

Leta shook her head, a smile lighting her features. "Of course you may ask my brother." She put her hands on her hips. "And if he refuses the offer, I'll give him a piece of my mind."

Buck laughed out loud. "You'll have your hands full, with him and Stella. I never saw two young people so anxious to grow up."

Narrowing his eyes, Pa looked in Stella's direction. "It looks like someone else has sparked her interest."

Stella was sharing strudel with Steve. Stella and Steve? A smile spread across Leta's face.

Tucking Leta's elbow beneath his arm, Buck steered her toward the stand of elm and oak trees. "I am taking a lady for a walk." The leaves had turned, a colorful canopy engulfing them with a momentary privacy. "Salem Ranch. I like that."

"I'll change my brand to a circle S—a symbol of eternity. Like a wedding ring." Blushing, she glanced at a plain gold band on her left ring finger. Under her breath, she recited, "Till death do us part."

Buck sucked in his breath. Did she still pine for her husband?

She twisted the ring another time and took it off her hand. "And death has parted Derrick and me. He's part of my past. A precious, important part—but it's time for me to move forward." She inched forward and raised her head to his.

Accepting the implied invitation, Buck pulled Leta into an embrace. "I was a lot like Andy when I was his age. I couldn't wait to get away from home and prove myself to people who didn't already love me."

She glanced down before lifting her eyes to his again. "Do

you still have wanderlust? How long do you want to be a Ranger?"

Her eyes reflected fear. He laid gentle fingers on her chin and tilted it to look at him. "Major Jones already knows that I intend to resign. He sent me away to see if I would change my mind. I didn't." He lowered his face to hers. "Like you, I want a new start. Here in Mason County. I've found a new challenge, one that's big enough to last a lifetime. As your husband, if you'll have me."

She tilted her head until her lips were a scant breath from his. "Yes, William Meino Morgan. With everything that is in me, yes."

EPILOGUE

WEST TEXAS FREE PRESS
October 7, 1876

We are looking for a part of Maj. Jones' company to be quartered among us to keep peace, but I do not know that they will come, as our Gov. may countermand the order as "there is no crime in the State, all mere sensational reports." I hope they may come and keep the grasshoppers company.

Mason County, Texas
March 1877

It was a beautiful spring day, full of sunshine and promise. Leta had convinced Buck to take a trip to town before their baby arrived. Mason was relatively quiet these days; the feud had moved to the county next door, Llano.

While they waited outside the schoolhouse, Leta perused a letter from her brother. He was doing well, looking forward to the birth of foals in the spring.

"What does Andy have to say for himself?"

"He's excited about the responsibility your father has given him caring for the new foals." Leta peeked at the envelope sitting in his lap. "What does your aunt Billie have to say?" Even without the postmark, Leta would recognize her distinctive handwriting.

"She says my cousin Alex is heading this way. Just turned eighteen and decided he wants to try something different. Maybe the wanderlust bit him the way it bit me." He felt a jab in his ribs. "Was that you or was that the baby kicking me?"

"It was the baby." Leta turned her wide smile on him. "Like his daddy, he's tired of staying put in one place."

"He's not . . . ? You're not . . . ?" Panic laced Buck's words.

Her skin rippled again, and she felt a twinge of pain in her back. "Uh, Buck? I think I might be having a baby."

"You mean?"

She nodded, a tremulous smile on her lips. "Go get Ricky and let's get home."

"Forget that. I'm taking you to the doctor."

Eve Hope Morgan entered the world before midnight.

Buck looked into the tiny, red face of his daughter. "A baby makes the world feel right again."

"A new baby for the hope of peace." The baby wrapped her tiny fingers around Buck's index finger.

"Peace I leave with you, my peace I give unto you: not as the world giveth, give I unto you." Leta looked at her husband, love and joy flooding her exhausted body.

Buck handed baby Eve back to her mother to nurse. "God with us, the Prince of peace. In a world of trouble, that's the only peace we need."

Excerpt from *Cowgirl Trail*

PROLOGUE

Rocking P Ranch, near Brady, Texas,
July 1877

The *princess* wants to ride this morning. Saddle up her horse." Jack Hubble, the ranch foreman, clapped Alex on the shoulder and walked past him into the barn.

Alex shot a glance toward the house, but the boss's daughter hadn't come out yet.

"Uh . . . which horse?"

"Duchess, of course. Come on, I'll show you her gear." Jack strode into the tack room, and Alex hurried after him.

"That's the chestnut mare out back?"

"That's right. Here's Miss Maggie's saddle." Jack laid a hand on the horn of a fancy stock saddle with tooled flowers and scrollwork on the skirts.

"She doesn't ride sidesaddle?"

"Nah. Maggie's been riding like a boy since she was a little kid. Her father lets her get away with it, so don't say anything."

Alex nodded. His own sisters rode astride around the home place, and no one thought a thing about it. Why should he expect the boss's thirteen-year-old daughter to behave differently? But he had. Maggie Porter was a pretty girl, blonde and blue-eyed. She'd looked like a china doll on Sunday morning, wearing a pink dress with gloves and a white straw bonnet when the family set out for church in the buckboard.

"Here's Duchess's bridle." Jack placed it in his hand.

"Just saddle the mare and take it out to her?" Alex asked.

"Get your horse ready, too."

Alex stared at him. "Me? You mean I'm going with her?" He'd been hired at the Rocking P less than two weeks earlier. Now wasn't the time to argue with his foreman, but it seemed a little strange.

Jack laughed. "You're low man around here. Oh, the fellas don't mind, but it gets kind of boring. It's an easy morning for you. And Maggie's a good kid. Let her go wherever she wants on Rocking P land, but make sure she doesn't do anything dangerous. Where's your gun?"

"In the bunkhouse."

"You'll want it today, just in case."

"In case of what?" Alex's first thought was Comanche, but the tribes were now confined to reservations—his parents had followed the saga of the Numinu with special interest.

"You never know, do you?" Jack said. "Snakes, wild hogs, drifters."

"All right. How long does she ride?"

"As long as she wants, but get her home by noon. Her mother gets fretful if she's late for dinner." Jack looked him up and down. "Oh, there's one other thing."

"What's that?"

"Maggie's young, but she's starting to notice you boys. Don't do anything to give her ideas."

"You mean—"

"I mean, she's a thirteen-year-old girl on an isolated ranch. She's cute, and she's smart. She's getting to the age, if you take my meaning."

"I'm not sure I do, sir."

"It's Jack," the foreman said. "My meaning is this: if you lay a finger on that girl, I'll tear you apart, and then her father will flay your hide. You got it?"

"Yes, sir. Jack."

"Good." Jack strode out to the corral.

Alex pulled in a deep breath and hefted Maggie's saddle.

Maggie watched the new cowpuncher saddle the horses. He'd sure taken long enough to get the tack out and hitch Duchess and his own mount in the corral. The rest of the hands were long gone, out toward the north range.

She stood outside the fence while he saddled Duchess, then a black-and-white pinto for himself. He never looked her way once while he worked. He wasn't very old—seventeen or eighteen, she guessed. And he was cute. If Carlotta were here, she'd swoon. Maybe sometime she'd ask Papa if the new cowboy could escort her as far as the Herreras' ranch.

Her cheeks heated at the idea. When had she started thinking about boys that way—and showing one off to her best friend? She supposed it was Carlotta's fault. She always chattered about the boys in town and the young men on the various ranches. Carlotta was a year older than Maggie, and her mother was talking of sending her to Mexico City to stay with her aunt for a year or two and finish her education. Maggie hoped she wouldn't go.

The cowboy finished adjusting the straps and then double-checked Duchess's cinch before he led the horses out of the corral.

"Here you go, Miss Porter."

"It's Maggie. You're Alex, aren't you?"

"That's right. Do you need a boost?"

She scowled at him. "Not since I was seven."

"Oh. Excuse me." He turned away and hid his smile.

It was a very nice smile, not mean or anything. Maggie wished she had let him help her, but she'd gotten to the age where Mama said she mustn't let any of the men boost her into the saddle. Except Papa, of course.

Alex swung onto the pinto's back. By the time Maggie was up and had smoothed her divided skirt and gathered the reins, he looked as though he'd sat there an age, waiting for her. His dark eyes intrigued her—he seemed to see everything and yet he didn't stare.

"Where are we goin'?" he asked.

The wind gusted and caught the brim of the felt hat she wore riding. She reached up and pulled it down over her ears. "I thought we'd head south. There's a pond there, and sometimes there are birds on the water."

"All right. I've never done this before. Do you want to lead the way, or what?"

She flushed again, and her embarrassment was compounded by the realization that he noticed. "You can ride beside me."

He nodded, and she couldn't read the expression in his eyes. Did he think she was too old to need a nursemaid? Or too young to be blushing when a cowboy looked her way?

They walked the horses for a few minutes, until they got off the road and onto the range. The grass was dry and brownish—it hadn't rained in weeks. But the wind never stopped blowing.

Alex didn't say anything, but matched his horse's stride to Duchess's when Maggie picked up a trot.

After a minute, she said, "I'm sorry to keep you from your regular work. I expect you'd rather be with Jack and the others."

He shrugged. "I don't mind riding. Beats sinking fence posts."

Maggie nodded. Some of the men complained about all the new fences they were stringing. Her father said they had to do it, so Jack told the men to put a lid on it—she'd heard him tell Harry and Nevada that.

"Some of the men think riding with kids is a waste of their time," she ventured.

"Well, I can see your pa not wanting you out here alone. It's a big range. My sisters aren't allowed to go far by themselves."

"You have sisters?"

"Two. One's about your age."

"What's her name?"

"Elena."

Maggie thought about that. Elena sounded Spanish, though Alex didn't look Mexican. He had brown hair and eyes, but not too dark, and not the olive-toned skin Carlotta and her family had.

"I wish I had a sister." Sometimes she felt the loneliness sharply. With only her parents and the ranch hands around, some days she thought she'd die of boredom. She'd never been to school—her mother taught her at home. But they did have regular church in Brady, and she saw the Bradleys or the Herreras once a month or so.

They came over a rise and looked down on the pond.

"Now, that's a pretty sight." Alex gazed down at the water and the trails leading over the prairie to it, the two cottonwoods on the far bank, and the waterfowl gliding on the surface.

Maggie smiled and squeezed Duchess a little with her legs. The mare pricked up her ears and tensed. "Race you there." She kicked Duchess, and they tore for the pond. A moment later, Alex and the pinto edged up beside them. He didn't tell her to be careful or to watch out for holes. He just sneaked that pinto past her inch by inch. He reached the pond first and turned to look at her, grinning.

Maggie laughed at the joy of it. Finally, someone to ride with who wouldn't let her win a race and wouldn't scold her or fuss over her. She was almost there when the wind seized her hat and blew it off.

"Whoa!" She pulled Duchess up and wheeled to see where her hat went. The wind buffeted it along like a tumbleweed. Before she could decide how best to fetch it, Alex's horse streaked past her.

At first she thought he'd fallen off—the saddle was empty. Then she saw his boot sticking over the cantle, and one hand clamped on the saddle horn. The next thing she knew, he'd galloped the pinto right up to the hat, reached down while hanging off the horse's side, and snatched it off the ground. Then he bounced up into his saddle, pivoted the horse on his haunches, and bounded back to her.

He halted next to Duchess and dusted off Maggie's hat with his cuff. Smiling, he bowed from the waist and held the Stetson out to her. "Your chapeau, Miss Maggie."

She stared at him, still not believing what she'd seen. "How did you learn to do that? Are you a circus rider?"

He chuckled, obviously pleased that he'd startled her. "My mother used to live with the Comanche, and she learned a lot of their riding tricks."

She eyed the tousle-haired boy keenly—because he seemed

more like a boy now than a hired man—and decided he was telling the truth. "That was amazing."

"Thank you, miss. Now where would you like to go?"

Maggie put her hat on and tugged it down. "Guess I need a string on this thing. Let's follow the stream up to the hills. There used to be buffalo bones up there."

Alex grinned. "Let's go. We just have to be back by noon." He glanced up at the sun.

Maggie fumbled inside her collar and pulled out the pendant watch her mother made her wear when she went out. It had a pretty enameled flower design on the back. She wouldn't mind, except that she *had* to wear it. She'd have liked it better if Mama didn't remind her all the time.

"It's not even ten o'clock. We've got ages." She set out gleefully, her heart singing. A friend. She would try not to think of him as a cute boy. But she could hardly wait to tell Carlotta about him.

A Morgan Family Series

LONE STAR TRAIL

paperback 978-0-8024-0583-8 e-book 978-0-8024-7873-3

After Wande Fleischers' fiancée marries someone else, the young fraulein determines to make new life for herself in Texas. With the help of Jud's sister Marion, Wande learns English and becomes a trusted friend to the entire Morgan family. As much as Jud dislikes the German invasion, he can't help admiring Wande. She is sweet and cheerful as she serves the Lord and all those around her. Can the rancher put aside his prejudice to forge a new future? Through Jud and Wande, we learn the powerful lessons of forgiveness and reconciliation among a diverse community of believers.

www.RiverNorthFiction.com

www.MoodyPublishers.com

A Morgan Family Series

CAPTIVE TRAIL

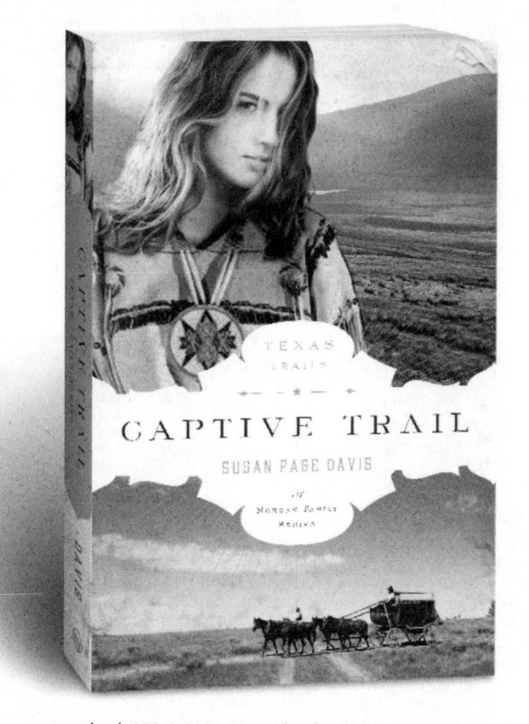

paperback 978-0-8024-0584-5 e-book 978-0-8024-7852-8

Taabe Waipu has run away from her Comanche village and is fleeing south in Texas on a horse she stole from a dowry left outside her family's teepee. The horse has an accident and she is left on foot, injured and exhausted. She staggers onto a road near Fort Chadbourne and collapses.

On one of the first runs through Texas, Butterfield Overland Mail Company driver Ned Bright carries two Ursuline nuns returning to their mission station. They come across a woman who is nearly dead from exposure and dehydration and take her to the mission. With some detective work, Ned discovers Taabe Waipu's identity.

www.RiverNorthFiction.com

www.MoodyPublishers.com

A Morgan Family Series

THE LONG TRAIL HOME

paperback 978-0-8024-0585-2 e-book 978-0-8024-7876-4

When Riley Morgan returns home after fighting in the War Between the States, he is excited to see his parents and fiancée again. But he soon learns that his parents are dead and the woman he loved is married. He takes a job at the Wilcox School for the Blind just to get by. He keeps his heart closed off but a pretty blind woman, Annie, threatens to steal it. When a greedy man tries to close the school, Riley and Annie band together to fight him and fall in love.

But when Riley learns the truth about Annie, he packs and prepares to leave the school that has become his home.

www.RiverNorthFiction.com

www.MoodyPublishers.com

A Morgan Family Series

Calling all book club members and leaders!

visit

TEXASTRAILSFICTION.COM

for discussion questions and special features

www.RiverNorthFiction.com

www.MoodyPublishers.com